WOLF

STOPE PACKS # 1

REBECCA ZANETTI

*Enjoy Wolf!
xo
RZ*

RAZ INK LLC

Copyright © 2022 by Rebecca Zanetti

All rights reserved.

No part of this book may be reproduced in any form or by any electronic or mechanical means, including information storage and retrieval systems, without written permission from the author, except for the use of brief quotations in a book review.

❦ Created with Vellum

For my Family

CHAPTER 1

A predator stared back at her.

Mia Stone set her face into calm lines, her hand inching to where her weapon used to sit on her hip. Only a leather belt existed there now. She shook off the unease. Jail bars. Many bars, evenly spaced, stood between her and the man currently meeting her gaze without expression.

She'd faced evil, good people who'd committed evil…yet she'd never really faced someone truly unreadable. She swallowed.

His gaze dropped to her throat.

An odd quaver wandered down her spine. What in the world was wrong with her? Maybe she'd been out of the game for too long. Focusing, she did her job and studied him.

Near the end of a cot, he lounged against the far wall of the cell. Most prisoners automatically sat when doing time in jail. Not this guy. He had to be, what? Early thirties? At least six and a half feet tall, he leaned his shoulders against the worn brick. His hair was a pure black and his features masculine and solid. Though his eyes were a mix of different blues—light to dark.

A scar ran down the right side of his jaw to disappear into

thick hair that almost reached his shoulders. Too rough to be called handsome, there was no doubt he was compelling.

Many killers were.

Mia cut her eyes to the quilt. Pink and homemade, the bed cover belonged in a jail cell as much as the diamond earrings she wore belonged in the small-town sheriff's office. But she'd promised her mother, and there hadn't been time for a fight before driving to the middle of nowhere. Still, she'd left her hair down to camouflage the sparkle.

She squared her shoulders and stepped up to the bars. "Mr. Volk, my name is Mia."

Upon arriving at the station, she'd asked to talk to the prisoner alone and had promised to stay in the hall. The sheriff had merely shaken his head and shut the door separating the main office from the two cells. Seeing the man in the cell, gratitude filled her that she hadn't pushed to go inside with Volk.

She tried to appear in control. "I was hoping we could talk."

Slowly, one dark eyebrow rose. "You're a cop."

"No, I'm not." She kept her face in pleasant lines, showing honesty.

"You reached for your weapon," he said softly.

Surprise had her stilling. "Yes. I used to be a cop. FBI, actually."

Volk straightened. "That makes you sad." Intense, he studied her.

The breath caught in her throat. She forced herself to exhale. This wasn't the first subject who'd tried to get inside her head. "Are *you* sad, Mr. Volk?"

"My father is Mr. Volk." Two long strides, and he stood much closer on the other side of the bars. The scent of wild sage came with him. "Call me Seth."

Courage had her lifting her chin and refusing to retreat. He could easily reach through and grab her. The last time she'd messed with a psychopath, she'd lost. "Seth."

He cocked his head to the side. Slowly. "I like how you say my name."

A warning trilled in the back of her mind. "So, you'll talk to me?"

"I am talking to you." Low, rough, his voice wrapped around the silence.

"Thank you." She'd learned early on that respect went a long way with killers and sociopaths. "As I said, I'm not a cop, but they've asked me to speak with you. If you're okay with that, we can talk."

He quirked his upper lip, making him seem approachable. Almost. "I want to talk to you."

She frowned. "Why?"

"Your voice is pretty." He rubbed the stubble on his chin. "Kind of like Ingrid Bergman's in *Casablanca*. Soft and classy with a hint of sass."

Warmth messed with caution in her chest. Bogie embodied everything she'd ever wanted in a man. Plus, that was her favorite movie.

"But your eyes are sad. Haunted." Seth's large hands wrapped around the bars. "Who hurt you, Mia?"

She jerked her head to the side. Instinct told her to run. "I'm asking the questions."

His expression went blank again. "You said you wanted to talk. Talking goes both ways."

This was no stupid country hick. She stared deeper into his eyes, seeing intelligence and…what else simmered in those dark depths? An emotion deep down. Anger. The guy was pissed. "Do you have a temper, Seth?"

"Yes." His knuckles whitened on the steel. "Did somebody hurt you?"

"Yes." She kept her arms loose at her sides, just in case he reached for her. "Do you harm women?"

"No." His jaw firmed. "Is the person who hurt you still alive?"

"No." She shoved emotion into a box. "Did you kill Ruby Redbird?"

His head cocked. "No. Why did you just lie to me?"

"I didn't."

Exhaling, he released the bars and turned his broad back to her. "Yes, you did." Faded jeans covered a hard butt and led up to a dark T-shirt. Those shoulders spread wider than a linebacker wearing pads. The flak boots on his feet were probably size fourteen, yet he moved with masculine grace. "You can go now."

Panic threatened to cut off her air. She needed to prove that she could still do the job. "I shot and killed the man who wanted to hurt me." When had she lost control of the conversation?

"And?"

Seth should've been the profiler. "I believe that man had a partner. If so, he's still alive." She could do this. Reveal her past pain to get to the truth.

Seth turned around. "I'm sorry."

"Doesn't matter—and most people think I'm wrong." The world centered again. "If you didn't kill Ruby, who did?"

"I don't know. But I will find out."

Now, *he* was lying. She didn't know how she knew that, but she did. What she didn't know was *the lie*. Had he killed Ruby? Or was he protecting the person who did? "I thought you disliked lying. That goes both ways, too."

His eyes darkened as his gaze traced every contour of her face.

Nerves sprang to life as if his fingers caressed her skin. She stepped even closer to the bars. "Have you killed before?"

"Yes." Thick boots clanged against metal as he took the final step toward her. Warmth from his massive body brushed her silk shirt. Only metal bars separated them…no air. "Besides the man you just mentioned, have you killed before?"

Her head jerked back. "No."

"Now, who's lying?" he asked softly, curiosity and an odd gentleness curving his bottom lip.

She blinked twice. Something about his voice was mesmerizing. A killer who hinted at safety right before murdering. His mouth caught her attention. Full, sexy, male. "I will find out who killed Ruby."

The moment stretched until her heartbeat echoed in her head.

"Step away from the cell," Seth said, taking a large stride back from the bars.

Keys rattled outside the exit door.

Startled, Mia shuffled across the rough concrete until her shoulders rested against worn brick on the opposite wall. There was no logical reason for her to obey his command.

Yet there she stood.

His gaze remained on her, dark and thoughtful, as the door opened.

Then a metamorphosis occurred. His expression went blank with boredom and a fierce insolence. He glanced at the two men striding toward them.

"Sheriff, you'd better have a decent reason for arresting Seth this time." A tall man in a sleek gray Armani suit led the way, his hair a perfect salt and pepper, his skin bronzed from sun obviously enjoyed away from Washington state.

The sheriff sighed. His hair was *more* salt than pepper, and grooves cut lines into the sides of his mouth. Apparently, Sheriff Pete Maxwell had spent some time at the local diner over the last year if the strain on his brown uniform was any indication. "Your client is a killer," he said shortly.

"That's slander," the tall guy said, stopping in front of Mia. "Who the hell are you?"

Seth stepped toward the bars.

Mia had the strangest urge to wave him back. She focused on the well-dressed man and extended her hand. "Mia Stone."

He took her hand, gripping tightly as they shook. "Prat Lenessee, Mr. Volk's attorney. I do hope you didn't question my client outside of my presence, Stone."

Mia slid her cop face into place, biting back a wince at the hard pressure. This wasn't the first asshole lawyer she'd dealt with. "I'm not a cop."

Lenessee released her. "If the police invited you here, then you're an agent of the police, so you're as good as a cop."

Yet she wasn't. She might not ever be a cop again. In any case, instead of wallowing, she allowed a slightly pissed-off smile to curve her lips with the unintimidating pink lipstick she'd chosen. "I've shaken a lot of men's hands, Mr. Lenessee. The ones with obvious insecurities,"—she dropped her gaze to his pressed pants and then traveled back up to his face—"always grip too hard."

Surprise opened his mouth, which he quickly snapped shut.

Her smirk widened just enough to let him know she saw the surprise. "*You* grip too hard."

In her peripheral vision, she caught a flash of Seth's grin.

The sheriff chortled, not even trying to hide his amusement.

Yeah. No doubt the lawyer thought she'd shake off the purposeful show of strength. She hadn't been the best profiler in DC for nothing…well, until they determined she'd grown crazier than the bastards she hunted. Throwing an attorney off track was half the fun of her former job.

He leaned over her in an obvious intimidation tactic. "Perhaps you're too soft to play with the big boys."

Seth hissed out a breath. "Lenessee, get me the hell out of here." His voice rumbled low with threat and danger.

The attorney straightened to stare at Seth. "Of course. Your bail has been posted, Mr. Volk." The lawyer's tone hinted at no deference, no affection, and no respect. If anything, he seemed indifferent to the point of condescension.

The sheriff exhaled loudly and unlocked the door, sliding it open.

Seth stepped out.

Lenessee retreated.

Interesting.

Mia glanced from Seth to the lawyer. The attorney was on guard. Just how dangerous was Seth that even his lawyer feared him?

He brushed by the attorney, heading down the hallway without another word.

Lenessee turned to the sheriff. "You had no basis to arrest him, and you know it. You might want to contact the county attorneys, because there will be a civil rights violation filed by the end of the day."

"No, there won't." Seth's low voice rumbled back before he shoved open the exit door and disappeared.

Lenessee inhaled, both nostrils flaring. Pivoting on Italian loafers, he strode after his client.

The sheriff raised an eyebrow. "Well?"

Mia shrugged. "I don't know. But I want to find out." Turning, she hustled away from the cells, moved through the small interior of the police station, and out to the waiting room.

The space held several worn leather chairs around a large coffee table displaying magazines about hunting, farming, and football. A wide wall of windows looked out onto the deserted Main Street.

Mia skirted the table and stared out the window.

Seth and his attorney spoke on the sidewalk, the lawyer keeping his distance. Well, the lawyer talked while Seth glanced around the quiet street. He stood next to a *No Parking* sign, his head nearly as tall as the placard.

His shoulders straightened, and he shifted his attention to her.

Finally, the lawyer wound down, turned on his heel, and headed for a Cadillac parked across the street.

Seth cocked his head to the side, his expression full of dare.

Mia shoved open the glass door. She should get a weapons permit if she continued to work in the state—not that she hadn't already stuck a small Glock 43 into her ankle holster. Several steps across a rough sidewalk had her close enough to smell wild sage. Her shoulders went back.

"You're very pretty, Mia."

Not what she'd expected. She frowned. "Who killed Ruby Redbird?"

Seth slowly shook his head, wrapping a hand around her biceps. "That's a mystery you're no longer involved in." His grip was warm and unbelievably strong.

He moved into a stride.

She tried to yank free.

His hold slid smoothly to the back of her elbow, effectively putting her in a position where she had to move, much like a parent with a wayward toddler. For the briefest of moments, she felt vulnerable—like a civilian and not a trained law enforcement officer. Confusion had her biting back an expletive. They'd traveled halfway down the block before she dug in her heels and turned to face him.

She swallowed, angling her head. Up close, he was even bigger than he'd seemed in the station. Heat cascaded off the man. "Stop manhandling me."

"Where's your car?" His harsh features held no expression.

She shook her head. "None of your business."

Sighing, he glanced toward the parking lot that served the entire block and pointed to her older Toyota. "That's the only one I don't recognize. You need to take your sweet butt over there and go home, wherever that might be."

Small chunks of concrete scattered when she settled her stance. "I'm trained, Volk."

His smile was instant and almost charming. "You're half my size, darlin'. And your training won't do you any good."

Something in his tone suggested she believe him. But she'd faced killers before, and she'd solved murders before. This was her chance to get back into the life she'd loved. "I'm not going anywhere until you tell me the truth."

He released her. Almost in slow motion, he reached out to run a thumb along her cheekbone. It was a whisper of a touch that swept a flash of heat through her body.

Shock kept her immobile.

His features were strong and somehow ruthless, but he dropped his hand and released her from his spell. "Please, leave."

"No."

Those blue eyes darkened to almost black. "Leave, or you'll be as dead as Ruby."

Mia retreated a step, her heart shooting into a gallop. "Is that a threat?"

"No." A veil dropped over his eyes. "That's a fact, Mia Stone."

CHAPTER 2

Only a strong voice calling her name allowed Mia to tear her gaze from Seth's. She turned to see the sheriff standing outside his door, one hand on the butt of his gun.

Seth sighed. "Say goodbye to the sheriff, and good luck to you, Mia." Quick strides had him across the road and jumping into a rugged Jeep.

Mia watched him speed off before turning on her heel and following the sheriff into the station, winding behind the battered counter. Apparently the receptionist was on vacation. Mia continued past the desks of the two full-time deputies, who were both out on calls.

Finally, she stepped into the sheriff's office.

"Did you find a place to live in Seattle?" He resettled the belt around his big belly as he sat behind his massive desk.

"Not yet. Mom and Aunt Dotty are at a hotel as we speak. Though I have a month to get them settled before I start work at Seattle PD—as a shrink and not a cop, unfortunately." Mia bit back a grin. "How's the food around here, anyway?"

Pete rolled his eyes. "Fantastic and stop making fun. You're nicer than that."

"Am not."

"Are, too."

"If you say so." Mia looked around the tiny office with the signed photograph of Roger Clemens proudly displayed on the side wall. The opposite wall held pictures of the small town, and the brick wall behind the sheriff held a wide window showing the forest outside. "I can't believe you came out of retirement in this tiny town."

Pete shrugged. "Me, either. As it turns out, being retired sucks, and the fishing around here isn't much better. When the New Age Coalition approached me to run for office, I thought...why not?"

"NAC?" Sounded like a bunch of vegans.

Pete shrugged. "Yes. They're an Eco-Group that's tired of the mine running the town. They organized—pretty well—and I won the election. Barely."

"Who lost?"

"Milt Jones. His family has worked for the mines for years, but he left town for a while to get a law degree. He's practicing now instead."

Still. To go from being a field supervisor in DC to a small-town sheriff was quite the stretch. Mia leaned forward, trying not to cringe as the metal folding chair protested. "Are you enjoying the job?"

"Sure." Shields dropped over Pete's faded blue eyes.

Mia cocked her head to the side. "That's the first time you've ever lied to me."

"No, it isn't." Pete folded his hands over his belly. "I lied years ago when I said you'd never make it as a behavioral scientist."

"No. That was a tactical move to inspire a young agent." One she had easily seen through. Without question, she never would've made it without his support and guidance. "You seem like you're holding something back."

"I'm not. Small towns are weird, and I'm nowhere near understanding this one. " His bushy eyebrows rose on the last.

"You've been a part of this town forever."

"No." He slowly shook his head, his lips pursing. "I've had a hunting cabin here for years. I'm not part of the town—at least I wasn't before taking this job."

Something in Pete's voice hinted that he still wasn't part of the town. So, they had mining people and Eco-villagers. Sounded like a recipe for problems. "Fair enough. Tell me about Seth Volk."

Pete tugged a file from a drawer, flipping it open to reveal a mug shot of Seth's strong face. "Seth is the eldest son of Benjamin Volk, the guy who owns the silver mines."

"So he's the largest employer in this small town."

"In the entire county." Pete frowned. "The Volk family has owned the mines since they were discovered centuries ago. The family has clout and power."

"Yet you arrested Seth."

"Tactical move. I wanted to see what happened."

"What was your basis for arrest?"

Pete flashed a grin. "I wanted to ask him questions about Ruby's death, and he refused. So I held him on the charge of impeding an investigation."

"Bogus charge."

"Yeah, and he's out now. No harm, no foul."

And Pete had wanted her to study Seth. There was something —a reason—he wasn't sharing with her. An odd hurt wandered down her spine. "We've known each other for years. Why aren't you leveling with me?"

Pete grimaced, yanking a large key ring from his back pocket to throw onto the table. "I need to lose weight."

She lifted an eyebrow.

He settled his bulk more comfortably in the worn leather chair. "I'm not hiding anything from you. Something odd is going on in this town, and I think Seth is involved. I wanted your expert take on him. It's nothing more than my gut instinct."

She'd bet her life on her old trainer's gut. "Why Seth?"

Pete scratched his wide jaw. "He's known as the Volk family's enforcer. If there's a problem, Seth steps in, and the problem goes away."

"Was Ruby Redbird a problem?"

"I don't know yet. But she was supposedly dating Erik Volk, the youngest son."

"So?"

Pete shrugged. "It's a connection." He slid another file across the desk.

Mia opened the folder. A young woman smiled from a photograph. Black eyes sparkled with fun, while a thick braid kept her dark hair in check. "Ruby was beautiful."

"Yes, and she was from the wrong side of the tracks."

Mia lifted an eyebrow. "There are tracks here?"

"Figuratively. Ruby's people are deep-earthers."

Intrigue had Mia running her finger over the photograph. "Deep-earthers?"

"Blue-collar, old-time miners. No college grads. Heck, no high school grads."

"They go right to work in the mines."

Pete nodded. "Most men in this town head to the mines the second they turn sixteen."

"Sixteen-year-old boys don't count as men."

"They do in this town."

"What about the women?" Mia flipped pictures over, pausing at one showing the dead woman lying on a rock formation over some wet leaves.

"They get married."

Mia nodded, studying the photographs. Spread-eagled and secured to the ground by shiny handcuffs attached to what looked like rock-climbing bolts, Ruby had been beaten across the neck and chest. A long, protruding spike remained embedded in her throat. Blood covered her denim shirt, neck, and face. Horror lined her smooth cheeks, even in death. "Handcuffs are an odd choice."

Pete nodded, reached into his back pocket, and tossed a shiny pair of cuffs onto the table. "Yeah. These are pure silver, as are the ones that bound Ruby."

Mia frowned. "Pure silver?" She fingered the smooth metal and leaned in to read a stamp in the middle. "Volk Mining."

"Yes. We have a box of them in the back room—all created and donated by the Volk Mining Company decades ago."

"That's so weird. Why?"

Pete rubbed his chin. "Some sort of odd tradition. When the mine first opened, there was no real law in the area. So they made up their own policing force and created handcuffs with silver from the mines. I guess the mold used today is the same as that used three hundred years ago."

"The cuffs are a huge arrow pointing to the mine." Maybe too big.

"Yeah, and that's not all." Pete pointed to the photograph. "Those are rock bolts in the ground—also from the mine. They're used to secure lines to the walls."

"Interesting. What about the stake in her throat?"

"The stake is actually drill steel. It's the big thing put in the drill to pound into the rock. This one is only two feet long—most are eight to ten. This one is well worn."

Mia shook her head. "It's as if the killer wanted us looking at the Volk family and their mine."

"Unless it *is* the Volk family, and they don't care if we know."

"What is this, the Wild West?" Mia fingered the photograph. "We can assume a man was the killer—an incredibly strong one to be able to shove that two-inch-thick drill steel into a human throat."

"Yes. Definitely a man."

Mia sucked in air. "Ruby was fully clothed."

"Yes."

"There was a lot of anger here." Mia could almost hear the screams. Or maybe those were memories. She shook her head. "Any signs of sexual assault?"

"No. But we should know more when we get the coroner's report tomorrow."

"Who found her?" Mia asked.

Pete grimaced. "A troop of Boy Scouts from Seattle trying to earn their survival badges. She wasn't quite dead when they found her."

Mia stilled. "You think they interrupted the killer?"

"Yeah. I do." Pete rubbed his whiskers. "The Scoutmaster had a pistol and drew it immediately. If the killer was still there, he left quickly. Ruby gasped a couple of times and then died in front of those boys."

Poor kids. The first death anybody witnessed scarred. "What do you know about the Volk men?"

Pete slid three folders toward her. "Not much. Seth was in the military, some sort of scout. Worked alone."

Mia flipped open the file to see a lot of paper...with most words blackened out. "Something tells me he was more than just a scout."

The phone rang, and Pete lifted the dented handset to his ear. "Sheriff." He nodded, his gaze slashing to Mia. "You have got to be kidding me." A red flush shot up from his neck to his thick cheekbones. "Find out how and get her back." He slammed down the phone.

"What?"

"Ruby Redbird's body was stolen from the Seattle coroner's office late last night." Pete stood, fury lighting his face. "I sent her to Seattle for an objective result. Apparently, the Volk family's reach is farther than I'd hoped."

"You'd better have more than your gut to go on if you make an accusation like that." Unease had Mia shifting in her chair.

"I know." Pete scrubbed both hands down his face. "I need a favor."

She sat back, exhaling slowly. "What?"

"Help me on this case. I'm no profiler, and you're the best."

Pete had trained her in combat and shooting, and she owed him. She sighed.

He pressed forward. "I know about your problems in DC. You catch a killer here, and you'll be back in—maybe work as a cop for Seattle instead of just a shrink. You're the best, kiddo. Please, help me."

She owed him. Without question, she owed him. "I don't know. I still need to find a home for Mom and Aunt Dotty. We're not even settled yet." Guilt choked her. They'd never be settled again.

"I know, and I have a solution. There's a cabin for rent near Lost Lake. It'll be quiet and peaceful—perfect for Gena as she recovers from her, ah…ordeal."

"Ordeal? That's one way to describe a kidnapping by a psychopath." Mia took a deep breath.

Pete nodded. "I know. How is she, anyway?"

Heat slid down Mia's throat. "Same. She's the same."

Pete cleared his throat. "How is Sister Dolores Catherine?"

Mia couldn't help the eye roll. "Aunt Dotty is fine…and she'll kick your butt if you call her that again. She hasn't been a nun for over a decade."

"I know. It makes me laugh to think of her as a nun. You never told me why she quit."

"No, I didn't." Mia glanced at the brick wall. A cabin by the lake might be good for them all. Quiet and peaceful…surrounded by beauty. Plus, she could assist Pete on the Ruby Redbird case. "You already had this planned. I mean, the cabin and all."

Pete raised an eyebrow and let the unanswered question about

Dotty go. "I was hopeful. Still am. I need you on this. You don't start work in Seattle for a month. We'll have the killer by then."

When was the last time anybody needed her professional skills? Mia bit her lip. A fresh start had been her intention when moving out west. "Show me the cabin."

CHAPTER 3

The log cabin was perfect. Sprawling on two levels, the fully furnished place held three bedrooms with attached baths, a large gathering room with a huge fireplace, and an updated kitchen with stainless steel appliances.

Within four hours of the sheriff showing it to her, Mia had signed the rental papers at the agency in town and fetched both her mother and Aunt Dotty from the small Seattle hotel. They'd all been relieved to leave the dismal place.

Of course, Gena had been tranquilized for the drive and move —and she'd probably sleep the entire night.

Mia peered into the still darkened bedroom at her mother sleeping peacefully on the antique wedding band quilt. In sleep, she looked less than her fifty years, her skin smooth, her eyelashes dark against her pale cheeks. Curly dark hair sprinkled with gray framed her pretty face. Even so, a sense of sadness clung to her.

When was the last time she'd smiled? Mia sagged against the doorframe for the tiniest of moments, allowing grief and guilt to engulf her. She'd repeatedly been warned to drop the case, but she couldn't stop once she was on a hunt. Maybe it was her childhood or even her training as an adult, but if a true predator was out there, she had to stop him.

Her mind flashed to Seth Volk. There was no doubt the muscled man was a predator, but every instinct in her body screamed that he had a code of honor. That didn't mean it was the same code she lived by. Curiosity about him wandered through her. He'd been compelling, and even though he might've threatened her, she wanted to know more about him. Maybe she was wrong again. Perhaps there was no code of honor. He was obviously strong enough to drive a spike into a human body.

Her mother gasped slightly in her sleep and rolled over as if to protect herself from a threat.

Mia pressed a hand to her chest at the pain. What had she done to her mother?

"Knock it off." Dotty hip-butted her, shoving her away from the door. She wore an avocado face mask matching a nightgown with odd pink lace down the sides. Her shoulders were broad, her waist surprisingly narrow, and her attitude…usually calm with an edge of strength. "What happened wasn't your fault, and it's time to stop wallowing."

Mia rolled her eyes, moving into the large gathering room. "My mother was taken hostage and tortured by a serial killer I couldn't catch. He took her because of me." She'd been hunting the bastard for so long that all she thought about was him. Apparently, he'd been learning about her, as well. She should've considered that he'd go after her family. Unfortunately, she had only realized that fear once she'd returned home to see her mother through the window. Mia had known instantly what was going on. "I should've known better, and I didn't. How the hell isn't her pain my fault?" She grimaced at the last sentence. Oops.

Dotty slammed both hands on her ample hips. "I may not be a nun any longer, but you really must watch your language."

Right. Like Dotty didn't swear like a judge on a binge. But she didn't use the h-word or take the Lord's name in vain. "I'm sorry."

Hazel-green eyes softened. "Thank you. Now, stop being an asshole."

Mia coughed out a laugh. "I'll try."

"Gena will be all right. That fancy psychologist you sent her to said it would take time. This is a great place to find the time." Dotty peered out at the quiet lake lit by the moon outside. "Peaceful in a totally out-there type of way."

"I guess."

Dotty studied her with her shrewd gaze. "You're more down than usual. Are you missing Kurt?"

"No." Interesting. She'd dated the FBI agent for nearly a year, and she hadn't thought about him once on the trip east. The guy hadn't exactly been supportive after her career blew up, although she had noticed a couple of missed calls on her phone from him. What was there to say? He had been more interested in protecting his career than their relationship. "I think I liked how he looked more than the way he acted."

Dotty snorted. "He did have the smooth guy look down, didn't he? I hope he loses his hair."

Amusement filtered through the exhaustion trying to weigh Mia down. "That's not nice." Kurt had really liked his thick, blond hair, that was for sure. "You know, I would often catch him checking himself out in store windows when we walked by." At the time, she'd thought it was humorous. Now, it was just annoying—plain and simple. She couldn't imagine Seth Volk watching himself in reflective surfaces. Though he'd likely be searching out threats while looking in windows. Of course, Seth was probably the biggest threat around.

But was he guilty of murder? More importantly, why was she comparing him to Kurt?

Mia turned to face her aunt more fully. "You and Mom need to be careful until I figure out this town, okay? There's a murderer here." The last thing she wanted was to put her loved ones in danger once again. "Please promise me." A chill skittered down her back.

Dotty patted her shoulder. "I promise. You know your mom will want to stick close to the cabin for a while, anyway. It's a nice and peaceful place." She peered into the quiet night for a moment, her tone thoughtful. "You can't worry so much and do your job. Right?"

Mia swallowed. "Right."

"Well, night, sweetie. I'll see you tomorrow." Dotty gave her a quick kiss on the cheek and headed to bed.

Mia nodded, her gaze remaining on the deep water outside. She needed to grab a cup of tea and do some thinking, and the deck seemed like a perfect spot for problem-solving. Hopefully, they could all heal here in this beautiful place.

A beautiful place where a murderer hid.

SETH VOLK JOGGED through the forest, each step pounding away the tension of the day. Moonlight winked through the trees, weak but determined, even at the midnight hour.

A slight breeze cooled his bare chest. Growling, he wiped his right hand on his running shorts. The feeling of Mia's soft skin under his thumb had haunted him all day. Beautiful and definitely lost, the former FBI agent's scent wouldn't leave his memory. She smelled like vanilla and lilacs—pure, wild, and sweet.

The woman had grit. The vulnerability in those deep emerald eyes had not only tugged at him but had also insisted he help. The one lesson Seth had learned without question in his life was not to help outsiders.

Pretty Mia was certainly an outsider.

She would be in definite danger if she stayed in his town. He'd warned her for her own safety and hoped like hell she followed his advice. His gut told him she wouldn't.

When Lenessee had threatened her, Seth had almost jumped through the bars and strangled the asshole. An odd reaction, to be sure. Although he'd only known Mia for a few minutes, he'd easily kill Lenessee for hurting her.

When had he become such a monster?

He stumbled on the familiar trail.

Shit, when had he worried about questions like that? He'd been born a monster—or he'd earned the title in his teens. Either way, it was entirely too late to ask such a question. Entirely too late to even think about being with a sweet thing like Mia.

She deserved better.

The trail wound through towering pines and evergreens, their strong scent failing to banish Mia's, which remained on his skin as if she'd claimed him for her own. Idly, he wondered about the man she'd killed. He'd never killed for a woman before. He'd kill for her.

With that disturbing thought, he sprinted into a full-out run.

Leaping over a rickety bridge spanning a small stream, his feet pounded dead leaves into moist earth. The wind picked up and brought the scent of rain—maybe hours away.

Footsteps echoed in the distance, and he shortened his stride to listen. Then he slowed to a stop, turning to view the trail. He smelled dark rum before his brother ran into view, his jeans ripped, and a scowl on his face.

Erik stopped and yanked branches from his shoulder-length blond hair. "What are you doing here?" he slurred.

"What are *you*?" Seth asked quietly.

Erik stumbled against a tree and rubbed his gut. "I want to see where she died. Where she took her last breath."

"You're drunk."

His brother snorted, bloodshot eyes blinking. "What's new?"

Seth ran both hands over his face. "This isn't smart."

"What isn't?" Erik wavered and regained his footing. "Me in

the woods where Ruby was found? Or you in the woods where she died?"

"Either."

"I loved her."

"Bullshit." The time for sympathy didn't exist—and it was damn well time his brother grew up. They had enough problems right now and needed to get on the same page. "You fucked her, just like all the others."

Erik lurched forward until they stood nose to nose—both tall, both broad. "You sound jealous, brother."

"Disgusted, actually." They shared height and their mama's blue eyes, and that was about it. "This behavior is embarrassing the family as well as endangering everything we believe in. Knock it off."

Erik's lips twisted. "Listen to the family bulldog—the Enforcer. You're just the old man's lapdog now, aren't you?"

"And you're his bitch."

The swing came from nowhere and planted hard in Seth's left cheek. He could've stopped it and chose not to do so. Sometimes, feeling pain was better than feeling nothing. Fire flared along his skin. Stars exploded behind his eyes. With a growl, he slammed both hands against Erik's shoulders and shoved.

His brother flew backward to land on his ass and skid several feet. His hands windmilled and then slapped the wet leaves, trying to stop his slide.

"Stay down," Seth growled, fury clenching his hands into fists. He'd been out of sorts since meeting Mia, and his body wanted a fight. His heart did not. "I mean it, Erik."

"Fuck you." Erik leapt up and slammed his head into Seth's gut in a hard tackle, sending them both sprawling into the bushes. His fists flew faster than his spewing words. "You might have five years on me, old man, but I'm all grown, brother."

Seth blocked several punches to his face and shot his forehead into his brother's cheek. "Then act like it." Asshole. It wasn't like being thirty made him old. He shoved Erik hard in the chest, putting power into it but not enough to break bones.

Erik spun end over end, slowly rising and brushing off his pants. Fury lit his eyes but failed to hide the torment glowing there. "If I acted like it, I'd have to kill you." With a low growl, he turned and ran back for the forest, increasing his speed until he was just a blur.

Seth stretched to his feet, wiping blood off his forehead and ignoring a sharp pang of loss as he eyed the now-empty trail. "I know."

He turned and started running north, his mind on his brother as he spat blood from his cut lip. He wouldn't be able to harm Erik —so he'd probably have to die. The inevitability of that fact spurred him to run faster, to enjoy the smell of the night while he could.

Another scent floated on the breeze, the one he'd been trying to vanquish. His feet turned of their own accord. He all but flew down the mountain, skirting the lake.

Then he saw her.

CHAPTER 4

Seth caught his breath at seeing the woman who wouldn't leave his thoughts.

Mia sat on the weathered deck, a cup in her hand, her gaze on the moonlight dancing across the water as it peeked between the clouds. She'd pulled her long, brown hair into a ponytail, showcasing classic cheekbones in a pale face. The darkness veiled the deep green of her eyes. She sighed.

Lonely.

Sad.

Stunning.

When he'd been young, very young, his mama had read him a book about a lost princess. She was beautiful and brave in a way that had haunted the hero…mainly because he couldn't have her. He couldn't save her.

Mia was a lost princess.

She perched silently in one of the worn wicker chairs, her bare feet on the wooden railing that skirted the deck. Her toenails were painted a light pink, only enhancing the fragility he saw in her. The cabin lay dark and quiet behind her. The strong scents of vanilla and woman wafted between them.

He silently crossed between pine trees, the shadows hiding him. He belonged in the darkness, while she should be in the light and not outside by herself. Did she have any idea the kinds of predators hunting the woods? Irritation clawed at him that she'd be so careless with her safety. If she were his, they'd be having a difficult discussion right now.

His entire body jolted. His? There was no way he could make the lovely agent his. The beast at his core roared in protest, and he shut it down. Hard. Unable to help himself, he nevertheless moved a little closer to her.

She stiffened, her gaze sharpening as she scanned the forest. Her feet dropped from the railing to the planks.

Good instincts there.

Slowly, he moved into the dim light, hands at his sides. It was impossible for him to look harmless, but he did his best, not wanting to spook her.

The sight of her lifting a gun from the bench next to her brought him up short. Against all rational thought, all need to survive, he smiled. His chest warmed, and his groin hardened. Need blasted through him with shocking heat. "I won't hurt you."

The woman stood, the gun pointed at him with steady hands. She was half his size and fragile, but her aim was true. "I may hurt you."

As words went, they had power. Icy fingers rippled down his spine. His chest chilled. Even so, he couldn't find it within himself to hide from her. "It'd be worth it," he whispered.

She tilted her head, her shoulders stiff, her stance set. "What did you say?"

His gaze on her wide eyes, he stepped lightly across wet leaves, hearing the drier ones crunch in protest. The need to get closer to her, even while she held a loaded gun, drove him hard. Just a little closer. "You won't shoot an unarmed man."

"You're armed without a weapon, Mr. Volk."

Make that *excellent* instincts. "Maybe. And it's Seth, Mia." He could be polite and call her *Ms. Stone*, but distance by manners bothered him. This once, with this woman, distance hurt. "Please."

She relaxed back onto her seat, the gun remaining trained on his chest. Her gaze was thoughtful and intelligent, drawing him even stronger toward her. "You out playing in the woods...Seth?"

The sound of his name on her lips made the distance vanish with an illogical ache. He couldn't have her, couldn't know her, yet deep down, where hope lived, something lit. Keeping his gait loose, he reached the bottom of the warped steps and planted one foot. "I often go for a jog at night to clear my head."

"Something bothering you?" Low, soft, her tone hinted at understanding and curiosity. Yeah, she felt whatever this was between them as strongly as he did. "Want to get the truth off your chest?"

"What's the truth?" he asked softly, willing to agree to anything to keep her talking to him. Her soft voice might even chase the nightmares away for one night. Maybe even two.

"You tell me."

That would never happen. Not really. "The truth is you need to get out of here. You don't belong."

"I've never belonged," she said quietly.

Her loneliness echoed throughout his body. His hand trembled with the need to smooth the hair back from her face. To soothe her. He wasn't a man who trembled—ever. So he shoved his hand into his pocket where it belonged. Touching her would be a colossal mistake he couldn't make. "I didn't kill Ruby." Damn it. Not what he wanted to say.

"Prove it." Her chin lifted as she met his gaze squarely.

"Can't." He shifted his weight, his breath catching at the alarm flaring in her emerald eyes. So he stepped back. Had he wiped off all the blood from his scuffle with Erik? Man, he hoped so. "Ruby was stabbed. Do you really think I need to stab a woman to kill her?"

"No." Mia's gaze wandered to his large hands and then back to his eyes. "Killings by stabbing can indicate sexual penetration. You have problems in that area?"

Unbelievable. The woman was actually profiling him. If she had any idea how quickly he could snatch the gun from her, she wouldn't be taking such a risk. His face heated, and he climbed the first three steps. "No, and I'd be happy to prove that to you."

Satisfaction twitched across her lips.

Yeah, she'd gotten to him. Against all logic, against his brain, he did something he should never have even considered.

He took the gun.

* * *

One second the gun was in her hand, and the next, Seth twirled it around his thumb. Even so, the threat came from the massive man, not the weapon. Nobody moved that quickly.

He dropped onto the matching wicker chair, which groaned beneath his substantial bulk. "Looks like I have the gun." Odd, but he sounded bemused, not threatening.

Mia swallowed. Her heart rate picked up. How had he gotten the weapon out of her hand so quickly? And so smoothly? More importantly, why wasn't she attacking or at least trying to flee? There was something about him she couldn't quite grasp. "Apparently you have quick reflexes."

The man wore loose shorts and no shirt. Hard angles showed defined muscles across his broad chest. Not muscles made in a gym, but natural, strong, more masculine—like those found in a wild animal. A light sheen of sweat glistened across his torso as if he'd been running for quite some time. Yet his breathing remained calm, and his sinewed body appeared relaxed.

He scratched his head and then released the clip into his other hand. "Is there one in the chamber?"

"Yes." Lying would accomplish nothing. In his hands, the weapon looked innocuous. Not needed and almost in the way.

Seth nodded, his eyes cutting through the darkness. Slowly, he handed the gun back to her—with one still in the chamber.

She took it, her hand shaking. The metal had warmed from the brief moments in his hands. Even with the powerful weapon returned to her possession, Seth posed the most danger. "How did you move so quickly?"

"Good reflexes."

That was the understatement of her life. The guy should play professional sports. Though there was no sense of play about him. "Why did you give it back?"

"So many questions, former FBI Special Agent Mia Stone," he murmured as he settled his bulk in the chair and turned to face her squarely. "Maybe I want you to feel safe around me."

Even without a murder between them, there was no way he inspired safety. Although appearing relaxed, a tension rolled off him that sped up her breath in a way she didn't understand. Had she ever felt more *feminine*? Instead of interesting her, that very sensation ticked her off. "Why would you want me to feel safe?"

"I don't know." His dark gaze studied her face, almost feeling like a caress. Intrigue and intensity glowered in the depths of those deep blue eyes, as if she were a puzzle he was driven to solve. As if in that one moment, she was all that existed. Such was his focus.

"I've had killers try to charm me before." She could admit to the effect he had on her body. In fact, she needed to acknowledge her reaction to him so she could protect herself.

His teeth flashed in a quick smile. "Charm?"

Oh, he had to know his wild features went beyond handsome…to sex and danger combined. The perfect combination to lure prey. The fact that he questioned the word *charm* instead of *killers* made the hairs on the back of her neck spring up. She should tell him to leave.

"You're in my town, Mia Stone," he said too softly.

Her shoulders straightened, and her breath caught. "So?"

"So I have to assume danger attracts you."

The guy was too much. Plus, danger had always attracted her—a sad but true statement of fact. "You're not dangerous." The lie nearly choked down her throat. She waited for his response and kept an eye on his breathing and facial expressions.

The smile took her by surprise. Genuine, almost boyish, the grin hinted at shared amusement. "Stop trying to profile me." He ran both broad hands through his hair, ruffling the thick mass. Was it as silky as it looked?

She had to profile him. There was absolutely no other reason she'd be talking to him under the luminous moon all by herself. The fact that she wanted to study his flat stomach and ripped abs was irrelevant. Who wouldn't? She hadn't realized men were made like this in real life. "Tell me the truth. If you didn't kill Ruby, who did?"

His eyes blanked again. "As I already said, whoever harmed Ruby will pay—I promise. We'll handle it internally."

"Internally? What does that mean?" Warning ticked down her spine.

He shrugged. "Small town, different rules. We take care of our own."

She grinned in challenge, wanting to smack him just to take him by surprise. But she didn't know how he'd react. Plus, she wasn't a big fan of battery. "So I'm on the outside looking in, huh?"

"Oh, baby, I'd let you in within seconds if you wanted." Low, masculine, his voice dropped to a whisper she felt along her skin, one that slid beneath to caress nerves she didn't realize could awaken. Those blue eyes darkened to almost black, intensity vibrating from him along with need.

Her lungs stuttered. "Flirting with me won't work."

Dark eyebrows arched. He kept her trapped with his gaze as if trying to read every secret she'd ever buried deep. "Is that what I'm doing?"

She didn't know what he was doing. The speeding of her heart rate and the increase in her breathing made her pause. She'd never reacted to a suspect like this. Sure, they challenged her...even intrigued her. But not once had she been attracted to one.

Until now.

CHAPTER 5

Mia gulped coffee, wincing as it burned down her throat. She should listen to her doctor and take those sleeping pills at night. After Seth had jogged back into the forest, she'd gone to bed and stared at the dark ceiling for hours.

The sun rose above the sparkling lake in a futile attempt to banish the morning cold. Stupid sun.

"Morning." Dotty swept onto the deck, a large mug in her hand. "My goodness. Isn't that view spectacular?"

"Humph."

"You're such a grump in the morning." Dotty sank her bulk into the nearest chair. Today, she'd worn bright pink leggings with an oversized Seattle Seahawks sweatshirt. Her eyeshadow was purple; her lips were peach.

Mia tried to blink. "Seahawks?"

"We were moving to Seattle." Dotty tossed platinum blond hair over one shoulder. She'd chosen the color for their trip. "I figured I'd fit in."

No way would the woman fit in. "That was a good idea."

"Yes." Delicate bone structure was still evident beneath the roundness of her classic face. Her hazel eyes were clear and shone with intelligence. "We should find the church in town so we know where to go on Sunday."

"Go right ahead." Mia stood and stretched her neck, straightening her sweater.

"You have to make peace with God, smart aleck." Dotty leaned forward, both hands around her mug.

A scuffling by the door saved Mia from having to answer. "Morning, Mom."

Gena hovered by the door, wearing a gray yoga outfit, her hair caught at the nape in a clip. Her hazel eyes widened as she took in the view. "Morning."

Mia gentled her voice. "Would you like to come outside? Just sit on the deck? It's a nice fall morning."

Gena glanced around. The classic bones in her face protruded, emphasizing how pale she still was. The yoga outfit hung on her frame. While she'd always been slender, now she was too thin. "I'm...maybe."

"Morning!" Pete skirted the edge of the deck.

Gena gasped and scurried back inside.

Pete stopped short. "Ah, shit. I'm sorry."

Dotty stood, placing her mug on the railing. "No worries. We're just in a no-fast-movements zone for a while. Good morning, Sheriff."

"Morning, Ms. Dolores Catherine."

Mia bit back a smile. If the man had been wearing a hat, he likely would've tipped it.

"It's good to see you again, Pete." Dotty gave Mia a tremulous smile. "I'll go make sure your mama eats breakfast. You get to work."

Mia nodded and cleared her throat. When would things improve? "Let's go."

Pete rubbed his clean-cut jaw and shifted his weight. "Ah, yeah. I really am sorry, Mia." He led the way around the cabin and tall weeds to his Lost Lake patrol car, which was a Mustang.

"Not your fault." Mia ran her hand along the sleek lines of the car. "This is amazing."

Pete nodded. "The city believes in its police force. It's kinda nice."

Mia slipped inside the vehicle and sank into the plush leather. "I bet this puppy moves." Too bad the sheriff had to drive it down the dirt road. The car had probably been spotless before.

Gunning the engine, Pete ripped out of the drive to the main lake road.

"Show-off." Mia secured her seatbelt.

The car easily took the twists and turns along the lake. Pete tapped his fingers on the steering wheel. "Is your mother going to be all right?"

"I think so." Mia stretched her neck. "She was kept hostage in the house while a serial killer I was hunting waited for me to come home. You know she had problems before."

"I know. But, I mean, she wasn't..."

"No. She wasn't raped or beaten. He tied her up and messed with her head." Bile rose in Mia's throat. "I got home and I shot him. Dead."

"Good for you."

Yeah, except the mental problems that had always plagued Gena came back three-fold. The woman wouldn't leave the house now. "Where are we going?"

"To the Volk house. I want your take on Ben, Erik, and Seth." The car ate up the asphalt as Pete continued following the lake until he turned up a long drive.

Pine trees lined the way, their needles falling to the ground in the colder weather. Carefully tended bushes lived between them, extending in every direction. Soon, a large ranch house came into view. Three stories, made of wood, the house sat at the base of a rising mountain. Snow dusted the very top of the peak.

"Wow." Mia took in the intricate stonework covering the bottom story of the house. "The Volks have serious money."

"Yeah." Pete pulled to a stop. "By the way, you're officially hired as deputy so you can help on this case. We can do the paperwork once we get back to the office." He jumped from the car.

Mia nodded, her gaze still on the imposing house. "Okay."

Pete scratched his head. "I talked to Ruby Redbird's best friend yesterday and then confirmed with Ruby's doctor. Guess what? Ruby was pregnant."

Mia stiffened. "Can you say *motive?*"

"Might not have been Erik Volk's baby." Pete ambled toward the wide double door.

"That's even more of a motive." The weight of the gun at her ankle lent her a sense of security. "I need a service weapon."

"Yep. I have a Glock 21 for you back at the station."

So she was Glock girl now. Good. She was comfortable with Glocks.

Pete rang the doorbell, which pealed throughout the entire house in an echo that bounced back. He scratched his head. "Why do rich people always have weird doorbells?"

"Dunno. Am I leading, or are you?"

"You're on after I introduce you."

A man wearing all black opened the door, his movements graceful and precise. He stood to at least six feet tall and was packing, the gun casually tucked in his waistband. His dark eyes surveyed them. "Sheriff Maxwell. The Volks have been expecting you."

A bodyguard? These people had bodyguards?

She cut her eyes toward the sheriff, following him through an entryway that went beyond opulent to *are you freakin' kidding me?* Priceless vases adorned antique tables while original oils from the masters lined the walls—mostly western paintings, several of them C.M. Russell's. Mia's feet twitched with the need to take off her shoes so she wouldn't stain the Persian rug partially covering the solid pine floor.

Instead, she kept her eyes on the bodyguard's broad back. The guy moved like an FBI sniper she'd met once. Spooky guy with great pecs.

He shoved open a pine door thicker than Mia's calf to what could only be called a gentleman's study. She had no clue where she'd heard that expression, but it certainly fit.

The scent of pipe tobacco hung in the air, providing a comforting vanilla whiskey smell as she stepped into the room. A wide desk sat over in the far corner, while a seating area made up of overstuffed chairs surrounding a large glass table filled the middle. Seth leaned against an intricate wood mantel adorning a tumbled rock fireplace big enough to step inside.

He wore faded jeans and a long-sleeved navy shirt with the flak boots she remembered. A two-day scruff lined his hard jaw. His bottom lip was swollen. No expression sat on his rugged face.

But the impact from those blue eyes slammed her hard in the solar plexus.

Two other men sat in chairs—one scowling and blond, the other about sixty with shrewd chocolate-colored eyes and gray hair. The door closed quietly behind the bodyguard.

The older gentleman stood. "Sheriff, how nice to see you again."

"Same to you, Mr. Volk. This is Mia Stone, who is working on the Ruby Redbird case."

"Benjamin, please." He glided forward, smoothly taking her hand in his rough one. Gently. "It's nice to meet you, Ms. Stone."

"Mia." She allowed him to pull her to sit in one of the plush chairs.

Benjamin Volk had straight, patrician features set in a cultured face. Thin lips, high cheekbones, and a direct stare. He moved with grace and a sense of strength. While he and Seth were about the same size, he lacked the wildness so apparent in his eldest son. But the edge of danger was there.

The blond stood, a charming smile flashing twin dimples in a handsome face he obviously inherited from his father. The similarities were striking. Though a bruise extended along his left cheekbone.

Had the Volk men been fighting? Why were they both bruised?

"I'm Erik." He leaned across the table to shake her hand.

The sheriff dropped into a chair. "Is your lawyer coming?"

"Why would we need a lawyer, Sheriff?" Seth drawled, his gaze remaining on Mia.

"No reason." Pete flashed a smile as both Ben and Erik retook their seats. "Mia just has a couple of questions."

Benjamin turned his focus on her. "You're a police officer?"

"No. I was an FBI Behavioral Scientist."

"Interesting." Something in his expression seemed off.

She studied the man behind the civilized mask and kept her face set in pleasant lines. "Really? Why is that?"

He cleared his throat and tapped his fingers on the armrest of his chair. "Well, after the trouble you had as a teenager, I figured law enforcement wouldn't be your first choice as a profession."

So Volk had already investigated her. That was quick. He must have decent connections. "You figured wrong."

"Still,"—his smile didn't quite reach his dark eyes—"to be accused of murder while just a young teen must've been difficult for you."

Seth shifted his stance. "She was exonerated. Let it go."

"Not quite true," Mia murmured. "There wasn't enough evidence to prosecute me. That's different than being exonerated." She met Benjamin's stare evenly.

The older man lifted a shoulder. "The file said you'd killed a foster parent who'd raped your foster sister and made a move on you."

Pete leaned forward to protest, and Mia waved him back.

"I know what the report said." She kept her body relaxed. This asshole wouldn't throw her off her game. "He made more than a move. He drove me to the middle of nowhere...and met with an unfortunate accident before he could hurt me."

"He ended up at the bottom of an abandoned well." Ben's eyes sparked with curiosity.

"The terrain in the middle of nowhere is uneven." Mia rested her hands in her lap, focusing on her responses and not the emotional reactions to that day.

Ben hissed out a breath. "Did you kill him?"

"Enough!" Seth's voice cracked across the room like a whip.

Erik jumped, and Pete set his hand on the butt of his gun.

Yet Mia and Benjamin remained calmly in place.

The older man nodded. "Yes. I apologize for the intrusion into your life. I try to know what's going on in my town."

Mia crossed her legs. "In that case, who killed Ruby Redbird?"

Benjamin relaxed back in his chair. "My best guess? The transient seen lurking around town all that week. We don't get many visitors here, and he stood out. After Ruby died, he disappeared."

Yeah. Wasn't it always the transient? Mia studied the Volk brothers from the corner of her eye. Erik had lost his smile and leaned away from both his father and Mia. Seth hadn't twitched. It was interesting that he'd remained standing. From his vantage point, he could intercept either her or the sheriff if one of them went for Benjamin.

She turned her focus on Erik. "You were dating Ruby?"

"No. We weren't dating." He crossed his legs. Wearing ripped jeans and a club shirt, and with his hair clasped at his neck, he looked like he was heading out for the bar scene in Seattle.

"What were you doing?" Mia asked softly.

Benjamin gave his son a look. "They weren't doing anything, Ms. Stone."

Erik opened his mouth and then shut it again.

Mia nodded. "Okay, let's start differently. Erik, did you know Ruby Redbird?"

"Yes." He ran a finger along the scruff at his jaw. "We live in a small town. Of course, I knew Ruby."

"Were you friends?"

"Sure. I'm friends with everybody." His upper lip twisted on the last.

Man, she'd like to get him alone and away from the two men currently flanking him. "I'm assuming a lot of people saw you and Ruby together in this small town. Did you take Ruby out?"

He sighed. "No. But we spent time together in a group."

"Tell me about her."

His eyebrows rose. "Ruby was a sweetheart. She worked over at the drug store, but she, ah, wanted to be a writer." His voice softened at the end.

"What kind of books did she write?" Mia asked.

Erik's shoulders lowered. "Mysteries. She really liked the suspense in a good mystery." He laughed, the sound lacking humor. "That's ironic now, isn't it?"

"Yes." Mia clasped her hands together. "Where did she live?"

"She lived in the apartment complex over on Main Street—by herself. No roommates."

Seth's shoulders straightened slightly, and Benjamin's head tilted. Erik seemed oblivious to the sudden tension.

Mia kept her focus on his blue eyes. This close, they appeared several shades lighter than Seth's. "What was her apartment like?"

"Clean. Ruby was a neat freak. And everything was gingham—lots of different colors of gingham." Erik scrubbed both hands down his face. "Somehow, it really worked. She had a gift."

So, he admitted to knowing Ruby, being friends, and seeing the inside of her apartment. "Was Ruby dating anybody?"

Erik paused and then licked his lips. "I don't think so, but I wouldn't really know. We weren't that close."

Liar. Mia nodded slowly. "Okay. When was the last time you saw Ruby?"

He swallowed. "Earlier the day she died. A bunch of us met to watch the football game over at Smiley's Tavern."

"What was she wearing?"

"Blue shorts, green top, and gold sandals," Erik said, his gaze darting to the floor.

Interesting he could remember that so clearly. "What were you wearing?"

He shrugged. "Probably jeans and a shirt. Who knows?"

"Did she leave with anybody?"

Erik drew air in through his nose, his gaze rising to meet hers. "Not that I know of."

Time for Mia to lie. "Witnesses said you walked out with her."

"No, they didn't." Erik lowered his chin, his gaze direct, a small smirk on his lips. "Nobody told you that."

"Because it isn't true, or because nobody would speak against you?" Mia asked, her gaze raking the wealth in the room.

"Does it matter?" Erik shot back.

Mia pressed her hands against her dark jeans. "I think it might." She'd never had money or understood people who had a bunch of it. Somehow, they thought little pieces of paper decorated with the faces of old presidents made the rules different for them. "Was Ruby drinking?"

"We had pitchers of beer on every table." Erik frowned. "But I don't think she drank any. For some reason, I remember her ordering a soda." He glanced at his wristwatch.

Mia lifted her gaze to Seth. "Were you there?"

"No." His voice was much lower and smoother than his brother's. The rumbling tone slid over her skin like silk.

Erik barked out a laugh. "Seth isn't interested in football games."

What *was* Seth Volk interested in? "Why not?"

"I'm busy." His hooded gaze was really beginning to annoy her.

"When was the last time you saw Ruby Redbird, Seth?" she asked.

Benjamin waved his hand. "No more questions about Ruby. We've answered them all."

"I don't remember the last time I saw Ruby," Seth said, ignoring his father. "Sorry."

Pete signaled her with a head tilt. Yeah, they were about done. The Volk men were finished answering questions for now, and the bodyguard would probably make an appearance any second.

Mia let out a breath. "I just have one more question. Do any of you know who fathered Ruby's baby?"

CHAPTER 6

Seth's entire body went cold.

Erik leapt to his feet, and his fingers curled into fists. A growl emanated from deep in his gut, sounding way too animalistic. "Ruby wasn't pregnant."

A low rumble echoed from Benjamin as he stood, his stance set and fury vibrating off his body. He might be in his sixties, but Benjamin Volk was all power and strength and would be for a very long time. It was impossible for anybody with a brain to mistake the threat he represented for anything but death. "Get out of my house." His voice had turned guttural.

Seth took two steps to put himself between his father and Mia, keeping them both in his sights. He didn't stop to ask himself which one of them he was protecting. "Everyone, calm down. What proof do you have that Ruby was with child?" Why hadn't the young woman said anything to him?

Mia stood, all grace, yet keeping her right leg free. The woman had a gun at her ankle. She eyed Erik but inched ever so slightly toward Seth—probably wasn't even aware she'd moved. Seth's tension ratcheted up more. He'd been trained since the age of six to protect his father…yet he was about to shield a woman he'd just met. What was it about this particular female?

The sheriff ambled to his feet, looking clumsy but seeming in perfect control of his body with his hand resting on the butt of his gun. He used the good ol' boy role to his advantage, but his gaze was sharp and missed nothing. "We spoke with Ruby's best friend, and we saw her calendar where she'd just had an appointment with a gynecologist in Seattle. A phone call to him confirmed the pregnancy."

Erik's hand trembled as he ran it through his hair. His face went pale, showing dark circles under his eyes. Even his lips leached of color. "Bullshit. This is bullshit." His tone had risen from the low growl, so at least he was in control of his body at the moment. But his emotions rocketed through the room in waves of shock and hurt.

"Keep it together, brother." Seth hadn't felt the need to provide cover for his brother in a long time, and the urge to do so now rode him hard. He felt as if he were being pulled in three different directions, so all he could do was stand in the middle of the storm and wait for whoever made a move. The only person he wasn't interested in protecting was the sheriff, and he was off to the side, surveying the entire scene. Safely.

Mia stepped toward Erik, looking small and graceful. "Would you like to revise your statement, Erik?"

Seth pivoted, putting his body slightly between them in case Erik struck. While Mia might think she had the advantage, considering her training and weapon at her ankle, she was dead wrong. If Erik lost control and showed his true face, she would be in even more danger. Benjamin would make sure of it. "Knock it off, Mia," Seth growled, his voice way too guttural for the moment. Energy coursed through him, sparking through his extremities. He rolled his neck to remain sane and in control. The idea of her in danger shouldn't be affecting him to this degree.

Erik's chin lowered. "You have no idea what you're talking about."

Benjamin shoved his son back into the chair with one hand on his shoulder, showing too much strength for his age. "I said to get out of my house." Pivoting, he moved toward Mia with the obvious intention of removing her bodily.

Without thought, Seth grabbed Mia's arm and turned them both toward the door. He tried to keep from bruising her, but when she attempted to pull away, he firmed his grip. There was no way she could evade him, but she didn't understand that as of yet. Without hesitating, he dragged her to the door, his senses filling with her unique scent. He'd know her anywhere in the world, even if she were blocks away from him. "Time to leave, pretty Mia."

The door swung open, and their housekeeper gestured toward the front door. About sixty and a permanent fixture in the house, her red hair had been tied to the side, revealing a wound in her upper shoulder. A raw one that had just begun to heal, which meant she'd probably sustained it the night before. Seth paused and then shook his head.

He gave Mia a slight push, releasing her arm. The loss of her touch hit him square in the gut, and it took every ounce of his impenetrable control to keep from reaching for her. She didn't belong there in the middle of his family's drama, especially since blood would most likely be shed. "Alice, please see Ms. Stone and Sheriff Maxwell out." He bent to whisper in Mia's ear. "Meet me at the diner three blocks down from the sheriff's office at noon for lunch."

She jerked her head away from him, her gaze on Alice. "Were you bitten by a dog?"

Alice pursed her thin lips. Her gaze was sharp, and her nostrils flared as she no doubt took in the tension surrounding them. "Yes, and I'm fine. Please let me show you out."

Mia gave Seth one last look and headed for the door. He let

her go, wanting nothing more than to follow her right out and touch that soft skin again. He needed some time to figure out why he was so drawn to her, especially since only danger surrounded him. There had to be a way for him to keep her safe, and that meant maintaining a close eye on her.

It would be their one and only date. He tried to convince himself of that truth and then gave up. While he had no problem lying to other people, he very rarely lied to himself. He wanted Mia Stone with a need that was frightening.

Erik's ragged breathing caught Seth's attention, so he schooled his features and returned to the study, shutting the door quietly even though he wanted to slam it. "Ruby was pregnant?"

Erik ran trembling hands over his face. His body shuddered, and for the briefest of seconds, he looked like that lost, five-year-old kid Seth used to protect. Bewilderment filled his blue eyes, and pain etched out from the corners in thin lines. "I didn't know she was pregnant."

Ben pierced them both with a narrow-eyed glare. "Whose baby was it? Seth?"

Fire exploded in Seth's gut. "What the hell?"

Almost in slow motion, Erik turned his head. Betrayal spread a crimson flush across his sharp cheekbones. "Did you sleep with Ruby?"

Jesus. Things were about to go seriously south. "No."

"Bullshit." Ben stood, his body vibrating. "Did you think I didn't know about your late-night visits with her? The times you spent with her when Erik was working? Did you honestly believe I'd let you roam this town free?"

"You bastard." Seth let a snarl loose. "You were following me?"

Ben puffed out his chest, his eyes narrowing to pinpoints. "I own this town, son. Don't you ever forget it."

"I'm not your son." Seth drew even closer to the line he'd been edging toward for over a year. "Don't *you* ever forget that."

"Yes, you are." Erik threw a pillow across the room and struggled to his feet. It appeared as if gravity were kicking the crap out of him. "You were legally adopted. Dad claimed you for his own, and that's the end of it. Why can't we all leave it at that?"

The rage and sorrow he'd lived with for too long exploded in Seth's chest. The only reason Ben had adopted and claimed him was because his mother wouldn't marry the bastard unless he did—a sad fact that Ben had admitted one night years ago while drunker than shit. "I'm not blood."

Ben kept silent.

Really...why not? There was nothing to dispute.

Erik headed for the bar in the corner and poured himself three fingers of scotch. Seconds later, he'd downed it. Turning around, his face still red, he glared. "Unfortunately, we have bigger problems to deal with right now than you two stubborn assholes. If Ruby really was pregnant, we just became even stronger suspects."

Funny. His brother got smarter when he drank. Seth rubbed his jaw. "They won't find her body."

"I know." Erik took a deep breath. His eyes darkened with a rare vulnerability. "I have to know. Did you screw her, Seth?"

"No. You have my word." How had he gotten to a point where his brother even had to ask a question like that? There was a time, years ago, when they'd been inseparable. Before Erik came of age, and Ben had begun grooming him to take over. There was only one way that could happen—when Seth died.

"Then what were you doing with Ruby?" Erik rested against the bar, his face flushed, his body too still.

"Nothing." Seth told the lie without blinking. Without feeling anything. A trick he'd learned from Ben when he'd been too young to know he'd spend his life perfecting the art.

"Bullshit." Ben grimaced as Erik turned back for more scotch. "By the time I caught on, you'd been meeting with her regularly—my bet is her babe was yours. Forget how to keep it in your pants, Seth?"

So Ben didn't know how long Seth had been meeting up with

Ruby. "You're wrong." He allowed a slight smirk to curl his upper lip. "What's up with the wound on Alice's neck? It looks like you're the one who forgot how to keep it in his pants, Benjamin."

Deep brown eyes narrowed to slits as Ben's shoulders went back. "You'll refer to me properly, or I'll kick the absolute shit out of you, boy."

A need to challenge the older man rose fast and hard up Seth's spine. A new need...one born of instinct, and something he didn't want. Mainly because he'd win—without a doubt. Destroying the old man was something he couldn't face. Yet. "We're not in public."

"I don't care," Ben snapped.

Was there hurt in those dark depths?

Seth shook his head. No. Ben had never given a shit about him. In fact, the old bastard's life would be a lot easier if Seth took a dirt nap. Easier than even Ben knew. For now, Seth had a date with the prettiest woman he'd ever met. If he were going to die soon, he would take at least one good memory with him. "I have to go. Ruby's body will be ready whenever you want it."

"Saturday night." Erik tossed back another full glass, pain cascading from him.

"Saturday night, it is." Seth pivoted and left the remnants of his family behind.

CHAPTER 7

Deep-fat-fried potatoes, burgers, chicken, and even vegetables scented the air like only a hometown diner could. Sparkly blue booths lined the windows, running parallel to the counter sporting several ripped stools that somehow looked comfortable. At noon, the place was about half-full.

A teenage waitress wearing bright blue eyeshadow had dropped a sweating glass of water next to Mia, saying she'd be right back.

What was she doing meeting Seth again?

Sure, she wanted to solve the case—and prove she was still good at her job. But it was something more. Seth was something more. One of those dangerous, tough-guy alpha types she read about in romance novels. Until now, she hadn't thought they really existed.

Too bad he might be a murderer.

She really, really didn't want him to be a murderer.

With a clang, the ancient glass door opened, and she sensed him before he came into view. The air vibrated with a different intensity, a sense of maleness that had the hairs on the back of her neck standing up.

Or maybe she was just freakin' crazy. The family history sure made that possible. Her mother had always skirted the line between reality and other worlds and had crossed over more than once.

Mia forced her body to relax into the booth as Seth stalked toward her. Most women probably either met him halfway or sat to full attention for him.

His gaze landed on her…even bluer and more intense than she remembered. It stayed as he maneuvered past the waitress and patrons lining the counter, his body moving with a sinewy grace surprising for such a large frame.

He slid onto the seat across from her. Sage mixed with his unique male scent surrounded her. A sense of intimacy filtered around them.

"Thank you for meeting me, Mia."

He said her name with a sense of satisfaction—possession. So she lifted her chin. "I'm hoping you have more information regarding Ruby."

"I know why you're here, darlin'." The slightest of twangs lifted his consonants.

She cocked her head to the side. "Where are you from originally?"

One dark eyebrow lifted. "I've always lived here."

"Liar." No heat echoed in her word. For some reason, she really didn't care. But the man was lying.

Now surprise had his eyes narrowing. "I'm an exceptionally good liar. Most people have no clue."

Interesting that he'd admit the skill so easily. "You're not that good."

The words hung between them. A slow smile spread across his face—sexy and sure. "Oh. I'm that good."

Heat slid up her chest, spreading across her neck until it warmed her face. The damn man had made her blush. She'd dealt with sexual innuendos her entire life. Yet Seth was a master at it. "Let's keep to the case, shall we?"

"I thought we were," he said blandly, his eyes darkening.

The man had absolutely no problem lying, now, did he? "How about you make me a promise?"

"What's that?"

"You don't lie to me for the rest of our lunch." Sure, he could lie about the promise, but something told Mia that if she got him to commit, he'd see it through.

Heat rolled from him, even across the table. "What would I get out of that?"

"What do you want?" Sure, the question held danger. But what the heck?

"I don't think you'll give me exactly what I want—right now, anyway." He sat back and ran a broad hand through his thick hair. "How about you tell me the story about the guy you shot recently?"

At least he'd asked about the recent shooting and not about her teenage years. He wanted to get inside her head as badly as she wanted to get into his. But she'd been trained by the best and had never lost in this kind of battle. "Okay."

His expression held the warning of a predator. "Excellent."

The waitress chose that moment to bop up to their table, her hips swaying in an unnatural attempt by a teenager to be a femme fatale. Thick mascaraed eyelashes fluttered in a purple parade of motion. "Hi there, Mr. Volk. It's so nice to see you again."

"You, too, Mandy." Seth smiled at the girl. "What's good today?"

The girl pouted her lip out in a style more suited to monkeys. "The special is a steak sandwich with homemade fries."

"We'll take two of those." Seth glanced at Mia, who gave a half shrug. Yeah, that sounded good.

The waitress nodded. "Anything for you, Seth." She paused and looked at Mia. "You're working on Ruby's case, right?"

Mia stiffened. "I am. Did you know her?"

"Not really, but nobody around here would kill her. You should let the sheriff do his job and go away." Then she flounced off, but not before taking a second to wink at Seth.

Mia fought the incredibly strong urge to roll her eyes.

"What?" Seth shoved the ketchup bottle out of the way so he could plant his forearms on the scarred wooden table.

"You're quite the catch around here, aren't you?" Mia unfolded the paper napkin to place on her lap.

"Things aren't always what they seem." A scowl twisted his upper lip. "In fact, around here, they're never what they seem." He glanced at the gold cross nestled against her chest. "You believe in God?"

She shrugged. "The jury's out on that one. How about you?"

"Maybe. For other people, I mean. If there's a God, he's not concerned with me." While matter-of-fact, the tone hinted at something else.

Most sociopaths either didn't believe in God or figured they were on par with a deity. Mia's shoulders stiffened. "Did you kill Ruby?"

"No. Who did you kill before fleeing west?"

Fleeing was as good a term as any. "Robert Joseph Delaney. He killed fifteen women by strangulation in a three-year time. All sex workers and easy marks. Picked them up, tortured them for seventy-two hours, and then killed them before dumping their bodies in DC dumpsters. I interviewed him…looked into his eyes…and knew he was guilty."

Seth watched her patiently, giving her the full focus of his attention. "You arrested him?"

"No. Couldn't get him to break—and there wasn't enough evidence. Mainly, he had an alibi for two of the murders. But time of death wasn't certain on either, so maybe not." Mia's gut began to roll. She'd forgotten her antacids.

"So, you let him go?"

"Yes." A sharp stomach pain replaced the roll. She needed those pills. "He turned all his attention on me and ended up mentally torturing my mother for several hours one night until I arrived home."

Mia remembered the night so vividly. The front porch light hadn't been on...and she'd known. She'd just known. So she'd taken out her gun, circled around the house, and saw them in the kitchen. No thought, no heroic measures to arrest him, nothing had entered her head. She'd taken aim through the window and shot him through the throat.

"His blood coated the pastel yellow curtains my mother had made. So much red—and I didn't feel a thing." More than anything, that still bothered her. No fear, no fury, just...nothing. As if for the tiniest of moments, she was the one who'd turned into the sociopath.

"You're not supposed to feel anything when you kill," Seth said softly.

The words took seconds to register. "How many times have you killed?"

"More than you." Seth nodded as Mandy set down the plates. "While I won't lie during lunch, I'm not confessing to any crimes here."

The man was smart. He hadn't really confessed to enough for her to get any type of warrant, yet he hadn't lied. "Have you committed many crimes?"

He shrugged. "Depends on whose laws you're talking about. Society's or nature's."

"Nature has the same laws."

"No. Natural law is much different than man-made laws," he murmured.

Great. A sexy, possible sociopathic philosopher. "Did you kill Ruby?"

"No." He took a big bite of his sandwich. "You mentioned that

Robert Joseph Delaney had a partner. Is that because he may have had an alibi for a couple of his murders?"

Wow. Seth had a good memory, too. She took a bite of her sandwich, fighting a low moan at the delicious flavors. There was nothing like a hometown diner. While in the city, she'd missed good, greasy food like this. "That was one of the reasons."

"And the other?"

"Instinct. I felt that he wasn't working alone. Pure instinct." She was the only one who'd thought that. The other FBI agents, the other profiler, her ex-boyfriend...they'd all thought she was off her game from the ordeal. She wasn't. Well, probably.

Seth chewed and then wiped his mouth with a napkin. "Do you have good instincts?"

"Usually." She sampled the fries. Excellent.

"Do you think I killed Ruby?"

She stopped eating, his gaze capturing hers. Centering herself, she opened all her senses, even the ones she didn't fully understand. Several deep breaths calmed her internally, and she studied him.

Blue eyes of many shades studied her back.

"No." But the word came out as more of a question. Her gut feeling was that he hadn't killed Ruby. But her gut might be influenced by both her newfound insecurity as well as the need for him to be innocent of the crime. How could she be so attracted to a suspect? "I've been wrong before."

Seth finished his sandwich.

Without thinking, Mia slid her unfinished half across the table. She was stuffed.

He stared at the meal for a moment before slowly picking up the sandwich. "I've never had a girlfriend."

Her breath caught. "You don't have one now."

His smile flashed a dimple that had been hidden. "I know. But the whole sharing of the meal thing...I've never done that."

She swallowed, her heart speeding up. Something about the hint of vulnerability in the dangerous guy screwed her up inside. She wasn't here to save him. "You know it can't happen between us, Seth."

His gaze traveled from the sandwich back to her eyes. Challenge darkened those dangerous blues. *"What* can't happen?"

Oh, he was not putting her on the spot like that. "Don't play dumb."

"I won't play dumb if you don't make stupid statements you can't back up." He took a manly sized bite of the thick meal.

"Stupid?" Her long-dormant temper began to stir. "You're calling me stupid?"

He lifted an eyebrow and finished swallowing. "No. You're smart. That statement was stupid."

Being caught off guard never sat well with her. "Were you the father of Ruby's baby?"

"No. If Ruby was pregnant, I wasn't the father. I never slept with her."

"What about Erik?"

"I haven't slept with him either."

Funny—and great deflection. It took more of an effort than Mia liked to keep from grinning. "Did he impregnate Ruby?"

"Ask Erik." Seth's mouth tightened into a forbidding line.

A chill swept across Mia's skin. "You having problems with your brother?"

"Define problems." The man didn't blink as he finished devouring the sandwich.

"You define problems."

"No."

Well, that wasn't a lie. "I don't find you very cooperative."

"As long as you find me." His grin failed to make him seem any less dangerous. It was doubtful that anything could soften the man. "Speaking of which, are you dating anybody, Mia Stone?"

"No. That includes you."

A wicked expression crossed his face—so knowing—so... carnal. "Does it, now?"

"Yes." She subtly took a breath to steady herself, keeping her expression bland to hide the turmoil he caused with only a glance. The man was either playing a game or declaring war. Either way, she wasn't easy to beat. "You're awful flirty for a man who wanted me out of town just yesterday."

He stared at the now-empty plate. "I like that you're not afraid of me." He lifted his chin, his gaze wandering across her features like a warm caress. "Though you should be."

The resigned loneliness in his tone resonated throughout her body. "I'm not afraid of much." Any demons she feared were from the inside, not out. "I've been trained by the best to take care of myself. To find evil and hide it away from the rest of humanity."

"Ah, sweetheart. Who defines evil?" He cocked his head to the side, stilling as he awaited her answer.

"Evil doesn't require defining. It just is," she said softly.

Slowly, as if he didn't want to spook her, he slid his broad hand across the table to run his thumb along her knuckles. "You really believe that."

"Yes." The spit in her mouth dried up. Fire flashed hard and fast through her, landing low in her abdomen. The gentle touch from the dangerous man caught her heart in a stutter. She swallowed, trying to force air from her lungs. "What are you playing at?" Her voice emerged much too weak.

He leaned forward, intensity carving grooves along his mouth. "I don't play. Ever." The warmth of his touch disappeared as he put his hand in his lap. "Protect yourself and *never* forget that."

As warnings went, it was a damn good one. So much so, she thought to return the favor. "I always catch the bad guy. No matter what it takes or what I must sacrifice, I take him down. You don't forget *that*."

"Fair enough." His gaze shuttered closed as he gestured for the bill. "Let's hope our goals stay the same, Mia Stone."

She thought about taking the bill but knew without a doubt he'd end up paying. "Why is that?"

Sadness filtered through his eyes before they blanked. "You don't want me for an enemy. It would be unfortunate for us both."

CHAPTER 8

*G*ena Trevano-Morrison-Hecklevy-Stone edged one foot out onto the warped deck. A slight breeze wandered in from the lake, skittering right up her spine. An hour after dinner seemed like the appropriate time to do this. Good thing Mia had decided to stay in town to meet the sheriff for a late dinner. It was nice to see her working again.

The wind slapped against Gena as if to shove her back inside.

Danger.

Evil.

Pain.

Anything and everything outside the cabin doorway would lead to something bad. She swallowed, the sound deafening.

No danger.

No evil.

No pain.

She repeated the mantra, sliding her foot farther outside. There was nothing bad on the deck. Her mind couldn't control her.

Yet, it did.

The lessons from the current shrink ran through her head, but the words didn't make sense. Plus, they were the same words—mainly anyway—from the other shrinks throughout the years.

"I am fucking crazy."

As she whispered the expletive, she smiled. A little.

Dotty was snoring softly on the flowered couch, her feet on the coffee table, her eyes closed to the episode of *Stargate Atlantis* playing on the television. The ex-nun couldn't hear Gena swear.

But her sister shouldn't be an ex-nun, now should she? If Gena had taken control of her life, if she'd been strong enough, then her sister wouldn't have had to quit her calling to take care of little Mia.

Now, Mia's life was fucked, too. All because of Gena.

For some reason, employing the f-word truly cheered Gena up. Gingerly picking up her other foot, she set it down on the deck.

Holy Mary Mother of God. She was standing outside.

Sure, her nails bit into the shredded wood of the doorframe, and her butt was still inside, but the rest of her body was outside. She glanced behind her. Nope. Her butt was outside, too. Man. When had she lost so much weight? She'd had curves at one time.

The sun was just beginning to dip behind the mountains. Darkness would arrive soon. She wanted to die before it was too dark.

The world was dark enough as it was.

She wanted to perform the sign of the cross but making the gesture would be unforgivable. Especially considering what she was about to do.

So she took two steps onto the deck.

Panic rippled through her stomach in a pain strong enough to make her teeth clench. But it was about to be over. She couldn't get the thought of that killer out of her head, or the image of his blood splattered all over her nice curtains.

Her daughter had done the right thing in saving her, but why did Mia have to be the one to save her? Why was she an FBI agent? Or an ex-agent. Did her need to balance the scales stem from her ordeals in foster care? That was Gena's fault.

If Gena had been strong enough, tough like Mia, she wouldn't have lost her daughter to the system more than once. Dotty had left the church to step in, and that had hurt *her*.

Gena caused hurt. She didn't mean to do it, but that was the result. Everyone would be better off with her gone.

She already felt gone most of the time. The surreal sense around her, when her brain played games, made the difference between reality and imagination hard to distinguish.

It was time for the reality to go away.

The trees rose high around her, opposing and deadly. The spit in her mouth dried up. Taking a deep breath, she shoved her body into motion.

Almost like a wind-up toy, she propelled herself across the deck and down the five steps. She counted each one in her head—they were the last steps she'd ever take. Too bad they were warped. The last steps someone took should be nice and smooth.

Story of her life.

The lake beckoned her. Mysterious, deep, and a dark blue...the water waited. Solitude and safety waited. Sand crunched under her feet, and oblivious to the cold, she kicked off her tennis shoes, remaining in her pink socks. Her gaze stayed on the still water.

A memory of a good day when Mia had been about five took hold. They'd gone to the lake and had a picnic, and the sun had been so bright. What a lovely day to remember right now. Gena would take it with her as she went.

She really did need to go.

Her baby would be better off without her. Her sister could finally go on with her life. And Gena wouldn't have to hurt any longer. She was so very tired.

Suddenly, she perched at the water's edge.

Cold.

The lake was so cold.

But warmth and peace slumbered beneath the surface. She just had to keep walking until nothing hurt anymore. The water would take away all the pain.

Straightening her shoulders, she took another step forward, and the chill spread through her socks and up her ankles.

A huge splash threw water to cover her shirt. She raised her hands in protest, jerking her face to keep from being doused. A low growl filtered across the water. Numb, she slowly turned her head to the side. The sight was too unbelievable to comprehend.

Snarling, dangerous, and golden-brown, a massive wolf bared its teeth and jumped right in front of her. More water splashed up, and she shut her eyes, holding up her hands.

Then, silence.

Trembling, she forced her eyelids open to see the animal as it blocked her way to death. Bigger than any wolf she'd ever seen in pictures, its fur stood up on its back.

The air hazed. She shook her head. "I'm hallucinating." Maybe she was already dead. Was it possible? Had she walked into the lake and then just blacked out? Shouldn't she remember struggling for air?

Water rippled toward her as the wolf kicked out one paw.

Cold. Really cold water. Dread slid down her throat, even as she removed herself from all feeling. Shouldn't she be running? Yes. She should be running. But the beast was between her and the deeper water. The blessed quiet of the water. "Get out of my way."

The beast snarled louder, blade-sharp canines flashing. Covered in golden-brown fur with eyes bluer than the water, the wolf had streaks of white extending from its muzzle on either side. The air vibrated around it as if tension came from the animal to assault the oxygen.

Gena tilted her head to the side. "Are you some spirit guide?" Yep. She was dead. As spirit guides went, hers was a little mean with sharp teeth.

The wolf huffed, shaking its head.

Ah. Well, apparently, she had killed herself…there'd be no heaven for her. The church teachings she'd learned young did have meaning. "Hmm. We going to hell?" Something in her should care about that, shouldn't it? At the very least, she should feel sorry that her sister, an ex-nun, wouldn't ever see her again and would probably know why. That was sad.

The wolf huffed again, somehow looking put out. A paw bigger than a man's hand splashed the water, sending small ripples toward her.

She couldn't help the smile. Sure, she'd been skirting the edges of insanity for years, but now it had finally arrived, and it didn't seem so bad. She'd probably need to be crazy to spend time in hell, and it'd be nice to have a pet there. Or perhaps the animal was just her guide to get there, and she was supposed to start following it.

It stared at her.

She stared back. "Well, if we're going somewhere, maybe you should lead the way." Hopefully, it was around the lake and not right through, considering she was absolutely freezing at this point. She'd figured she wouldn't feel anything, but it seemed she'd been wrong. "Come on. Let's get going."

The wolf took a step toward her, his snout sniffing the air.

She took a step back. Apparently, instinct still ruled. Then the breeze whipped into action, slapping her in the face. Realization had her stumbling back.

Oh, God. The wolf was real.

Slowly, the animal stalked her, taking a step forward and waiting until she stepped back before taking another one. The sand squished between her toes. She shivered, her eyes wide and focused on the animal. Why wasn't it attacking?

Minutes passed as they continued their odd dance. One step back. A matching step. Then another. Its eyes remained steadfastly on hers, and she had the oddest sensation it was being patient with her. Or *he*. Yeah. She figured the wolf was a he, and she didn't want to think of him as an *it* any longer. "You're a he," she whispered.

He nodded slightly.

She giggled. Was she actually having a conversation with her wolf spirit guide? Or just a plain old wolf in the woods? Didn't they eat people?

The edge of the stairs finally smacked against her ankles. She sank to the third one, and the worn wood chilled her butt. If the animal was going to rip out her throat, why herd her back to the house? Any rational explanation for that was out of her reach.

What in the world? Her mind fuzzing, her skin chilling, she held out a trembling hand to the beast. It was as if he'd saved her. The least she could do was thank him.

The animal edged toward her and lowered his powerful head under her palm in a moment of absolute trust.

Her heart swelled.

Letting loose a small laugh, she ran her hand through the thick pelt between his ears. His fur was softer than she would've imagined, even with the droplets of water clinging to it. "I don't understand what's going on." She should be scared to death. In fact, she should be dead—either in the lake or by his huge canines. "Why did you save me?"

With a snuffle, the wolf huffed and lay down, stretched out on the coarse sand.

She slid down to the bottom step so she could continue petting him without having to lean over so far. The last thing she wanted was to lose her balance and land on the wild beast. He probably wouldn't take too kindly to such a surprise.

Those wild blue eyes closed, and he gave a contented snort as she continued stroking him. His butt shimmied a little, and he stretched his hind legs out as if in perfect contentment.

Gena shook her head. How long had it been since she'd had a friend? If this was crazy, she never wanted to be sane again.

CHAPTER 9

Mia shoved the empty pizza carton to the far side of the conference table. The chairs were plush leather, the walls brick, and the table oak. Comfortable and oddly luxurious for the only combination conference/interrogation room in the sheriff's office. "You can't be serious."

Pete shrugged, stretching his neck. "The medical examiner's building burned down about ten years ago with all the records."

That was too convenient. Ruby's killing was too ritualistic—there might be similar crimes. They needed the old records. "Okay. So, it was the county medical examiner's office—there had to be computer backups."

Pete rubbed his whiskered chin. "No computers. Old Riley hated them, apparently."

"Old Riley?"

"The county coroner. He died in the fire."

Weird. Mia mulled over the issue. "If he hated computers, my guess is he kept a backup somewhere."

Pete shrugged. "I guess it's possible. There are boxes of manilla files in the basement here. It's dirty and dusty, but we can go through them tomorrow. For now, I need to double-check the messages since Loraine has been out sick for a week. Be right back." Stretching to his feet, he ambled from the room.

Mia kicked back to view the corkboard covering one wall. It held Ruby's picture as well as photos of all three Volk men. Against her will, her gaze kept returning to Seth's unreadable eyes. It was almost as if the picture watched her back.

A chill swept up her arm. "Who are you?" she whispered. She'd never underestimated an opponent. Doing so could get an agent killed. But she'd never overestimated one, either. Something about Seth seemed larger than life...and it related to the timing of the case. She was off her game after everything that had happened in DC. Seth was no tougher, no smarter, no more dangerous than any other human being out there.

Those blue eyes seemed to mock her.

She'd dated a Navy Seal before. At the time, she'd thought he was a dangerous man. Now, she wasn't so sure.

The air swished as Pete loped back into the room. "I had two messages about cats getting caught in trees. Hopefully, the callers either got ahold of the voluntary fire department, or the damn cats jumped down. I'm not heading out for cats." The leather chair fluffed out as Pete sat. "And you're not going to believe this, but we've been invited to a ball."

"A *ball?*" Mia wrinkled her nose.

"Yes. I was on the phone earlier with my friend Spike, the Seattle coroner, and he mentioned the mayor having a ball tomorrow night. I asked if we could get tickets, and he just left a message saying he got them for us. The Volk men should be there, and I figured we could get a bead on them away from their little fiefdom here." Pete waggled his eyebrows up and down. "Whaddya say, Cinderella?"

She sat back in the chair. "Well, it'd be nice to observe the Volks in public and see how they interact. It'd also be really interesting to see their reaction to finding us on their turf." She already knew they wouldn't like seeing her or the sheriff in Seattle, where they no doubt let down their hair.

"Exactly. *We're watching you…*" Pete snorted. "Rich assholes."

Maybe Benjamin and Erik. But Seth seemed anything but wealthy. Lost, maybe. Though tickets to something like that usually cost a bundle. "How is Spike getting us tickets?"

"Spike's granddaughter is the mayor's social planner." Pete scooted papers together into a nice pile, his thick hands wrinkling several pieces. "So? We goin'?"

"Yeah. We're going." The sudden rush of adrenaline she felt had nothing to do with the idea of seeing Seth in a social setting. What would the handsome man look like in a suit, anyway? Like a rough James Bond? "By the way, the waitress earlier thought I should leave you to do your job and basically told me to get out of town. Her name tag said *Mandy*. I guess you have a fan."

Pete shook his head. "No kidding? You'd be talking about Mandy Fulsome, who was Ruby Redbird's second cousin."

Mia stilled. "Interesting that neither Mandy nor Seth mentioned that at lunch. In fact, when I asked Mandy if she knew Ruby, she said, 'not really.' The girl lied to me." More importantly, Seth hadn't corrected the girl. Why would he have let that lie stand? It was easy enough to find out the truth. "It's odd she lied, right?"

Pete shrugged. "Not really, considering you're an outsider here. So am I, but apparently, Mandy is thinking I can solve a crime—which is an improvement for me, at least. If you want, I could bring her in for questioning about why she lied to you. Maybe she knows something about Ruby's murder. Or at least about Ruby's life before she died."

"No. She won't break. She's more loyal to this town or the Volks than she would be to you or me, and bringing her in formally would only make her angry or scared or both." Mia bit her lip and glanced at her watch. "Tomorrow, I want to head over to that bar where Ruby was last seen and check things out. For now, I need to get going. Maybe I'll try to track Mandy down first to talk to her in an informal setting. Where do the teenagers hang out in this town, anyway?"

"Same diner. They can't go to the bar, so they hang out in the back room there. There are some dartboards and an air hockey table." Pete stood and shifted his belly over his belt. "Want me to go with you?"

"No. I'll approach her woman-to-woman." Then Mia needed to get home to her mom. Darkness still scared the older woman. Standing, Mia glanced again at the photo of Ruby staked to the ground. "The handcuffs have significance."

"Probably." Pete reached into his back pocket and tossed a pair to her. "You're on the payroll as a deputy—you'll need cuffs. Just in case." Then he opened a drawer and drew out the Glock 21. "You have a holster?"

"Yes."

He handed it over.

"Thanks. I'll let you know how it goes with Mandy." Mia checked the weapon and then slid it into her waistband. Then she headed through the quiet office and outside to the deserted street. Thunder rolled in the distance as the wind scattered dead leaves around her boots. Fall was fading to winter too quickly. She drew her blazer tighter around her body. Sighing, she walked past dark storefronts for three blocks until she reached the diner, its neon blue sign glowing through the sudden murk. A storm was headed their way.

She ignored the cold and walked around the building to the rear exit. Several cars were parked on the dirt, their metal shining under a strong streetlight. A laundromat to the north and a bank to the south also backed up to the makeshift parking area. She glanced at the ATM and the bank building. Had Pete requested surveillance tapes? It was something to check out the next day.

For now, she stalked back to the front of the building. Warmth smacked against her chilled face as she yanked open the door and headed inside. Other than a couple of weathered men in flannels sitting in a booth, the front of the diner was empty. She nodded at the patrons and maneuvered past the counter to the back room. Four booths lined the far wall, all full of teenagers drinking soda or what looked like strawberry milkshakes. A couple of boys dressed in all black threw darts over to the left, while on the other side, two cheerleaders in full outfits smacked the puck across an air hockey table with speed and grace.

All eyes turned toward Mia.

She settled her stance, zeroing in on Mandy. "Hello, Mandy."

The teenager sat in a booth next to a boy with a pierced nose and had been giggling before Mia appeared. Now she paled and lost the smile. Whispering to the kid, she scooted out and headed toward Mia. Grabbing Mia's arm, she tugged her into the main room and dropped into a booth.

Mia sat on the plush seat and smiled. "You want to talk?"

"God, no." Mandy hunched her shoulders, her eyes darting toward the far room and her friends. "You shouldn't be here."

Mia followed the glance to see the boy in the booth talking on a cell phone. Instincts flared, and she focused on the girl. "Yet, I *am* here. Why didn't you tell me you were related to Ruby?"

"Why would I?"

Good point. Mia studied the girl. "I just want to help find who killed your cousin."

Mandy shook her head, sending thick, black hair flying. Tonight she'd donned green mascara and dark red lipstick. "Listen. You're a friend of Seth's, kind of, so people will be nice to you for now. But you really need to go back to wherever you came from. You totally don't belong here."

Mia lowered her chin. "Why not?"

Mandy gave a frustrated huff. "This is a small town where everyone has known each other forever. New people aren't welcome—and we like it that way." Her eyes narrowed, and she suddenly looked ten years older. "I understand how hot Seth is and how much a city girl might think he needs saving or redeeming or whatever you think he needs. He doesn't. Seth is one of us, and we take care of our own. Which you are not. Believe me, you don't have a shot with him. No chance in hell. So, go home."

"I kind of like it here." Mia stretched out. "Everyone is so dang friendly."

Mandy snorted and gave what looked like an unwilling smile. "I know. But things are the way they are, and you don't belong. I'm, ah, sorry." She sighed and shoved the sleeves of her white sweater up her arms. "I'm not tryin' to be mean." Sincerity coated the girl's words.

Mia nodded. "I know."

"So, you're a cop, a real FBI agent, huh?" Mandy picked apart a paper napkin.

"I'm on a break, but I have worked for the FBI." Mia softened her voice.

"That's cool." Mandy shrugged. "I bet you know a lot of neat stuff."

Mia studied the teenager. "What about you? What do you want to do after high school?"

Mandy breathed out, her lip twisting. "Nothing. I mean, I may dream a bit in my diary, but I'll probably get married, maybe keep working in the diner, but I'm not going anywhere." Resignation filled her eyes.

Mia frowned. The entire town was trapped in the dark ages. "Why not? You can get scholarships or financial aid to go anywhere you want. Don't you want to see the world a little bit?"

The sad smile lifted the girl's lips. "That's not how it works here. Believe me." The boy from the booth gestured to her. "I need to get back to my friends."

"Why do you think Ruby was killed, Mandy?"

Mandy sighed. "Ruby was killed because she wanted to be something she could never be."

"What does that mean?"

A motorcycle roared to a stop outside the window, and Mandy straightened her shoulders. She grabbed Mia's hand in a surprisingly strong grip. "You're really nice. Please, believe me…you have to get out of this town while you still can."

The door jangled open, and Mia knew who it was before looking.

Mandy released her and slid from the booth. "Bye."

Before Mia could follow suit, a large body blocked her way. She glanced up. "Hello there, Seth. Fancy seeing you here."

CHAPTER 10

Mia tried to keep her body still as Seth looked down at her, no expression on his chiseled face. She'd expected frustration or even anger, but the lack of expression was more terrifying than either.

"Let's go," he said softly—too softly.

She swallowed. "I'm good right now, but thanks."

His hand wrapped entirely around her upper arm. "You're anything but good right now. Don't make me carry you out." There was no doubt he could, and she knew it.

"You're flirting with another arrest," she said, scooting from the booth. Oh, she was ready to fight him, but she didn't want to do it in front of a bunch of kids. So she allowed him to lead her from the restaurant and into the chilly air, biting her tongue the entire time. She could take him down with a kick to the knee, but creating a scene at this point seemed counter-productive. Yet as they escaped the warmth of the diner and faced each other on the windy sidewalk, she wrenched free. "Who called you?"

He shrugged, shoving both hands into faded jean pockets. "Does it matter?"

"Not really." She tucked her hair behind one ear to keep it

from her eyes. "Watch yourself, Volk. I've been deputized, and you don't want to be charged with assaulting a police officer."

"The laws are different here, Mia."

"Meaning what?"

He stepped into her, bringing warmth and banishing the wind. "I make the laws."

She shoved him hard with both hands and moved him two feet. There was no question he allowed it to happen. His chest was a solid wall of rock against her hands. She lifted her chin and studied him.

Black and fierce, his eyebrows frowned low on a face cut hard and sharp. The worn leather jacket over a white T-shirt covered broad shoulders that tapered to a narrow waist. Standing with legs apart in front of a gleaming Harley, he was every girl's version of a bad boy.

Except there was nothing boyish about him.

The night was dark…the man darker.

She allowed the scene to wash over her, allowed herself to take one moment and appreciate his primal beauty. "You're a killer."

"Without question."

"I read your military file."

His expression didn't change. "I seriously doubt that."

Good point. Most of the file had been redacted, hadn't it? "You're a lost soul, Volk."

His low chuckle lacked amusement. "Look who's talking."

The wind whipped into her face, making her blink several times. "Meaning what?"

A soft exhale accompanied his eyelids dropping to half-mast. Slowly, he reached out and ran one finger down her face. The pad was calloused and the touch gentle. "I have a feeling you were a lost little girl long before the problems in DC, weren't you?"

Fire ripped through her gut, and she knocked his hand away. Rage heated the air in her lungs. "Fuck you."

Any civility stripped from his face. Grabbing her arms, he

hauled her up until they stood nose to nose. "That's an offer I'll accept." Then his mouth took hers.

Heat and need spiraled down her so quickly her knees went weak. Hard and relentless, his mouth claimed. No gentleness, no persuasion, he just took. Angry and demanding, the kiss tasted of lust. Of desire.

Her mind blanked for two seconds.

Then she took him down.

Nailing him in the balls, she hooked her other leg around his knee. They crashed onto the dusty sidewalk. She landed on his hard chest, the breath whooshing from her lungs. Scrambling for the handcuffs in her back pocket, she whipped them out.

With a growl, he smacked her hand, and the cuffs spun into the road. Then he flipped her over with a sudden, brutal strength, pinning her. A heartbeat later, he captured both her wrists in one hand, extending her arms above her head.

She struggled against the cold concrete, trying to maneuver her heels under his hips to flip him.

He pressed down harder—groin to groin.

Every hard line of his body was pressed against her, and wicked heat settled low in her abdomen. "You're under arrest, asshole," she ground out.

He levered up, nostrils flaring. "I don't think so."

"Assault and battery," she gasped.

"That kiss was neither." He spoke slowly, his grip loosening just enough to ease the bite. "When you kick a guy in the balls, expect to be taken down. The charges will never stick, and you know it."

Well. When he put it like that. Apparently, the military had taught Volk decent moves. "Let me up."

His eyebrows rose. "I like you here."

For goodness sakes. They were on a public sidewalk outside a diner full of kids. While the street was quiet except for the whipping wind, somebody would be coming out soon. "Now."

He gracefully stretched to his feet, pulling her with him until they stood. Stepping back, he released her wrists. "Stay away from Mandy, stay away from my family, and the next time you try to cuff me, you'll be wearing silver." His voice lowered along with his chin. "I'd like to see you restrained, sweetheart."

Her heart beat hard enough to hurt. "Like Ruby?"

Temper flared hot and bright in his eyes. "You like to push, don't you?"

"Yes." This time, *she* closed the distance between them. "And I won't stop until I know what happened to that poor woman."

"Don't make me stop you, Mia." His unexpected plea was as surprising as the quick flash of vulnerability crossing his expression.

"Were the cuffs yours, Seth?" She reached out to finger the zipper on his jacket. Two could play at his game.

"No. But if you want cuffs, I'll get some." He captured her hand. "Don't touch unless you mean it, darlin'."

She ignored the sudden warm comfort of his hand cradling hers. "Where would you get silver handcuffs? At the mine?"

"Yes." He lifted an eyebrow. "You want a tour?"

"Yes."

"Now?"

She freed her hand and stuck it into her blazer pocket. "No. In the daytime."

"Tomorrow, then."

"Friday." She pivoted and dodged into the street for her cuffs. Plunking them into her back pocket, she headed toward her car at the sheriff's station. "I'm busy tomorrow."

"Doing what?" Seth called after her.

With a shrug, she kept walking. Her back heated from what had to be his gaze.

But she didn't turn around.

* * *

Mia drove home, her mind spinning from the confrontation with Seth. So he liked to cuff women, huh? Or was he just messing with her? His easy strength in defending himself had shot wild butterflies into her abdomen, and she so didn't want to be impressed by him. But she was. Once again, she'd ended up aroused after a tousle with him.

Maybe she was losing her mind. After the year she'd just had, it was entirely possible.

She parked and eased into the cabin, stopping short at seeing the women watching a black and white movie on the couch. The scent of popcorn hung comfortably in the air. "What are you two doing still up?"

Dotty snorted and decreased the volume. "What is she, our mother?"

Gena chuckled. "She's not drunk enough to be our mother."

Mia paused in dropping her blazer onto a chair. Had her mom just made a joke? Her mind reeling, she tossed the cuffs onto the end table and sat, reaching for a handful of popcorn as casually as she could. "What's playing?"

Gena nodded toward the screen. "Clark Gable. Doesn't matter what movie." She grinned.

A knot she hadn't consciously recognized began to unravel in Mia's gut. Her mother was on the mend and looked both at peace and calm. "So true."

Dotty shoved the popcorn bowl onto Mia's lap. "How's the case going?"

"Not good." Mia blew out air, unwilling to tell them about Seth or her visceral reaction to the man. "In the morning, I'm going through old boxes in the sheriff's basement, and then tomorrow night, I'm attending the mayor's ball in Seattle."

Four eyes widened, and two mouths dropped open as the older women gave her their full attention.

"The ball?" Gena whispered.

Mia shifted in her seat. "Um, yeah. It's actually for the case…

but I'm going." Why did they look so excited? She was attending because of a case and it would be a work night.

Gena clapped her hands together. "How fun. What are you going to wear?"

"Well, ah." Mia cleared her throat. "I was thinking my black pantsuit. You know, the pin-striped one?"

Dotty gasped in horror. "No. You can't wear a pantsuit to a ball. You just can't."

Mia pushed the bowl onto the table and tried to ignore the silky, florescent lime dress covering Dotty's body. "I'm going to the ball for work." Plus, the pantsuit was the nicest thing she owned. She didn't have time to buy a dress and wouldn't know what to get anyway. She'd never been good at that kind of thing.

"No." Gena stood and hustled from the room, heading back to her room. Minutes later, she returned holding a long, black bag. "I have the perfect thing."

Dread skittered down Mia's spine. "I don't think so."

Gena nodded. "Remember Giuseppe Linette? I dated him for a year or so in the nineties. He designed clothing." She slowly unzipped the bag.

Mia shook her head. "I don't remember him, and I'm not wearing a dress from the nineties." Sure, her pantsuit was old, but at least it fit. Plus, her pants were wide enough to hide her ankle gun, and she could run quickly in them if necessary. It was the perfect outfit for a ball.

Gena drew out an evening gown, carefully tugging the shiny material free from the bag.

Dotty sighed, standing and fingering the sleek material. "Oh, my goodness. It's gorgeous."

Mia swallowed. The dress truly was stunning. Orange and red commingled in a pattern that looked like dancing fire. Glittering copper stones lined the top of a sophisticated corset that narrowed to a small waist banded by more sparkles. The dress danced to the floor with a slit high up on one side. "I can't wear that," she breathed.

"Sure, you can." Gena shoved the dress toward her. "Go try it on."

Mia gingerly reached out to take the hanger, her eyes wide. "My purpose is to stand in the background and watch. This dress won't stay in the background."

Gena lifted her chin. "You're not meant for the background, sweetie. It's time to stop hiding...time to live. *In this dress.*"

Mia shook her head, even as she headed up to her bedroom. "I don't want to stand out."

"Every woman wants to stand out," Dotty muttered.

Panic had Mia's knees weakening as she walked into the room. The excitement in her mom's eyes wouldn't be denied. No way could Mia quash that sudden will to live. Maybe the dress wouldn't fit. She dropped her clothes and stepped into the cool material. The side zipper easily slid home.

She pivoted in front of the antique, oval mirror, her feet moving silently on the quilted rug.

The dress fit perfectly, almost as if it had been hand-sewn just for her body—from the way the corset pushed up her breasts to the slit that arrived high on her thigh. If she were somebody else, she'd love it.

Twin gasps echoed from the doorway.

Turning slowly, Mia prepared herself for the delight in Gena's eyes as well as the anticipation in Dotty's.

Gena twirled a pair of copper high-heeled sandals. "You'll wear your hair down."

"And smoky eyes with muted lipstick." Dotty nodded solemnly.

"I can't wear this dress," Mia whispered.

"You are going to wear that dress." Gena slammed both hands on her too-thin hips. "We've all been half-living, and that's over.

You're going to a ball, you're wearing that dress, and you're going to *enjoy* standing out."

Dotty scratched her chin. "If you're going for work, you want to make an impact. Shake somebody up, right?"

Mia narrowed her eyes. "Maybe."

"Excellent. It's settled, then." Gena glanced at Dotty. "You know she doesn't have the right makeup. We'll have to pool ours together for the maximum effect."

Dotty nodded and followed her down the hall.

Mia turned back toward the mirror and sighed. So much for her pantsuit. Where in the world could she fit her gun?

CHAPTER 11

*H*er morning latte hadn't contained enough caffeine. The basement of the sheriff's office smelled like dusty, decomposing raccoons. Mia found several of the dead creatures in a corner of the rectangular room, which had made identifying the stink easier.

Pete had shucked them up the stairs and outside. "Poor critters must've found a way in last winter and thought they'd warm up. Probably died of starvation."

Mia fought a shiver. As always, death had a smell. Shaking off unease, she surveyed the one long room that ran the length of the entire building. Brick made up the walls, while concrete covered the floor. Boxes were stacked along the east wall, papers protruding.

Opening the first box, she fought a sneeze as dust wafted up. "Handcuffs." Tons of the silver handcuffs emblazoned with the Volk Mining logo filled the box.

Sighing, she reached for the next one. Case files were arranged in alphabetical order by year, all beginning years and years ago. She smiled. "I found the backups."

Pete hitched his belt over his big belly while dropping to the floor. "Let's get to work, then."

Hours passed as they attacked box after box, working backward by date. Mia sighed and stretched her neck. "By the way, have you requested any surveillance tapes from the bank near the tavern where Ruby was last seen?"

Pete shook his head. "The bank doesn't have cameras."

Mia set a dusty notebook down and frowned. "Really? That's weird."

"Yes, it is. In fact, there are no surveillance cameras in town." Pete sneezed twice.

Mia's mind clicked facts into place. "But there's an ATM on the back wall."

"So?"

"They have cameras built in. Even if this bank branch doesn't use surveillance, I bet the cash machine records somewhere." She wiped more dust off her chin.

Pete straightened. "I hadn't thought of that." A smile spread across his face. "I'll call the bank headquarters in Seattle on Monday. See? I'm glad you're here."

Yeah? Well, she wasn't. The dusty file folders made her eyes water. Sniffing, she turned and opened another box of records. Finally, her breath caught as she found files dealing with cases about fifteen years old. She pulled one out, making dust fly. "Ashlynn Volk."

"Seth and Erik's mother." Pete turned away and sneezed.

Mia's heart rate picked up. Slowly opening the file, she blew dust away. "Do you know how she died?"

"No."

Squinting to decipher the scrawled handwriting, Mia read out loud. "Definite homicide, most likely suspect..." The breath chilled in her chest. "Seth Volk."

Turning the page, her gut dropped at the faded photograph of the crime scene. The picture showed a woman spread-eagle on hard rock, handcuffed to spikes with drill steel stuck in her throat. Her black hair cascaded around her head, and there was no mistaking the deep blue eyes. The myriad of colors were exactly like Seth's.

Pete reached for the accompanying case folder and read through several sheets of paper. "Seth was cleared."

"Why would he have been a suspect in his own mother's death?" Mia whispered.

Pete scratched his chin. "According to the police report, Seth was the one who found her and called it in. He was with a friend named Tyler Bankston, and they were out in the woods after several hours of partying."

"So?" Mia asked.

Pete kept reading. "Seth was a troubled teen. Lots of drinking, some vandalism, plenty of fights. He had a public argument with his mother the day before when she tried to get him to leave a party. He refused. Reading this, I think the sheriff just didn't like the kid."

"But he was cleared for the night of the murder?" Mia asked.

"Yes." Pete grimaced. "Melissa Redbird came forward and gave him an alibi for the time of death, which happened several hours before Seth and Tyler found Seth's mother."

Mia's eyebrows shot up. "Melissa Redbird? What's the relation to Ruby?"

"Her mother. Ruby would've been about five years old at the time, and apparently Melissa was a single mom. She was a teacher at the school who lost her job after giving Seth the alibi, considering she had a relationship with him."

Mia blinked. "A relationship with Seth? As in sexual?"

Pete kept reading. "Yeah. Very much so. At that time, he was seventeen, which was the legal age of consent."

"Even so, a teacher sleeping with a student had to be illegal, right?" If not, it should be. "So Seth had a relationship with Melissa Redbird and must've known Ruby as a young child. Now,

Ruby ends up dead, the same as Seth's mother." Mia's stomach rolled over. "What happened to Melissa after the school fired her?"

Pete shook his head. "She found a new job quickly."

"Don't tell me, she found a job at the Volk mine." There were circles around circles in this case.

Pete nodded soberly. "Yep. She gave Seth the alibi, he was cleared, and then she started working as a secretary at the mine for at least double, if not triple her teaching salary."

Now that didn't sound suspicious. Mia rubbed dust off her hands. "Small towns, man."

"No kidding." Pete flipped over pages and read some more. He stiffened. "About a week after the alibi, two more women were murdered—same way."

Mia jolted. "Two additional women were shackled with silver to the ground and staked through the throat? Seriously?" Why was this such a secret?

"Yeah," Pete said. "I haven't heard a hint of this in town, even after Ruby was found. Why wouldn't somebody at least draw the connections between the murders thirteen years ago? It wasn't that long ago."

"It's like nobody wants this case to be solved," Mia muttered. "Why? Who would the entire town protect?"

"The Volks," Pete said grimly. "They own the mine, so they own the town. Erik was too young to have killed the three women thirteen years ago, but Benjamin and Seth could've done it."

Mia nodded. "If Benjamin had killed his wife more than a decade ago, why would he have killed two more women after that?" She turned her head and sneezed again. Darn dust. "More recently, what if he'd found out about Ruby's baby? What if he didn't want Erik to have a child with Ruby Redbird."

Pete dug into his pocket and handed over a small plastic bag of tissues. "Benjamin Volk is an ass, and I have no doubt he could kill a woman. We need more than our dislike to bring him in for questioning."

Wasn't that the truth? Mia took a tissue and wiped her eyes. It was way too dusty in the basement. "For now, tell me about the other two dead women found thirteen years ago."

Pete shook his head. "According to a quick notation from the sheriff in Seth's file, both women had rap sheets for prostitution and drugs from Seattle. There's no record of how or why they ended up in Lost Lake, and no next of kin was ever found."

"I wonder if the authorities even looked?" Mia frowned. None of this made sense. "The cases just went cold?"

"No." Pete kept reading. "A man named Eddy Johnson was arrested and sent away for all three murders." He scratched his chin. "I was in DC at the time but still coming out here for summer fishing, and not once did I hear about any of this. That's weird, right?"

"Very weird. You'd think the Seattle newspapers would've covered the murders, at the very least."

"Not if the murders weren't reported beyond this little town." Pete read more. "Not even the trial made the Seattle news. While Eddy Johnson was arrested, and there was a local trial, he was found incompetent and sent to a psychiatric hospital. There's no mention of any of this in the local newspaper records. I already looked back just to make sure, right after Ruby Redbird's body was found."

Mia glanced over at the old records. "Why was Eddy arrested?"

"He was seen in town bothering Ashlynn Volk and was also found to be nuttier than a fruitcake. Though he proclaimed his innocence to the very end. He was convicted and sent to the Lost Asylum."

"Which is?" she asked.

"A loony bin on the far side of the county," Pete muttered.

Mia sighed. "Is it just me, or does all of this seem too nicely wrapped up?"

"Very nicely," Pete muttered. "No publicity, no real defense, no true answers. We wouldn't even know any of this if you hadn't suggested looking through old files."

Mia shifted her weight on the hard floor. "I find it odd that Seth and his family failed to mention that Ashlynn Volk died the same way as Ruby Redbird. What are they all hiding?" And why did it hurt her that Seth was hiding something this big? He was wild, and it would be painful to put him in a cell, but if he killed Ruby Redbird, then he'd go to prison. "I don't see Seth having killed his own mother."

"Why not?" Pete asked.

She twirled a file folder on the dusty floor with one finger. "I don't know. I've made him angry several times, and while he's bossy and evasive, he hasn't lost his temper once."

Pete watched the spinning folder. "These kills are planned out and meticulous, if bloody. Don't you think?"

"Yeah," she whispered. "You're right. No temper involved in any of the four killings." She swallowed over her suddenly dry throat. "Even so, I don't see that in Seth. Oh, he's a planner, and I have no doubt he could get his hands bloody. But to harm women like this? I just don't see it."

Pete lifted his gaze to zero in on her. "You like the guy?"

"No." Yes. Maybe. "I just don't read him like a man who'd kill women." Though there was no doubt he'd killed before, and she wasn't entirely sure his activities had been limited to the military.

"The sheriff thought he was strong enough to have done all three killings thirteen years ago, and the kid did have a problem with both his mother and authority," Pete said. "You need to keep an open mind here."

"I'm aware of that," she said, closing the file folder. "We need to visit Eddy at the asylum." She leaned over. "Where's the case file for his charging and trial?"

"There isn't one here," Pete said. "I only know about him from the notation in Seth's file once it was closed. We need to get the court file from the courthouse tomorrow. I'll take care of it."

That was at least a decent place to start. Mia took out her phone and sent off a quick text. "I'll have one of my few remaining friends in the DC FBI office do a deep dive and see if there are any similar crimes in the US going back the last twenty years." She frowned and typed again. "Make that forty years. If Benjamin is a decent suspect, we should go back that far."

Pete sighed. "I can't believe we don't have Ruby's body. We need to find out if Ashlynn Volk and the other two women were buried here. Maybe we could exhume them and have a decent crime lab look for evidence."

"That's a good idea."

Pete studied her. "Do you really think there's a second serial killer associated with that Delaney?"

"I don't know, and there's nothing I can do about it until something happens. We went through all the records, and any hint of evidence we could find, and there truly was nothing but my gut instincts." Right now, she had a current case to worry about. She rubbed dust off her chin. "I'd like to talk to Melissa Redbird. Where is she now?"

"She died of cancer three years ago. Ruby didn't have any other family." Pete closed the file. "This is quite the coincidence, the way Ashlynn Volk, the other two women, and now Ruby Redbird died."

"There's no such thing." The answers Mia needed were lost with four murdered women, the town, and the Volk men. She had to get Seth to talk.

For now, she had to hurry home and get ready for the ball.

CHAPTER 12

Mia took a deep breath, her arm through the sheriff's as they entered the opulent ballroom. A row of blazing chandeliers hung from the ornate ceiling in an intricate pattern. Tables covered in white and black linen were scattered throughout, with some people sitting, while many people stood at higher tables or meandered, working the room. A dance floor spread out before a raised dais holding a full orchestra.

Pete tugged on his striped tie. "You look freakin' amazing, Mia."

"Thanks." She tried not to grin at her old friend in the black suit. He'd slicked back his hair and had even shaved. "You look very dashing."

"Thanks. It's hard to believe we don't get chow with the cost of these tickets." He escorted her into the crowd.

She nodded. "Classy parties like this have little munchies instead."

"That's dumb."

Yeah, it was. Diamonds and jewels sparkled throughout the room on women wearing sophisticated black sheaths. There were some blues and an occasional muted green. Nobody wore orange—except her. She straightened her shoulders. "Let's find the Volk men."

"Nah. Let's get a drink." Pete escorted her toward a long bar against the far wall.

"Pete Maxwell, you sexy man." A sixty-something woman in a black dress and shiny shawl leaned in to kiss Pete's cheek. "I was hoping you'd be here."

Pete turned a nice shade of red. "Uh, hi, Judith. Um, this is my friend, Mia."

Mia held out a hand. "I'm a work colleague of Pete's." No sense ruining things for the guy if he had a chance at romance.

"It's so nice to meet you." Feisty, dark eyes took her measure. "You're a cop?"

"Yes." For now, anyway. "And you?"

"Ah, dearie, I'm divorced. Several times now." Good humor lifted Judith's bright red lips. Her pale skin was smooth, her age impossible to tell. Score one for Botox. "I believe I've made a career out of it." She eyed Pete and licked her lips.

Pete handed both Mia and Judith a glass of champagne, ordering brandy for himself.

Mia glanced around and stopped her glass almost to her lips as people parted and Seth came into view.

He was in profile, talking to several men. Untamed and raw, he stood in an Armani tuxedo that failed to camouflage the power beneath the smooth lines. The change from the relaxed country man in faded jeans to the animal in sleek black set something alight in her abdomen. He was James Bond to the nth power.

Judith cackled out a laugh. "Oh, sweetheart, good luck. Many a woman has tried to wrestle that man to the ground."

Mia couldn't help the slight smile that tickled her lips. She'd done exactly that the night before. "I'm sure. Is he seeing anyone?" She asked for the case, of course.

Judith shook her coiffed head. "No. At least, I don't think so.

He dated the mayor's niece for a little while—talk about a barracuda, that one. These days, Seth stays pretty close to his power base at home. Though there were rumors about him and some gal from his town, but I never heard a name." She patted Mia's free hand, diamond rings flashing. "Don't get your hopes up. Rumor has it he's one cold bastard."

"So I've heard." A pang caught in Mia's chest. She couldn't be jealous, could she? Man, she was so screwed up. "Did he come to the party with the mayor's niece?"

Judith leaned in, the delight of gossip flashing across her face. "No. Get this—his brother came with Shelly."

Mia frowned. "Erik brought Seth's ex-girlfriend to the ball?"

Judith nodded vigorously. "Rumor has it those boys like to share women. I don't know if it's true or not, though, and I just hate to gossip."

Why did people who loved to gossip always deny it? More importantly, if the brothers liked to share women, had the Volk men both been seeing Ruby Redbird?

A woman on stage began crooning *Someone to Watch Over Me*, and Mia fought a sigh. She loved classic movies that played the song.

Seth stiffened, slowly turning his head like a predator catching a scent. Blue eyes captured hers, and everybody else disappeared. Seth said something to the man next to him and pivoted, heading her way. People moved from his path like the instinctual animals they all were.

"Oh, my," Judith breathed next to her.

Reaching Mia, Seth took her glass and placed it on the bar. The scent of sage surrounded her. "Dance with me." Without waiting for an answer, he captured her hand.

Stunned, she followed him through the crowd to the dance floor, walking carefully in the high heels but keeping up with him. This was a mistake. She knew it and suddenly didn't care. Once there, he turned and slid one hand to the small of her back, tucking her close. "You look beyond beautiful," he breathed against her hair.

She tried to swallow, her mind reeling. Even in the heels, her head barely reached his chin. So she placed her cheek against his chest as the music surrounded them. "This is a temporary peaceful moment, Seth."

"Life is about moments, green eyes." His palm spread across her lower back, burning through the dress. "I hadn't realized how small you are."

"Don't mistake small for weak." Heat and the scent of man had her body relaxing into following his steps. She closed her eyes. "You're a good dancer."

"Only with the right partner. We fit."

She wanted to argue, but they moved together like they'd been doing it for a lifetime. "I have questions for you."

His grip tightened on her hand. "Not now. Not here."

The beauty of the song wound down her spine. Muscles shifted beneath her cheek, and heat flared in her abdomen that slid beyond desire to need. She breathed deeply. "We'll talk after we dance."

"Then we'd better make it good." His cheek rubbed against her temple, the scrape of a five o'clock shadow reminding her of his maleness. "Why are you here?"

"I was invited," she said dreamily, allowing herself this brief moment of bliss.

"Hmmm." His voice dropped to a huskiness she felt along her skin. "Are you a regular at political balls?"

Humor had her slightly shaking her head. "Ah, no. This is my first ball."

He whipped her around as the music sped up and then slowed them in perfect time to the beat. "No fancy parties growing up?"

"No. There wasn't a lot of stability growing up. My mother had, er, problems, and I spent some time in foster care. Well, until my aunt came to live with us." Mia shook off the unease about the past.

"I see. Don't worry, I'm not going to ask you about the early murder charge. Tonight, anyway." Somehow, he pulled her closer into warmth and shelter. A safety of sorts. "How old were you when your aunt arrived?"

"Fourteen."

He exhaled, his breath stirring her hair. "Who protects you, Mia?"

The old-fashioned question went right along with the romantic song. His world was so much different than hers. "I protect myself." She gripped his hand tighter, allowing herself the rare luxury of enjoying somebody else's strength. A man's strength. "What's your purpose here tonight, anyway?"

He stiffened just a tiny bit. "I believe my father is arranging a merger of sorts. Or, at least he thinks he is."

"Really? Interesting. Business?"

"Business and family, I believe." Seth spoke next to her temple, his breath heating her skin. "You really are stunning tonight, Mia Stone."

They quieted, moving in tune in perfect time. Seth was right. Life was about moments, and right or wrong, she was enjoying this one.

The melody slowly ended with the singer's mournful plea for someone to watch over her.

Mia lifted her head.

Instantly, the woman's amazing voice began to croon *I'll Be Seeing You*, and Mia stilled. She loved old war movies and had spent hours dreaming to the music.

Seth drew her close again, his lips brushing her forehead. "Just one more song."

Unable to resist, Mia relaxed again into his strength.

* * *

Seth drew Mia closer, inhaling her fresh scents of lilac and vanilla. When he'd turned and spotted her in the crowd, he'd almost swallowed his tongue. She was a wild flame in a sea of black—vibrant and alive. There was no doubt she would burn him. No doubt at all.

Right at the moment, he couldn't find it in himself to care.

Her fragility confused him. For some reason, she'd seemed bigger—even stronger. Her personality created an illusion. The bones beneath his touch were fine and delicate, and he could easily span her waist with his hands. He shouldn't have wrestled on the chilled ground with her. "Did I hurt you last night?"

"Of course not," she murmured against his chest, her voice soft and dreamy. "Did I hurt you?"

"No." The idea was unthinkable that she could hurt him. How was he going to protect her? The woman had no clue. If he had half a soul, he'd drop her hand and walk away right now.

Too bad he didn't have a soul.

Instead, he pulled her even closer, not caring that she'd be up against his erection. She stiffened and then softened against him again. Yeah. It was going to happen. He'd face hell afterward, but it would happen. *They* would happen. He'd protect her with everything he had. Nothing would harm the delicate woman now in his arms. He wouldn't let it. "I'm sorry your childhood was difficult."

"Wasn't yours?" Her smooth shoulders shrugged, beckoning his mouth.

He grimaced to keep his lips where they belonged and not on that delicate skin. "Yes. My mother married Ben when I was six and then died when I was seventeen. I miss her still."

"I'm sorry."

Guilt had him nearly coughing, but he wouldn't let her go right now. Even if that was the best move for his family. "Ben has protected me my entire life. I owe him."

Mia patted his back, sending comfort far deeper than she'd probably intended. "I'm sure you've been a good son."

Now that was debatable. Seth looked down at the pliant woman in his arms. Her willingness to follow his lead sent lust straight through his entire body. What would she be like in bed, all spread out for his pleasure? What would life be like if he had her trust? "This just became my favorite song."

"The music is beautiful, isn't it?" She tilted her head to meet his eyes. "Have you ever wondered if you were born in the wrong time?"

He frowned, captured by the myriad of greens and golds in her spectacular eyes. The music from another time wound around them, creating a cocoon of intimacy. One full of peace and worlds away from the bloody life he'd lived. "No. You?"

"Maybe. The song feels right...like I should've lived years ago instead of now." Her expression was unguarded for the first time, and pure sweetness lit her smile.

That easily, that quickly, she ripped out his heart.

The emotional pain had him almost gasping. When she closed her eyes and rested against him again, he closed his. Her hair tickled his chin while her scent filled him. Reeling, he struggled to make sense of the world. Even confused, his body continued to move with hers naturally, and his senses clocked every possible threat to her from any direction. Nobody could get past him to her. He didn't belong at the civilized ball, but for now, he felt like he belonged on the dance floor.

With Mia Stone.

Then a prickle flared on the nape of his neck. The world rushed back, and his mind cleared. Turning them, he surveyed the far wall. Benjamin watched Mia, heat and anger in his dark eyes. Seth raised his head just enough to make his intentions clear, staring at the older man without blinking. The line had just been drawn with a flame-colored marker as bright as her sparkling dress.

Ben shook his head, threat flaring his nostrils.

Seth slid his hand up Mia's back, his palm flattening until his fingers spread far enough to reach her shoulder blades. He might as well have yelled the word *mine*.

His father snarled and turned away.

Slowly, Seth turned his head to the other side of the dance floor, where his brother danced with Shelly, shrewd eyes watching the interaction. Seth raised an eyebrow. Erik stared back with no expression.

That wasn't good.

Mia sighed against Seth's chest, and he turned them again to enjoy the moment.

They probably wouldn't have many.

CHAPTER 13

Mia crossed her legs under the table, fully aware of the amount of skin her dress showed. So was Seth, if the flare of interest in his eyes was any indication. The glitter there was all lust, and her body reacted with a slow shudder she couldn't mask.

After dancing, they'd meandered outside to the covered patio after grabbing a bottle of champagne and two glasses. Lights glimmered off boats in the Washington Sound, while torch heaters scattered strategically throughout the patio kept it somewhat warm. The band was in full swing, so few people had headed into the quiet of the outside.

Seth poured two glasses of champagne. "Is there any chance I can keep you from asking about your case tonight?"

Mia reached for her flute. "No."

He sat back. "Why not?"

For some odd reason, she felt compelled to give him the truth. "Because right now, I want nothing more than to clear you."

"I didn't kill Ruby."

"How many people know about the earlier killings with the

same MO?" As she cut hard with the question, she couldn't help the sympathetic grimace.

To his credit, Seth didn't bat an eyelash. "What killings?"

She huffed out a breath. "Don't play dumb."

He took a drink of the champagne, the muscles in his neck moving. "We live in a very small county and an even smaller town. Everybody over the age of twenty knows about the earlier killings...as well as the fact that the murderer was caught and put away."

"Yet nobody told me about the similarities," she murmured.

He shrugged. "Like I said, we handle problems internally." Reaching out, he brushed a wayward curl off her cheek, the pads of his fingers rough but his movements gentle. "While I'd like to change the fact, you're still an outsider in my town, darlin'."

The warmth from his touch spiraled down to her abdomen. "How exactly would you change that?" Good God. She was going beyond flirting to challenging the man. While she may not know him well, there was no doubt he'd accept a challenge. He was that type of guy.

Downing the rest of his glass, he poured another. "Not in any way you'd like, sweetheart."

Her hand tightened around the flute. "This whole situation with Ruby's death and how she died has to be difficult for you."

"My mother's murderer was caught." Seth flattened his free hand on the white tablecloth. "Whoever killed Ruby is just a copycat."

"Unless Eddy Johnson wasn't really the killer." Mia took a sip of the expensive bubbly, allowing it to cool her throat. "He never stopped proclaiming his innocence."

"He was guilty and crazy as hell," Seth said flatly.

"Okay. Well, then, why do you think Ruby was killed in the same manner?"

Seth shrugged. "I assume the killer wants the police off track with the questions about the old case. Whoever killed Ruby wanted Ruby dead. We don't have another serial killer running loose—no matter how much you need to catch one to get your job back."

"That's a low blow," she said.

"I'm sorry." He didn't look sorry. He looked irritated and suddenly very uncomfortable in the expensive tux. Like a panther forced to wear a collar when he was too wild to tame.

Mia set down her glass. "Was Erik the father of Ruby's baby?"

A rustle sounded from behind her. "Why don't you ask me that extremely rude question?"

Erik Volk looked almost as dashing as Seth in a black tuxedo. He stepped closer to the table, his arm around a brunette wearing a tight, black sequined dress.

Mia sat back. "Were you the father?"

"No." Erik nodded at his brother. "Seth, you remember Shelly?"

Seth half-rose from his seat, his face settling into unreadable lines. "Of course. It's nice to see you, Shelly. Mia Stone, please meet Shelly Wentworth."

So this was the ex. Mia couldn't see her with Seth.

Shelly held out a slender hand to Mia. The woman shook it like a fish, and Mia quickly released her hand.

"It's so nice to see you again, Seth," Shelly murmured, her thickly made-up eyelashes fluttering. Diamonds glittered from her ears, neck, wrists, and fingers. Probably enough to pawn and feed all of eastern DC.

Erik drew a chair free from the table. "Mind if we join you?"

"Yes." Seth retook his seat. "We were having a private conversation."

Erik gently nudged Shelly into the seat. "We don't mind." He leaned over and whispered into her ear. "I'll fetch us a couple of drinks." Then he strode away and soon disappeared back into the crowd.

Benjamin stalked through the double doors with a twenty-something blonde on his arm. The woman had white-blond hair and dark eyes. She was tall with a lot of leg and a very narrow waist. In a gold dress with her pale skin, she looked like a goddess.

Benjamin paused next to Seth. "Seth, your date is finally here."

Mia stilled. He had a date?

Seth threw her an apologetic look and rose. "Hi, Emily. It's been a long time. This is Mia, Shelly, and of course, you know Erik."

Emily smiled, flashing perfect teeth. Her pink lips curved in what appeared to be amusement at the entire situation.

Ben patted her hand. "Emily's father would like a word, Seth. Darling, have a seat here with Mia and Shelly. I promise Seth won't be long." Casting Mia an inscrutable look, he settled Emily in Seth's chair.

Mia sent Seth a you're-kidding-me glare. What in the world was he up to dancing with her like that and having a date?

"I'll be right back," he growled and turned to follow his father.

Emily grinned. "Who was that snarled promise meant for, anyway?"

Shelly sighed and tilted her head toward Mia. "Her, I think." She wrinkled her nose as if the thought stank.

Emily reached for the bottle and refilled Seth's glass, taking a long swallow. "I'm not his date, you know."

Mia leaned back in her chair. "No?"

"No." The blonde rolled her eyes. "Our fathers have some crazy idea about merging the mining empires. It's not going to happen. Well, probably." She blew out a breath and frowned. "They can get fairly determined."

Shelly traced a pattern on the tablecloth with one red-tipped nail. "You're Philip Nightsom's daughter, right?"

"That's me," Emily said.

Shelly nodded. "Your mine holdings are almost as vast as the Volk conglomerate. People solidify empires or political allies with marriages all the time. Better get on board now." Slowly, she lifted her gaze to land on Mia. "I don't suppose that's your future, huh?"

"No." Mia returned the woman's stare evenly. She wouldn't let some snob from Seattle make her uncomfortable.

Emily leaned across the table and topped off Mia's glass. "What do you do, Mia?"

"She's a cop." Shelly said the words as if they tasted bad.

"Cool." Emily smoothed down her dress. "What kind of cop?"

"Profiler." Mia studied the woman's expression. She seemed genuinely interested.

"Like of serial killers?" At Mia's nod, Emily smiled. "I'm a writer—romantic suspense. Maybe someday I could pick your brain."

"Anytime." Mia relaxed against the chair. "I don't suppose you know anything about the recent murder in Lost Lake? The death of Ruby Redbird?"

Emily shook her head. "No. Sorry."

Shelly sniffed. "According to Erik, Mia's looking at either Seth or Erik for the murder. How dumb is that?"

Emily shrugged. "Depends on if they did it or not."

Mia's breath picked up. "Do you think either Erik or Seth could've killed somebody?"

"Sure." Emily's eyes darkened. "We live in a dangerous world. I'm sure they could've killed. But a helpless woman in the middle of the forest? I don't think so."

"It sounds like you *do* know a little about the murder," Mia said thoughtfully.

Emily lifted a toned shoulder. "Rumors travel fast. But that's all I heard."

"Have you heard that Ruby's body was stolen from the morgue?" Mia asked.

No expression of surprise crossed Emily's face. "No kidding. Well, that's weird."

Mia took another sip, her instincts humming. "It is weird. Tell me, as an author, why would somebody steal a body from a morgue?"

Emily wrinkled her nose, her gaze on the lights in the distance. "I can't think of any good reason somebody would take a body." As a liar, she wasn't bad. But lying she was.

"I think you do know," Mia said softly.

Amusement lit Emily's dark eyes when she glanced back at Mia. "Prove it." No heat existed in the words, but Emily's chin tilted in challenge.

Mia frowned, studying the gorgeous blonde. She knew something. What was the big secret with these people, anyway? The commonality between Ruby Redbird and Emily was one of mining—they both lived in strong mining communities. Was something wrong with the mines? Could it be an environmental issue that would've been discovered in an autopsy?

"I'm heading inside." Shelly stood in a flash of sparkles and sauntered back into the ballroom.

"I like it out here," Emily breathed, tilting her head and inhaling the salt air. "Don't you, Mia?"

Mia shifted in her seat. "Yes." The breeze wafted around them in the darkness, lending a sense of security to the deck.

"What's going on with you and Seth?" Emily asked.

"Nothing." No matter how good she'd felt in his arms.

Emily's lip quirked. "You don't really believe that, do you? I saw you two on the dance floor. Talk about combustible."

Whatever had happened on the dance floor was over now. Mia hid a yawn behind her hand. The hour had to be almost midnight. Maybe she should find the sheriff and head on home.

Raised voices at the end of the deck caught her attention. Two figures stood next to a staircase leading down to the beach.

"You're being a bitch," slurred a large man in a white tuxedo.

"Screw you." A woman in four-inch heels shoved the guy.

The guy instantly grabbed her by the neck, pushing her against the building.

Mia was out of her chair and between them within seconds. Her heels tottered against the uneven deck. "Knock it off."

"Get the fuck out of my way." The guy pushed her to the side.

Irritation flashing through her, she hooked the guy's knee, twisted, and sent him down. A yank of his arm behind his back had him huffing in pain as she leaned over his shoulder. "Now that just wasn't nice, was it?"

Out of nowhere, a fist connected with her jaw.

Stars exploded behind her eyes, but she kept her hold on the guy.

She turned in time to see Emily grab the guy's date and put her in a headlock.

"Sorry. She moved fast," Emily muttered. Holding the struggling woman, Emily looked like an avenging angel in her gold sequined dress.

The captured woman stuttered, her eyes watering. "Leave us alone," she slurred.

"Maybe it's a game these drunk assholes play," Emily said. She shook the woman. "You just assaulted a cop, dumbass."

Mia breathed out. She was a cop out of her jurisdiction, and she may have just interrupted a silly couple's spat. Releasing the guy, she hauled him up and shoved him toward the stairs. "You go that way."

Nodding at Emily to release the woman, Mia said, "You go through the ballroom. If you idiots meet up on the other side, I don't want to hear about it."

The guy muttered expletives as he stomped down the stairs and into the darkness, while his date huffed in irritation and whirled back to the ballroom, her pink high heels scraping on the deck.

Mia stretched her neck, gaze on Emily. Now that was interesting. "Thanks for the assist."

"No problem." Emily dusted off her hands. "You had the tougher takedown."

"I doubt most authors know how to put a drunk in a headlock." Who was this woman?

Emily snorted, pivoting to glide back to their table. "I doubt most authors had a bodyguard growing up who liked to teach various martial arts moves for fun."

What kind of a world had Mia just entered? "Bodyguard?" She retook her seat.

"Yep. Mining can be a dangerous business."

A rustle sounded by the door, and the sheriff hustled onto the deck. "We need to go," he said.

Adrenaline ripped through Mia's veins, and she stood. "Why?"

The circles under Pete's eyes deepened. "We have another body."

CHAPTER 14

The stench of decaying leaves assaulted Mia's nostrils as she stood under the spotlight's glare, her gaze on the dead girl. After dropping by the cabin to change clothes, she and Pete had hurried to the crime scene, which was halfway up the mountain off a hunting trail. Three pale and shocked elk hunters huddled under a rustling Cottonwood. They'd found the body when one of the guys had headed away from camp to take a leak.

Sorrow and rage flared through Mia's skin at the sight of Mandy Fulsome spread-eagle on the damp rock formation, silver handcuffs securing her to embedded posts. Her blue eyes were wide in death, a glimmer of shock still in the horrified depths.

Mia's boots slid in the wet mud as she dropped to her haunches, and she quickly righted herself. "Oh, no."

Fully clothed, the girl had been beaten repeatedly about the neck and chest and had a two-foot-long drill bit embedded in her throat. The killer had also yanked a muddy chain around Mandy's neck.

Mia leaned in for a closer inspection. "We'll need confirmation on death—there's enough blood that I think it was by shoving the drill steel through her neck. But he strangled her first—just not to death. Or he brought her back afterward and then stabbed her."

Pete nodded, scribbling on a spiral notebook. One of his deputies maneuvered the huge spotlight into position, while the other deputy gathered evidence from the scene. Dawn remained several hours away, and clouds covered a full moon that still glowed through. Eerie and ominous. The frowning county coroner stood by a pine tree, waiting for the okay to take the body.

Mia shook her head. "What time did he determine for death?"

"Body temp showed she died around eight tonight," Pete said.

"If the Volk men were in tuxes at the ball by nine, it's highly unlikely one of them had time to kill Mandy, get changed, and drive at least two hours to Seattle," Mia murmured, her shoulders loosening.

"Not unless they flew. And considering the limos I saw, I doubt that. But I'll double-check," Pete said.

Mia studied the body. "No signs of rape, but what is the significance of the silver handcuffs?" They were a symbol of domination...and the mines. Silver had several symbolic meanings, as well. Most well-known were the *thirty pieces of silver* that denoted betrayal. "Who did you betray, sweetheart?" Mia murmured.

Pete rubbed his chin. "You think we're dealing with a serial killer?"

Mia stood and wiped her muddy hands on her jeans. "I don't know. We had a killing, and Mandy was the only person in town willing to talk to the authorities. It may be a serial or just one killer messing with us."

"How will we know?" he asked.

Dread trickled down Mia's spine. "We'll know if there's another homicide."

"Do you think she's dead because she talked to us?" Pete jerked his head to give the coroner permission to take the body.

"Yes." Guilt tasted like acid in Mia's mouth. "She was targeted because of me. I just don't know if she was killed to cover up the first murder or if we have a multiple murderer." Either way, it really didn't matter. "We'll find whoever it is and take them down." Things had just gotten personal.

In the distance, a wolf bayed at the moon, the sound low and mournful.

Mia shivered. The glittering ballroom seemed years away instead of mere hours. "We'll need to find out how the Volk men got to the ball, and I'd like to go through Mandy's room. Teenage girls keep diaries."

The body was too fresh to smell, but death had a presence. The air felt heavy.

Evil had weight.

Pete stepped back as the coroner carefully wrapped Mandy's body in a shiny, black bag. "I'll try. Right now, I need to make the notification."

Mia blinked and took a deep breath. "I'll come with you."

"No. You go home and put some ice on that shiner. I can't believe you got in a brawl while wearing a dress," Pete said, stress lines bracketing his mouth.

Mia shrugged. "The dress had nothing to do with it. I should go with you for the notification."

"No. Right now, you're more of an outsider than I am, kid. I have to do this alone," he said.

Relief swamped Mia. Moments didn't get any more terrible than having to tell parents their child was dead. Even so, she hated being an outsider. What would it be like to belong? This once, it meant she didn't have to do the notification. "I'm sorry, Pete."

* * *

MIA PUSHED OPEN the cabin door and kicked out of her boots. The sensation of being too close to death clung to her clothing, but a shower would wake her mother and aunt. Sighing, she padded through the entryway to the kitchen and made herself a cup of tea.

A breeze filtered through her hair.

She stiffened, turning toward the open sliding glass door.

Pushing the teacup onto the counter, she grabbed her gun from her waistband. Her heartbeat echoed in her ears. With stealth, she maneuvered around the counter and stepped lightly toward the exit.

Her socks caught on the wooden deck as she slipped outside—and stopped cold.

Gena sat in a wicker chair, a massive wolf at her feet.

Oh, God. Mia steadied her aim with the gun. "Mom, hang tight. Don't move," she whispered.

Gena started. "Mia Eloise Stone, you put that gun away right now." Fire flashed in Gena's eyes.

The wolf lifted one eyelid to reveal a shockingly blue eyeball. With a snort, he went back to sleep.

Mia stumbled. "That's a wolf."

"I know. He's my friend." Gena leaned down to scratch the beast between the ears. The wolf rumbled in contentment.

"You're outside." Mia shifted her gaze to her mother.

"Sure." Gena shrugged, her gaze on the stunning wolf. "I can't hide forever."

Okay. Life was throwing Mia curveballs, and her bat had a hole in it. "I need a drink."

Gena snorted. "I've found that alcohol doesn't help in the long run...but it's still worth a try. Get me one, too."

"You can't have one on your medication," Mia said.

"Oh, yeah, I forgot. Hmmm. Well, when I'm finally off the brain drugs, then I'm drinking again." Gena closed her eyes while stroking the thick pelt. "You need to know, I will be off the drugs soon. I'm better, Mia."

Mia had heard those words before. "That's great, Mom.

Though I have to ask, what's up with the deadly beast at your feet?"

"We met the other day, and he needed a companion."

Most likely, Gena needed a companion. "Are you sure he's safe?"

Gena sighed. "Of course, he isn't safe. Nobody and nothing is *safe*, Mia. You have to know that."

Unfortunately, she did. "Okay."

"How was the ball?" her mom asked.

"It was work." At Gena's disappointed frown, Mia sighed. "Though I did dance with probably the sexiest man I've ever met. For two songs."

Gena's face lit up. "Will you see him again?"

"Absolutely." Hopefully, not in a situation where she had to arrest him. "We, uh, found another victim in the woods tonight. Please be careful and don't head out on your own."

"I won't."

The mere thought of her mother being well enough to leave the house and investigate their new surroundings simultaneously filled Mia with relief and dread.

Creepy and somehow nearly human, the wolf flipped open his eyelids to watch her—to study her. Curiosity seemed to illuminate the blue from within.

Mia took a step closer, and the wolf bared his teeth.

She faltered.

With a loud snort, the animal shut his eyes again. What the heck? It was almost as if the wolf was laughing at her.

Gena giggled. "He's funny, isn't he?"

Not really. "What's his name?"

"He hasn't told me." Gena continued rubbing the thick pelt.

Mia ran a shaking hand through her hair. Maybe her mother needed an adjustment on her medication. "Um, does he talk to you?"

Gena rolled her eyes. "Of course, he doesn't talk to me, Mia.

Geez. Do you think I'm that off my rocker?" Her shoulders stiffened, and she looked up. "Oh. Well, I guess I can see how you'd think that. I really am sorry. I mean, given all the problems when you were young."

Mia leaned against the doorframe, her hand remaining steady on the gun in case she needed to shoot the beast. "Mental illness isn't anyone's fault, Mom. I'm just sorry it took so long for the doctors to figure out the best regimen for you."

"Remember that shirt you tie-dyed for me when you were eighteen?" Gena grinned.

"Yes. Schizophrenia sucks—at least that's what the voices say." Mia laughed. "You got such a kick out of it."

Gena shoved the wolf gently, and he stretched to his feet before loping off the deck and into the forest. "I figured if we could laugh about it, then everything would be okay." She stood and smoothed down her pants. "Everything is still going to be all right, Mia El."

"I know, Mom," Mia said softly. "I've always known."

Gena's smile erased Mia's lingering doubts. "Then maybe it's time we both started living again. You know, have some fun."

"Sure." Mia forced an answering smile.

Gena studied her. "By the way, I believe in you. If you say there's another psycho out there after you, then there is one. Trust your instincts, sweetheart."

"I want to be wrong." Mia relaxed her hold on her gun.

"You're not."

Mia shuffled her feet. "But what if—?"

"You do not have schizophrenia, Mia. Stop worrying about that happening to you." Gena shook her head.

"It's hereditary." Mia tried to breathe normally.

"Yeah, maybe in some families. In others, the inflicted person did so many drugs as a teenager, the brain malfunction happens organically." Gena flushed. "I did drugs. I've told you that."

"I know." But, what if? What if the paranoia and fear were

organic—and not real? "Sweet dreams." Mia shuffled across the worn planks and dropped onto a chair. "I want to stare at the lake for a bit."

Gena nodded and plodded back inside. "Night."

"Night," Mia whispered, watching the darkness and trying to relax. The night pressed in with a hint of a chill.

The lake lay quiet and dark, barely lit by the moon's valiant effort to pierce the cloud cover.

Seth moved into the moonlight like an elemental piece of the night. She knew he'd show up. She had no clue how she understood him so well. But as an investigator, she'd learned to trust her instincts. As a woman...well, now. There had been no question the man would show.

He stood under the filtering rays of the moon, his face in shadow, his focus on her. Somewhere between the fancy ball and the evening of death, he'd changed into faded jeans and a worn T-shirt. All predator, he was big, quick, and dangerous...and she wanted nothing more than to take him on right now—to share the wild anger ripping through her.

She dropped her feet to the rough wooden planks. "Mandy's dead."

He stalked forward, purposefully striding over the warped steps before dropping into the matching wicker chair. "I know."

"Who killed her?"

"That, I don't know." Seth scrubbed both hands over his face. "My father offered condolences to her parents an hour ago. Pete was there."

Benjamin Volk knew about the notification awfully quick. "I find that odd," Mia said.

"What?" Seth asked.

"That your father would go visit a grieving family before dawn even broke. I mean, just when the sheriff was making the notification." She leaned toward Seth. "How did you find out so fast?"

His rugged face remained expressionless, as usual. "This is a small town, and I've already told you, my father runs it. He probably knew before you did." A low tenor of sorrow rode Seth's dark tone.

"Did you offer your, ah, condolences, as well?" she asked.

"No. My place is outside in such situations. Ben is the person they need to hear from." Now, Seth's tone turned matter-of-fact.

"Outside flanking the door, huh?" Mia shook her head. She didn't have time for anger…she needed answers. Seth was a damn good source, whether he liked it or not. "I need to go meet the parents later this morning and look through Mandy's room. What can you tell me about them?"

"Nothing."

"That's not true."

"You're right. I can tell you not to go see them later this morning. They don't need to be bothered by the cops. It's not your place, Mia," he said.

Her breath heated. "It *is* my place. I'm investigating the girl's death. I'm going."

"They won't talk to you," he murmured.

"They will if you escort me."

He turned to face her fully, leaving half his face in shadow. A low growl erupted from his chest. Reaching for her, he grasped her chin and tilted her head into the waning moonlight. "What happened to your face?"

His grip was gentle and firm at the same time.

She frowned and then winced as her cheek protested. "I got in the middle of a lovers' spat. No big deal."

"Somebody *hit* you?" His voice quieted to a tone that made her shiver.

She exhaled slowly. "I'm a cop. I get hit."

"Not in my town." His thumb swept gently across the bruise. "Who punched you?"

"Why?" Her smirk made the injury hurt more. "You going to go beat them up for me?"

"Yes."

She lost her amusement and studied him. He didn't move an inch. He was serious. An odd warmth filled her chest. Nobody had ever stood between her and danger before. Even so, she could take care of herself. "I don't need a protector."

"You need a protector more than any woman I've ever met." He sighed. "Now, tell me who marked your face, or I'll find out on my own. Trust me, it'll be better if you just say."

"Oh, for Pete's sake. At the ball, on the deck, a couple was having a spat. I took the guy down, and the woman hit me. I'm fine."

Seth's shoulders straightened. He smoothed a curl away from her face. "I'm sorry I left you alone on the deck. It won't happen again."

She leaned back and relaxed when he released her. "You know I'm a cop, right?"

"You're a woman first, darlin'." He stood and tucked his hands into his pockets. With the moon at his back, his entire face was hidden now. "I'll pick you up at eight this morning to visit the Fulsomes, and then we'll tour the mine I promised to show you."

A chill swept over her once he moved away. "Are you protecting Mandy's parents from me…or me from them?"

"I don't know. Maybe both." He half-turned, making his strong profile visible. "Either way, be ready in a few hours." Smoothly, almost silently, he descended the steps and disappeared into the night.

Far in the distance, a wolf howled a mournful tune to the disappearing moon.

CHAPTER 15

The morning sun appeared as weak as Mia's legs felt. After staring at her ceiling for a couple of hours, she'd finally meandered into the shower. Both Gena and Dotty were still asleep, and the quiet in the cabin's kitchen balmed her frazzled nerves. Hot coffee burned down her throat as she stared out the kitchen window.

A black truck rolled to a stop on the gravel drive. Apparently Seth had multiple vehicles. She'd expected the Jeep. Seth stretched out, his long legs encased in faded jeans over battered cowboy boots.

Wow. She'd always had a thing for men in cowboy boots. Her cell phone buzzed, and she pressed it to her ear, keeping her gaze on the man loping toward the cabin. "Yes?"

"It's Pete. I have news."

She stood up straighter. "Well?"

"A limo driver and three security cameras have Seth and his father arriving at the ball last night at nine in full monkey suits. There's no way one of them could've killed Mandy, changed into their tux, and driven to Seattle in an hour. It's a two-hour drive, even speeding."

Relief that she should probably examine later washed through her. "One of them could've flown, changed into a tux, and had a limo show up at the airport."

"Yes, except the security cam at the old folks' home right outside of town caught them leaving Lost Lake at seven. Windows down, drinking what looked like scotch."

Yeah, that was a pretty good alibi—and a darn good camera. "What about Erik?"

Pete exhaled. "Well, now, that's another story. He wasn't with them."

"Have you talked to him?"

"Not yet. Erik has his pilot's license just like Seth and Ben do, and they have more than one corporate plane."

Seth disappeared around the side of the cabin.

"I'll see what I can find out. I'm headed over to the Fulsome's before taking a tour of the mine," Mia said.

A quiet knock sounded on the door.

Pete cleared his throat. "The Fulsomes are pretty torn up, of course. Though I told them to expect you today. Who's giving you the tour?"

"Seth Volk." Mia hustled to open the door, grabbing her bag on the way.

"Be careful, Mia," Pete muttered. "Just because he didn't kill Mandy doesn't mean he didn't murder Ruby. The Volk men could be working together."

She smiled at Seth. "I'm fully aware of that." Every instinct she possessed told her that Seth wasn't the killer. Erik was another story, however. "Bye, Pete." She ended the call and looked up—way up—into a face Lady Luck had spent some serious time sculpting. "Morning."

"Morning." Deep and low, Seth's quiet response hinted at an intimacy that was a bad idea. "Pete? What did the sheriff want so early in the morning?"

Mia gestured outside. "Pete confirmed your alibi for last night. Apparently, you didn't kill Mandy."

"That's a relief," Seth said dryly. He pulled the door closed behind them and took her elbow as they maneuvered around the cabin. "I like your FBI look."

She stumbled and glanced down. Pressed jeans, white shirt, and navy blazer. Hmm. It was her standard FBI uniform. Some habits died hard. "Uh, thanks." The hand at her elbow held strength and assurance. They reached the truck.

Seth opened the door. "Ralph Fulsome is a big guy, and he's devastated. I'll let you talk to him but stay by me."

No, this wasn't how investigations worked. Mia took a deep breath. "We need to get a couple of things straight."

Seth rested his arm along the top of the door, his dark T-shirt stretching tightly across his broad chest. He cocked his head to the side. "Like what?"

"I have a gun at my waist and one in my ankle holster. I'm an excellent shot."

Puzzlement filtered through his frown. "Okay."

"I'm the cop. You're the civilian. If there's a situation, you get out of the way and let me handle it," she said.

His smile was full of amusement. "I know you're a cop, and I'm glad you can shoot. But, sweetheart, do you really think I'd let you step between me and some pissed-off guy? Ever?"

"Yes." Exasperation drew out the word on a hiss. She settled her stance. They needed to understand each other. "It's my job. Period."

"No." His jaw firmed as his thumb brushed the now-purpling bruise on her cheekbone.

The man didn't understand anything. "Yes." Okay, now they were resorting to playground jargon. "If you can't handle it, I'll go see the Fulsomes by myself."

"They won't see you unless I pave the way." Quick as a whip, Seth grabbed her waist and lifted her into the truck. "You're with me right now, Mia, which means I protect you. Deal with it." The door slammed shut with an irritating echo.

Exasperation had her wanting to lock the doors out of principle. They'd devolved to the Middle Ages in Lost Lake. While oddly sweet, his attitude was totally inappropriate and needed a serious adjustment. Now. If he were anyone else, she'd just take him to the ground and immobilize him. But last time she'd tried to cuff Seth, she'd ended up on her back on a cold sidewalk—darn his military training.

His door opened, and he settled himself in the driver's seat, firing the ignition.

"You need to listen." Mia fastened her seat belt.

He blew out a sigh and drove onto the main lake road. "What do you want from me?"

"I want you to treat me like a cop," she said evenly.

"If I treated you like a cop, I wouldn't be talking to you, dancing with you, or taking you anywhere—especially to the mine." He drove easily on the country road.

His implacable profile tempted her to punch him in the nose. Even so, she could understand why he didn't like cops. "I read the file on the earlier killings, and I get why you don't like the police. But I'm different."

"That's my point."

So much for being reasonable. "Okay, let's try this. If you get in my way, I'll arrest you for impeding an ongoing investigation," she said.

"Okay."

She would have to arrest him—she just knew it. "You're impossible."

He flicked on the heater. "On that note, and considering I'm no longer a suspect, how about we go on that date we've been avoiding?"

"Date?" Heat spiraled down her torso. "What date?"

He glanced her way, the deep intensity of his eyes mesmerizing. "Dinner at a restaurant before I take you home, spread you out on my bed, and feast until my name is the only sound on your lips."

Fire slammed into her abdomen, and her head jerked back. "What is *wrong* with you?"

His shoulder lifted before he concentrated on the winding road once more. "I'm not good with subtlety or games."

"No kidding."

"When we danced, you felt it as much as I did. We may be temporary, and this truce between us short-lived, but I want you. There's something here, and I don't want to always wonder." He rubbed his chin. "I like you, Mia. Not just because you're beautiful and delicate, but because you're also smart and way too gutsy."

She choked, trying not to appreciate that he found her beautiful. "Is that all?"

"No. You're as lost as I am," he said softly.

She stilled. The truth of that quiet statement shot her vulnerability front and center. "You're courting pain—for us both."

"I know." He drove the truck past town to the east. "But life is full of pain. You'd make the hurt worth it."

His matter-of-fact tone made something ache in her solar plexus. She reached out and rubbed her hand down his muscled arm. "Life doesn't have to be full of pain. It really doesn't."

His eyes turned velvet soft. "Prove it."

She dropped her hand. That was the problem, now, wasn't it? She *couldn't* prove it. "I'll think about the date."

"Thank you."

His honesty tempted her much more than she'd like. Sure, he could be trying to manipulate her into protecting his brother, but...he wasn't. She had to believe that he wasn't tricking her.

She settled into the plush leather seat. "Tell me about the Fulsomes."

"Too late." Seth drove quickly down a dirt road to park in front of a small house surrounded by overgrown pine trees. "We're here."

Mia slowly jumped from the truck, her gaze on the quiet home. The white paint had faded, and the front porch was missing a step. A sense of depression hung over the building with an oppressive presence. Maybe that was just her imagination, considering she knew what the occupants must be dealing with. She straightened her shoulders and wound around mud puddles to climb the steps, stretching over the missing one.

Seth beat her to the door and knocked quietly.

A little girl, about four years old, pulled it open. Sloppy braids captured her dark hair, and her nose and eyes were red. Her resemblance to Mandy was obvious, even in the threadbare dress. She looked at Mia and then tilted her head to stare up at Seth. She jumped for him. "Seth!"

He caught her easily and cuddled her close. "Hi, Juliet."

The girl levered back and put both tiny hands on his face. "Manda's dead."

"I know, sweetheart," Seth murmured. "I'm sorry."

"Ruby's dead, too," Juliet said with a sniff.

"I know," Seth said.

Juliet shook her head. "No more dead peoples, Seth. No more."

Seth inhaled, his face remaining calm, but his blue eyes burned with a fire that he briefly failed to bank. Then nothing glittered there. He tilted his head toward Mia. "This is Mia. She's my friend."

Juliet turned serious eyes toward Mia. "Okay."

A slight woman wearing a faded black dress pulled the door open farther. "Hi, Seth."

Seth tightened his hold around Juliet and leaned to hug the woman with his free arm. "I'm so sorry, Claire."

Claire nodded, her eyes blank, her black hair up in a bun. "I know. You didn't have to stay outside when Ben was here earlier, you know. You're our choice—"

"That's all right." Seth cut her off.

Claire put a trembling hand to her head and glanced at Mia. "Oh. Um, the doctor gave me a sedative, and my head is spinning."

Her pupils were huge, though shock still glimmered in their depths. What in the world had she been about to say? Mia would have to question Seth later.

Mia stepped closer. "I'm Mia, and I'm also so very sorry for your loss. I met Mandy. She seemed like a wonderful girl."

"She was." Claire's lips trembled. Her skin was smooth, and she looked to be in her early thirties. "My husband went to take care of arrangements with Ben, and I, uh, I just can't go through another interview right now. I'm sorry."

"That's all right," Seth said smoothly. "We can come back later."

"Actually," Mia kept her voice soothing, "I was hoping I could take a look at Mandy's room. Just to get an idea of what was going on with her lately."

Claire frowned. "I don't see why. I mean, the Volks will—"

"Help with the arrangements," Seth finished for her.

Claire's shoulders jerked. "Oh. Yeah. Help with the arrangements. I, um, I should go lie down."

"Could I take a quick tour? I'd like to see if Mandy kept a diary." Mia asked softly, edging between Seth and Claire, her irritation with Seth growing. That was the second time he'd interrupted Claire. What secrets was he hiding now?

"Mandy didn't keep a diary. Um, I don't know about a tour." Claire looked up at Seth, almost as if waiting for permission.

He was silent for a moment and then answered. "If it's okay, Mia will just take a few minutes."

"Okay," Claire said doubtfully, backing up so they could all enter the main room of the house.

The smell of chocolate brownies hung in the air. The place was threadbare but very clean. The avocado shag carpet was freshly vacuumed, and homemade slipcovers adorned the two couches. An older television sat on the floor near the far wall.

Claire gestured to a hallway on the right. "Mandy's room is at the end of the hall." She took Juliet from Seth and wandered to the couch. "I can't go in there yet."

Mia paused. "Seth, why don't you keep Claire company? I'll be right back."

Seth frowned, but before he could respond, Juliet piped up that he could sit by her. He gave Mia a look. "You have five minutes."

She smiled sweetly and hurried down a hallway lined with school pictures. Three boys and it looked like three girls...all with dark hair and their mama's blue eyes. Mandy appeared to be the oldest.

Mia passed a boy's room holding bunk beds, a little girl's room with twin beds, and then found Mandy's room at the end. The master bedroom must've been on the other side of the house.

Mandy's room held a queen bed decorated with peace signs that matched the deep purple walls. A desk sat to the right, covered with candid pictures of Mandy and her friends. Makeup was scattered across the desk in organized chaos. Mia quickly glanced through the drawers and found ordinary office supplies and more makeup. A quick look under the bed and between the mattresses uncovered nothing. She headed for the small closet to just find clothes and two pairs of shoes.

Maybe Mandy hadn't kept a diary. But hadn't she mentioned one that first night? Mia sat on the bed, sorrow compressing her lungs. The girl had been so young. She could've done anything with her life. Who would've killed her like that?

An odd-looking baseboard near the closet caught Mia's eye. Her heart thrummed. She moved and dropped to her knees.

"Mia?" Seth called. "Time to go."

She grabbed the board and tugged, the sound of Seth stalking down the hallway filling her head. Her fingers brushed a bound book. She tugged it out and shoved it into her bag, smacking the board back into place. A second later, she met Seth at the door.

He lifted an eyebrow. "Find anything?"

"No." She shrugged. "But I do have a better understanding of Mandy and her friends…what was important to her."

Seth scanned the room. "Okay. Let's go." He took her arm and led her down the hallway.

They said their goodbyes to Claire and Juliet, Seth keeping his hand on Mia until they'd exited the house, crossed the porch, and reached the truck. Once there, he opened her door. "What did you find?"

She looked him in the eye. "Nothing."

"Humph." He helped her into the truck and shut the door.

Mia held her purse closer. She'd wait until after the mine tour to go through Mandy's diary. Hopefully, there'd be a clue in there somewhere.

Seth jumped into the truck and ignited the engine. "Someday, you're going to trust me, Mia Stone."

CHAPTER 16

The road to the mine was barely a lane and a half with torn asphalt, lined by spruce, fir, and pine trees. Gentle twists and turns mellowed the steep incline as they traveled up the canyon. Nature thrived, raw and untamed, around them.

Mia straightened in her seat. Something about the wildness in the land seemed reflected in the people of Lost Lake. As if the terrain shaped the people instead of the other way around. "Sometimes, I think you live in a different world than the rest of us."

Seth shrugged, his gaze on the road and hidden by dark sunglasses. "Maybe you live in a different world."

"Maybe." Darn it. She'd forgotten her sunglasses again. "What did Claire Fulsome mean when she said you were their choice?"

"Nothing—"

"Please, stop," Mia said quietly. "Just level with me for once. Stop keeping so many weird secrets."

Seth exhaled. "Fine. Ben is going to step down at the mine sometime in the near future, and by rights, Erik will take over. There's a small contingent in town that wants me to take over."

That was a bizarre situation. Shouldn't the best, qualified

person for the job *get* the job? She'd never understood family dynamics since hers had been a little, well...odd. In Lost Lake's case, it appeared as if running the mine meant running the town. The cop in her didn't like that. "A lot of power comes with running the mine," she said.

"Yes."

Then the person in charge should have the entire town's best interests in mind, right? "Do you think Erik can handle it?" From what Mia had seen, Erik wasn't quite there. The people seemed to really like Seth—trust him.

"Erik can handle anything, and he's a decent guy, which matters." Seth maneuvered the truck through a narrow, gated entrance lined with massive wooden posts holding a *Volk Mining* sign about nine feet off the ground.

Yeah, but Seth was a natural leader. Even though she didn't trust him, not yet anyway, the town did. "Why don't you take over?" she asked.

"It's Ben's silver mine, and Erik is Ben's son," Seth said flatly. He pointed to a galvanized metal building probably built in the fifties. "That's our mill, where we take the raw material and process it before sending it to refining."

She circulated through the quick research she'd done about mining the other night on her laptop. "You don't refine?"

"We do." Seth drove farther and pointed to a massive smelter stack. "Most mines can't conduct their own smelting because of EPA regulations, but we're grandfathered in since we've done it for so long."

"What's smelting?" she asked, captured by the process. She hadn't made it that far in her Google search.

"That's when we take the refined material and actually make a finished product. We make silver bars." He looked around, scouting the area. For what?

"You also mold silver handcuffs."

Seth grinned. "Yeah, but just for Lost Lake, and only for tradition's sake. We don't make them for anywhere else." He pulled the truck in front of a hand-cut cedar building weathered by at least a century. Several lifted and dirty trucks were parked in the lot. "My office is in there...and over to the right is the entrance to the mine."

Mia craned her neck to see a building no bigger than a couple of outhouses set into the rock. "The entrance is just that small shack?"

"Yep. The lift is beyond the door, and you head on down. There's another entrance over to the north where we take in the dump trucks and other equipment that's too large for this lift. This is just for people."

He jumped out and crossed around to assist her out of the truck, his hold firm until her feet touched the ground.

Three men came out of the building, all dirty and wearing tattered flannels. The man in front stopped short, his shoulders shooting back. Everyone froze. A heartbeat later, he rushed Seth.

Seth pivoted and shoved Mia behind him.

The men impacted each other with a sound like thunder. Seth smashed to the side and into the truck. Metal buckled with a loud crunch.

Mia sidled away and reached for the gun at her waist.

Seth turned and captured the guy in a headlock, lowering his head to hiss, "You'll want to do this later, Barnby. Much later." A hard shove had Barnby smacking into the other two men, who quickly righted him.

Barnby whirled around, his face red, his eyes blazing. "What the fuck are you doing, Volk? You took this cop to bother the Fulsomes after their daughter was murdered?"

"Back away, asshole," Seth muttered as he kept his body between Mia and the threat.

"No. That girl's death is on your head, and you know it," Barnby spat.

"I'm aware of that," Seth said quietly. "Now go home and get a handle on yourself."

Indignation ripped through Mia so quickly that her breath caught. "Mandy's death is the killer's fault, not Seth's. The mere thought that you expect him to protect you all from everything is not only ridiculous but unfair."

Seth jerked, surprise crossing his face.

The shock infuriated Mia further. Had nobody ever stood up for the guy? She elbowed him in the side to angle herself in front of him. "We all know I could arrest you for battery, but since Seth probably won't press charges, I'm not going to waste my time. Though you need to understand if you bother him again, you'll have me to deal with."

Barnby stepped toward her, and she angled her right leg back, settling into a fighting stance. Oh, she'd love to knock this guy on his ass.

Tobacco-stained teeth flashed when he snarled. "You're as much to blame for the little girl's death as the Enforcer here. Don't worry; you'll get yours."

Who were these people? They actually admitted that Seth was the enforcer of whatever the mine wanted? The idea gave her a headache. "I'll get mine? You dumbass. How so, Barnby?" she asked.

"Oh, you'll find out. When your lapdog isn't behind you." The man's belly rolled over his pants, but his chest was broad, and his arms muscled.

She'd need at least two good moves to disable him. Mia sneered. "You want to go, asshole? Let's go."

At that point, everything happened too quickly to exist in reality.

Barnby shot forward just as an impossibly hard arm banded around Mia's waist and jerked her off her feet. Before she could take a breath, Seth had her safely out of the way and Barnby on the ground. Face down, nose shoved into crumbled asphalt, arm twisted up behind his back.

The bone broke with a devastating crack.

Mia gasped, her stomach dropping.

Seth jerked Barnby to his feet by the damaged arm. Barnby cried out, his face sheeting white. Seth shoved him toward his buddies—again.

They righted him, their jaws hard, their mouths closed.

Mia's heartbeat ripped into action. Seth had just broken the guy's arm! She was a cop...and should probably do something. Indecision froze her in place.

Seth vibrated. "You challenge me again, Frank Barnby, and you're dead. One hundred percent, I'll rip out your fucking throat. And you know it."

Barnby somehow paled more.

Seth grabbed Mia's arm and tugged her into his side. His eyes blazed the blue of the hottest fire, and his jaw seemed cut from raw steel. "Make sure everyone knows...if Mia Stone is harmed in any way, I'll show no mercy. None."

Barnby gasped. "You're making a claim? With her?"

Seth growled. "I've said what you need to know. Pass the word."

Barnby's buddy grabbed his good arm and hauled him toward a battered Chevy. Seconds later, they'd loaded and zoomed out of the parking area.

Probably for the hospital.

Mia shrugged free of Seth's hold. "What just happened?"

Seth rubbed his chin. "I apparently have some issues to deal with. Your tour of the mine will have to wait." Without waiting for an answer, he opened her door and lifted her inside.

She shook her head to regain her bearings. "You broke that guy's arm."

Seth slammed the door and stalked around the truck to slide inside. "He deserved more than a broken arm, but I didn't want to risk getting arrested by you." Seth flashed a grin full of malice, absent any amusement.

"What did he mean by you making a claim?" Mia struggled to keep her voice level. The archaic language fit the ass-backwardness of the entire freaking town.

Seth shrugged. "He's an asshole who doesn't understand that hurting women is unacceptable. If he thinks you're mine and I'll kill him if he comes near you…well, I'm fine with that."

"I'm not." She'd never get their respect as a cop if Seth kept acting like they lived in the fifties. "Seriously. You really have to stop this posturing. Enough is enough."

"You were okay fighting that guy, and he had at least a hundred pounds on you, Mia. That's unacceptable." Seth's knuckles tightened on the steering wheel, and he increased the truck's speed.

"So what? I've trained to take down guys that size." Mia fastened her seat belt.

Seth shook his head. "Barnby's tougher than he looks. Believe me."

"Whatever." Sure, it was a lame line. But, sometimes, it fit.

Seth sighed. "How about dinner tonight? There's a new restaurant right outside of town that has Italian and Greek food."

The switch from violence to a dinner invitation threw her. Hard. "I don't think so."

"Why not?"

"Because you don't respect me." Not to mention that he'd just broken a guy's arm without even a second's hesitation.

His head jerked and then swiveled. "How can you say that? I won't let anyone mess with you. I respect you."

"Not as a cop. Or you'd let me handle my own problems," she said.

Seth drove through the gated entrance. "This town is different. I've tried to explain that."

"I know, and it's just a cop-out. So, you're all hillbillies. Time to enter the current century," she muttered.

"Do you want to be with a guy who'd let another guy ram into you? I mean, really?" he muttered right back.

"That's beside the point." Why did he have to reduce every single argument to fundamentals? "I'm a cop, and you need to understand that and get out of the way," she said.

"I'm with the woman, not the cop. *You* need to understand that," he growled.

There was the rub. No distinction existed between the woman and the cop. "Dinner would be a bad idea," she finally said.

He chuckled. "Of course, it'd be a bad idea. So, we should go. Come on, Mia. Haven't you ever done something just for the experience, knowing you'd get bitten but that it might be worth it? Take a chance, darlin'."

"What are you, sixteen?" She'd lost her interest in bad boys years ago. Of course, if that were true, she probably wouldn't be so tempted right now. "What does an enforcer do?"

"Nothing interesting."

More like nothing he would tell her about. "Do you break the law, Seth?"

"Define *law*," he drawled.

Yeah. Exactly.

"Come on, Mia. You have to eat." His expression hinted at vulnerability for the briefest of seconds before being quickly blanked.

Why did that draw her? Why did he? Besides, what could dinner hurt? "If we go to dinner, I fully plan on questioning you further about the case."

"Hmmm." He rubbed the shadow on his chin. "Let's make a deal, then. You can question me before and after dinner...but not during. During dinner, we talk about anything except murder and Lost Lake."

The profiler inside her tilted her head while the woman inside stood at full attention. "Anything?"

"Anything."

"Okay. Pick me up at seven," she said.

CHAPTER 17

Mia's head spun as she tried to figure out what to wear for her date. A date she should *so* not be going on. She'd tried to convince herself that she'd only accepted because of the case, for the opportunity to question Seth when he let down his formidable guard. But she'd learned years ago not to lie to herself. The case was only half the reason.

The other was pure curiosity. She'd never been intrigued by a man before, and she had to figure out what draw Seth held for her. She'd met plenty of good-looking men, even dangerous ones, but he was unique in a way she couldn't describe. Instinct had ruled her entire life, something she'd honed through hard work and training. Being caught off guard by anybody was rare for her these days. Maybe she had lost it after the shooting. Perhaps her instincts now stank, and she should find another line of work. Either way, she was taking the opportunity to figure him out.

Mia finally took the time to take Mandy's diary out of her bag and scan through it as the afternoon crawled by.

She read the last few entries, her heart rate picking up as she paced around her room. Apparently, Mandy had known about Ruby's pregnancy, and she knew that Erik was the father. Okay.

Definite motive for Erik to murder the teenager. Mia flipped a page, her heart sinking. Mandy was out to prove it and had started tailing the younger Volk. What had the kid been thinking?

She kept reading, making notes as she went. Finally, she placed the diary on the top of her dresser. She should call Pete.

Her phone buzzed, and she snatched it off the dresser. Maybe Seth was canceling. "Stone," she answered.

"Mia? Hello," Kurt Colbey said, horns blaring in the background.

She paused. "Kurt? What's going on?" Their breakup had been more gradual than an actual moment. Odd that she'd barely thought about him while in Lost Lake.

"Hi. How are you doing?"

She didn't have time for chitchat. "I only have a minute. What can I do for you?" Had she forgotten some of her belongings at his place?

He cleared his throat. "We've had another murder. Another woman like the rest."

She stepped back and sank to the bed. Her stomach lurched. "You're saying Robert Delaney had a partner."

"No—no, I'm not saying that. It's entirely possible we have a copycat on our hands. You know that happens more often than not." Another horn blared, and he grumbled a curse.

She pushed wayward curls off her cheek, and her hand trembled. "Then why are you calling me?"

"I thought you should be kept in the loop." His voice lowered. "And I've missed you."

Huh. "I appreciate the heads-up. Where was the body found?" Delaney had chosen each place carefully, and Mia had factored in the kill sites while creating the profile that had ultimately led to catching him.

"Frankfort, Kentucky."

She blinked. This was the first murder outside of DC. "He moved locations?"

"As I said, it's a copycat. Delaney is dead, and nobody thinks he had an accomplice." The sound of a garage door opening came over the line. He must have had his windows down, even though DC was experiencing an odd heat wave.

"Except me," she whispered.

"Even you're not sure about that, and after your ordeal, it's understandable that you weren't at top form." Clothing rustled, and a car door shut quietly. He cleared his throat. "If I can get you assigned to this *new* case, will you come home?"

Her eyebrows rose. "The FBI let me go. You can't get me assigned to anything."

"You don't know that."

She cocked her head, studying the lake outside her window. It was calm during the late afternoon, the depths a mysterious midnight color. "You stepped back the second they investigated me, and now you want to help me? Why?"

"I've missed you." Another door opened, and his heavy footsteps echoed across the tiled floor of his kitchen.

She'd spent plenty of time there cooking with him, even though it had been his hobby and not hers—she didn't much enjoy cooking. "I don't know how to answer that."

"We were together for two years. Don't you miss what we had?"

Two years. Seven hundred and thirty days, more or less. Yet when she'd needed him, he'd protected his career. Her mind flashed to Seth Volk. When she'd needed *him*, he'd jumped in front of her and taken a tackle from a guy built like a bear. Yet she kept fighting him on every front. This was confusing. She rubbed her head. He couldn't be a killer, could he?

"Mia?" Kurt asked.

She jerked back to the moment. "Tell me about the case."

He paused. "I can't tell you unless you come back in."

"Not true." Yeah, it was true. "Just bounce ideas off me. How similar was the crime?" She looked toward the bottom drawer of her dresser where she had stashed her case file, the only one she'd brought with her across the country—in case she'd been correct, and Delaney indeed had a partner. "Exactly the same?"

"No. Vic's name was Linda Keelson. The media has it and is running with the story."

In other words, Kurt wouldn't break any confidences by telling her anything. He was still protecting his career.

Mia pushed farther back on the bed and crossed her legs beneath her. "And?"

"She went missing around five a.m. on Monday and was found by ten p.m. on Tuesday. She'd been dead already for several hours when discovered."

Mia plucked at a loose string on the bedspread. "So he didn't stick to the seventy-two-hour timeframe as before." Perhaps it *was* a copycat. "Was she strangled?"

"Yeah. Tortured and strangled like the others. She was also left in a back-alley dumpster outside of a steak restaurant. Like most of the others." They'd all been found in dumpsters, but the locations had ranged from outside restaurants to ones in the woods used by campers.

"DNA?"

"Don't know yet," Kurt said.

There hadn't been DNA on the others, but if this was a copycat, maybe he had slipped up. "Was she a sex worker?"

"Yeah."

Just like the others. "Who found her?"

"Restaurant worker taking out the trash after a busy shift. This is different, Mia. Delaney never strayed from DC, and now we're talking two states over."

That was true. Delaney's hunting grounds were limited. "I'm in the middle of a case right now." She wanted back in the FBI. Didn't she? But Gena was doing so well in the small cabin, and dragging her back to the city would likely be a colossal mistake. "I need more time here."

His sigh was familiar. "Because of your mother?"

"Yes."

"You can't live your whole life centered around her just because she's not all there," he said. Again.

Irritation clawed down Mia's back. "She's all there, and I don't appreciate your statement." She stood and moved toward the dresser, taking out the thick case file. "Keep me informed, and if you need background on Delaney, give me a call."

"What's your hurry? I thought we could talk." Ice clinked in a glass over the line.

"Can't. I have a date. Thanks for calling." She clicked off, checking the time. The cabin was quiet since Dotty and Gena had gone shopping for new jeans. Her heart filled with hope that her mother was healing from her ordeal.

Holding the file folder, Mia padded through the cabin and went onto the back deck. She had a couple of hours before Seth arrived, so she might as well go through her notes for the thousandth time. It was odd that an accomplice of Delaney's would move out of the DC area, but perhaps the shackles were now off the second killer. There was no doubt in her mind that Delaney would've been the dominant partner in a killing duo, and DC was his home base.

She sat at the wooden table and spread out her notes, wishing she had grabbed her sunglasses. A light cloud cover wafted over the sun, spreading out like cotton batting. Mumbling to herself, she read through the notes from the last kill.

Movement near the tree line caught her attention, and she stilled.

The massive golden-brown wolf strode from between trees. Its ears were up, its fur flat, and the sun sparkling off the pelt made it look more amber than brown. He moved toward her, looking so much bigger than wolves did on television.

Her breath caught.

The beast kept coming, padding up the stairs and moving slowly toward her, his blue eyes mellow.

She almost told him that her mother wasn't around. That was freaking crazy. She was losing her mind. "I don't have any food for you." Should she go and grab her gun?

He shuffled closer and then stretched out, flopping flat on his stomach near her feet.

She looked down at his wide head. "You're weird."

He sneezed.

"Bless you," she said automatically.

His ear twitched.

Was he actually somebody's pet? Did people keep wolves for pets? "While I appreciate the fact that you've befriended my mother, maybe you shouldn't hang out on our deck." She was talking to a wolf like it could understand her. Yet there was something oddly sweet about the deadly animal. He looked mellow and kind of lonely.

Resting on his belly, he looked up at her as if trying to appear harmless.

She lifted one eyebrow. "I don't think you're harmless."

His tongue lolled out of his mouth.

"If you're going to keep coming around, you need a name," she mused. Maybe he was a pet. He certainly seemed domesticated. "How about Henry?"

He tossed his head in the air.

"Not a Henry." She grinned. This was the most fun she'd had in a while. "Snookums?"

Did he just roll his eyes? No. She was imagining things. "Fine. We'll name you later. For now, let me get back to work."

He just watched her.

She watched him back. Usually, she talked to herself when trying to figure things out, but what the heck? "I think there's a killer out there who might want to finish the job his partner started." It made sense that if she had been Delaney's target, she'd be his partner's, as well.

The wolf tilted his head.

She leaned toward him and scratched behind his ears, unable to help herself. His fur was thick and silky. He closed his eyes, and a low rumble of pleasure came from him. "Yeah. I've kept off the radar, but I can't do it forever. It's easy to find people these days." She kept petting the wolf. "Unless I'm wrong."

He opened his blue eyes.

She nodded. "I could be wrong. The killer might not have had a partner, which means that any new cases are the work of a copycat and have nothing to do with me. But a similar case could get me back into the FBI." She leaned back.

The wolf yawned.

Man, those canines looked sharp. She rubbed her neck. "If I even want to go back to the FBI. It has been my goal, but perhaps I could work out of the Seattle office." Yet to do so, she needed to get back in and find success. "I don't want to go back to DC to do this, but it might be the only way."

The wolf sneezed again.

"Bless you." She looked down at her myriad notes. "I'm not sure I could leave my mom and aunt." Then she grinned. "Even if they're under your watchful gaze."

He panted again, almost looking like he was grinning.

Well, she had a willing listener. "All right. Let's talk this through." She started at the beginning of the case and ran through everything, making more notes as she drew connections between the victims, but coming at the situation from the point of view of Delaney's submissive partner.

The wolf listened intently as if actually paying attention. In fact, he was the best listener Mia had ever worked with, and when she wound down, the case was clearer in her mind than it had been even a month before. Finally, she gathered all her new notes to put with the others. "I still don't have an answer, but gut instinct says this isn't a copycat." She had no proof of that statement, but she felt it in her bones.

The wolf gave a short nod.

She chuckled. It was as if the animal actually understood. She'd need to buy him treats if he kept coming around. He deserved it. She glanced at her watch and then jolted. Seth would be there in less than thirty minutes. She had to hurry.

CHAPTER 18

Mia borrowed another dress from Gena for dinner—this one a straight, black, backless sheath. She paired it with whimsical red pumps, a pretty golden cross necklace, and simple gold earrings. The shoes were Gena's and the jewelry Dotty's. Maybe someday she should go shopping for her own clothing and accessories.

Upon hearing Seth's truck roll to a stop outside, she hustled through the door and down the walkway to the vehicle. Now was not the time for Seth to meet Gena and Dotty. Never would be a good time. They'd returned from shopping and were putting away their new clothing.

He'd stretched from the truck and met her at the passenger side door. "You look beautiful."

Maybe. But he looked better. Black slacks encased powerful legs, while a white dress shirt emphasized his strong chest. With his blue eyes and dark hair, he looked like something out of every girl's fantasy.

"Thank you." She accepted his hand to step up and into the truck.

He leaned in and brushed his lips over her cheek. "Relax." The door closed with a soft click.

Okay, so she may be a bit tense. Unclenching her hands on her lap, she visualized her body relaxing from her shoulders to her feet. They were well on the way around the lake road before she finally felt like herself.

She took a deep breath. "Tell me about this restaurant."

He tapped his fingers on the steering wheel, a relaxed smile sliding across his face. "A retired couple from New York opened it. He's Greek, and she's Italian. They have the best food in the county." Seth winked. "And they're proof that opposites attract."

Mia fought a snort. "I'd hardly call them opposites."

"Neither are we."

Man, this was a bad idea. There was no way she could justify the fancy dinner to herself—her accepting his invitation had nothing to do with the Ruby Redbird case. She needed to ask him to take her home so she could get back to work on the Delaney partner case.

His cell rang, and he drew it to his ear. Suddenly, his entire body tensed, and his foot slammed against the accelerator. "I'll be right there."

Mia clutched the dash, her mind spinning. "What's going on?"

"The ranch is on fire." Seth's face darkened, even in profile.

She gasped as the trees flew by outside. "On fire?"

"Yes." He fishtailed the truck around a bend and quickly righted it. "I'd take you home, but there isn't time."

"Is everybody out of the house?" she asked, tensing.

"Yes. That was Alice, our housekeeper. She said they're all out." Seth shot through the entrance to the ranch, and a faint glow hinted on the horizon. The glow turned bright orange with a blaze rippling across the north side of the house. Erik and Ben held hoses, squirting water onto the rippling fire. Ben's was connected to the house, Erik's to the nearby shop.

Alice stood to the side, her face and sexy nightgown black with soot, shock on her smooth features.

Seth yanked to a stop and propelled out of the vehicle before the engine stopped sputtering. "Are you sure nobody else is in the house?" he yelled.

Ben nodded. "We're clear." Tears and burns marred his silk pajama bottoms, while the bare skin on his chest had reddened. Seth ran and kicked open the shop door, emerging with a large bucket. Dodging around the edge of the building, he returned with it full of sloshing water. Graceful as ever, he rushed toward the fire to quench the flames before hurrying back for more water.

Mia slid from the truck and ran to Alice. Tucking an arm around the older woman, she angled them both away from the fire. Alice's jerky movements slowed their progress, but Mia finally helped the housekeeper into the truck, standing next to the passenger side door with it remaining open. "Just take several deep breaths," she said, patting the woman's arm. The fire crackled with an evil mirth while sirens trilled in the distance.

The exterior wall buckled out with an angry growl. Heat rushed toward her, and she jerked back, her breath catching.

Flaming shingles and boards crumpled. Erik shouted and bent at the waist, covering his head. Flames danced down his back. He cried out, flailing around, trying to pat his shoulders.

Seth bellowed and ran full-bore for his brother, bringing him down with a powerful tackle. Flipping him around, Seth smacked the flames away with his bare hands.

Mia grabbed a blue Afghan throw from the back seat and ran toward the men, ditching her heels on the way. Reaching Seth, she tossed him the blanket. He quickly smothered any remaining flames.

Erik levered up to his knees, sighing in relief. Soot marred his blond hair, turning it dark. "Thanks. That was close."

Burning shingles wafted down to the earth. The night filled

with swirling red and blue as the fire trucks screeched to a stop. Firefighters jumped out, grabbing hoses and hooking them up to the hydrant.

Seth hauled his brother up and reached for Mia's arm. "Let's get out of the way."

Mia shrugged him off and grabbed his hands. "How badly are you burned?"

He started and glanced down at his sooty hands. "I'm not. My hands are fine."

Mia flipped his hand over and sighed in relief. It was dirty but not burned. How odd. A small cinder singed her arm, and she yelped.

Seth turned her by the shoulders and gently shoved her toward the truck. "Please go make sure Alice is all right."

Mia nodded, ducking her head to keep from breathing smoke. She stumbled along the uneven ground and grabbed her shoes as she went. Finally, she jumped into the driver's seat in the truck and shut the door.

Alice sneezed. "You all right?"

Mia glanced at the older woman. Soot covered her hair and chin, and the strap of her negligee was ripped. Apparently, there was more than a professional relationship between the housekeeper and Benjamin Volk. "Yes. You?"

"Yes." Alice wiped her bloodshot eyes. "Are the boys okay?"

"I believe so." Mia turned to watch the firefighters battling the blaze. Seth and Erik continued using the hoses, while Benjamin spoke to a man wearing a fire marshal's badge. Mia coughed out smoke. "I think Seth kept Erik from being burned too badly."

Alice hugged herself and rubbed her arms. "Seth has always protected that boy. Always."

The man was rather protective. He worked in tandem with his brother, both of them angling their water streams for the best coverage, not speaking but fighting the fire in perfect sync and staying out of the way of the larger fire hose. They were both muscled and strong looking, battling the flames with a gracefulness that reminded Mia of wild animals. "They seem close."

Alice nodded, her voice softening in the quiet cab. "They are, though the age difference seems much larger than their mere five years. Seth saved Erik's life once, you know."

Mia straightened up, her gaze on Seth. "He did?"

"Yes." Alice crossed her legs. "Erik was eight, and Seth was thirteen. It was winter, and Erik decided to skid across the north pond at the beginning of the season. He fell through the ice."

Mia breathed out. "Were you there?"

"No. Just a bunch of the kids were out there, but we've all heard the story." Alice scrubbed at some soot on her hand. "Seth reacted and ran across the ice, breaking it as he went because, even then, he was large. Then he dove in, no thought for his safety."

Mia swallowed. "What happened?"

"Seth dragged them both toward the shore, punched up, and broke through the ice." Alice shook her head. "So brave, even then. His strength is beyond the norm. He'd make such a good leader." Regret lowered her voice.

Irritation snapped Mia's spine into alignment. "Are you talking about the mine?"

"Of course."

The time of family empires and firstborn male heirs was over. Wasn't it? "Why can't they both work at the mine?"

"That's not how we do things," Alice said quietly. "There can only be one leader. It's not like we have a CEO and a COO or whatever."

What was Mia missing? "I really don't get it. Start another mine. Have the brothers work together."

Alice sadly shook her head.

"Fine. Even saying that things have to be the way you say—which makes no sense, by the way—Seth could lead the mine and this entire backwoods community. It's silly that he wouldn't be chosen if he's the best candidate."

"No. Blood matters around here, Ms. Stone." Alice's mouth firmed into a white line. "You wouldn't understand."

Now that was a true statement. "There's a lot I don't get about this town. For one thing, why won't anybody level with me about Ruby Redbird? Everyone seems to know more than they're saying."

Alice lifted a delicate shoulder. "You're not one of us. Sorry." She glanced at Mia's dress. "You and Seth are temporary…you have to know that, right?"

Mia's head jerked up. "Like you and Benjamin?"

A sly smile slid across Alice's face. "Temporary? I don't think so. We've been together much longer than anyone knows."

So why not commit? Curiosity almost prompted Mia to ask the rude question, but good manners won out.

The fire gave up the fight.

It took another hour for the Volk men and the firefighters to go through the house to determine that the north side had sustained the most damage. The bedrooms sat at the farthest south corner, so everyone could remain at home for the night and probably even while the home was rebuilt.

Mia slipped on her shoes and levered from the truck when the fire marshal came back into view. Her heels caught in the rocky ground, but she finally reached his side. She stood about eye-to-eye with him. He was tight and fit, and probably about fifty. "Marshal?"

He nodded and wiped soot from his gray hair. "Deputy Stone, I take it?"

Nice how word got around so easily about her. Too bad there were so many other secrets. "Yes. Tell me about the fire, please."

"Definitely arson. Fire from a bottle, as they say," the marshal said.

Dread slid down her spine. "Any ideas who?"

He shrugged. "No. My official report will be available Monday. Good night." Turning on his heel, he loped toward a firetruck.

Ben hurried over to fetch Alice and was gentle with her as he wrapped an arm around her shoulders and led her back into the home.

Seth stalked close enough to grasp Mia's arm. Soot covered his hair, his face, his entire body. Weariness cut grooves on either side of his mouth. "Some date, huh?"

She nodded, noting the tension in his expression and the fury in his eyes. "Arson?"

"I guess." Gently yet firmly, he led her back to the driver's side of the truck and helped her in, waiting until she'd scooted over before settling his bulk in the seat. "You hungry?"

"No." Her head ached from the smoke, and the last thing she wanted was food. "I think I'll head home."

He turned his head slowly, the blue of his eyes cutting through the darkness. "How about you come to my house?"

CHAPTER 19

The fire cast a heated glow. Warmth slid against her skin, and shadows swayed on the cedar walls, darkening the indentations and hiding the grooves.

Seth's place was a secluded cabin in a quiet bay of the lake. Mia shook her head, settling more comfortably into the leather cushions. Why had she agreed to come here? She knew exactly why. After arriving at the cabin, Seth had made a fire and then hustled into the shower to wash off the smoke and soot.

A large kitchen sat silent to the left, and the bedroom lay to the right. The comfortable main room held the huge fireplace, a TV, and a shotgun by the door.

Seth suddenly filled the bedroom doorway. His wet hair curled at his nape while his broad chest gleamed in the dim light. He'd yanked on faded sweats and was barefoot. Even his feet looked strong.

His gaze on her, he stalked forward and sat. Mia tipped toward him and quickly straightened herself.

"No." He turned and lifted her to straddle his lap.

She teetered, gasping as her dress rode up, and his thighs heated hers.

He brushed her hair back from her face with both hands. "From the first second I saw you, I imagined you here, lit by fire. You're beautiful." The low rumble of his voice sparked her blood hotter than the crackling flames.

Her hand trembling, she slid her palm along his sharp jaw. So much strength. Men like him didn't exist. How was he possible? So masculine, so deadly.

Blue eyes pierced hers. "Why did you come with me tonight?"

She took a deep breath, her gaze dropping to the strong cords of his neck. "You're dangerous and scary...and yet you make me feel safe." Of course, it didn't make sense. *They* didn't make sense. "And you're lonely. That made me feel needed."

Vulnerability shrugged her shoulders forward, but she didn't know any other way to be with him. The truth mattered. Instinct whispered that the moment held importance.

She swallowed. "Why did you ask me to come with you?"

He tugged her hands and trapped them on her thighs, his palms warming her knuckles. "I've never wanted anything as much as I want you. When we danced at the ball, when you smiled at me, you changed me." The corner of his mouth quirked. "And you're right—I am lonely."

She shook her head. "I can't fill you."

"You already do."

Such sweetness from the man she'd seen pulverize a bully and fearlessly fight a fire tempted her to let go. Completely. "We're not a good match."

This time, sadness marred his smile. "I'm fully aware of that, ex-FBI agent Mia Stone. I don't care."

"I don't either." She tried to tug free to touch him again.

Wickedness darkened the blue hue. "Here we play my way, sweetheart."

Her lungs trapped the air as well as Seth had trapped her hands. She breathed out. "Um, I'm not exactly the tie-me-up type of gal. Let me go."

"I don't need to tie you up." Quicker than possible, he captured both her wrists in one broad hand. The other dug into her hair, pulling back.

Her neck elongated. She struggled to keep her balance. "Seth..."

"Relax your body, Mia. I won't let you fall." The unrelenting grip tightened at her nape.

She didn't have much of a choice. Her nipples peaked. Arousal heated her core. The display of dominance was too natural to be a game, and for some reason, it was sexy as hell. Dangerous and sexy. Slowly, she relaxed her muscles and allowed him to hold her in place. "I'm not the submissive type."

His lids lowered to half-mast. "Then when you submit, the moment will be all the more rewarding."

The arrogance and absolute belief in his tone spurred her temper. She opened her mouth to argue, and his descended.

It wasn't a kiss.

His heated mouth captured hers, and then he conquered. The hand at her nape immobilized as he took. Strong and insistent, he delved deep.

Lava boiled through her veins. Her heartbeat echoed in her ears. With a groan, she accepted him.

He freed her hands, encircling her waist and yanking her flush against him, his mouth claiming. Pressed along his hard length, her sex softened. Even through his sweats and her dress, his erection pulsed. Quicker than an impulse, her mind blanked. Her body instinctively relaxed into his demand. All training, all intelligence fled as he forced her under.

Nearly gasping, she wrenched her mouth free, needing to breathe. He allowed her a couple of inches of space but no more.

Opening her eyes, she struggled to think. One look at his face, and she gave up all rational thought.

Midnight lit his eyes while a hard flush covered his high cheekbones. Need, want, lust, demand all hinted in the strong line of his jaw. Purely masculine, definitely deadly, there was no way in hell he was letting her go.

The absolute truth of that shivered down her torso and ended with a blast of heat that had her swaying. Desire was too simple a word to describe the raw need spiraling under her skin. She could easily lose herself in him, and for once, she didn't give a damn. There was no turning away. No hiding.

Tethering her with his gaze and the hand tangled in her hair, he glanced down. A growl rumbled as he lowered his head, nuzzling the tops of her breasts. Then he leaned her back.

"Seth—"

"Shh," he whispered against her skin. "I have you."

And he did. Femininity stretched awake inside her, cautious and hopeful. For the first time in her life, Mia Stone let somebody take over. Relaxing into his hold, she trusted.

He stopped for the briefest of seconds, and somehow his cock hardened even more against her. Warm air rushed against her back as he pushed her dress down to her hips. With a moan of appreciation, he ducked his head, and his tongue flicked over her nipple, sending electricity straight to her clit.

Inhaling sharply, she rubbed against him, trying to dispel some of the ache.

Pure heat engulfed her breast as his mouth surrounded her, and she stilled. How was he so hot? On fire, she shot both hands through his thick hair, digging in, holding him in place. More. She needed more.

He chuckled, nearly sending her over the edge.

The world tilted, and she found her legs wrapped around his hips, moving through the cabin. Finally. There had to be a bed somewhere. Levering forward, she pressed her lips along the hard column of his neck. Salt and man filled her senses. The masculinity of the rough cords made her head spin.

With a satisfied smile, she licked her way up and under his cut jawline.

A warning growl hissed from his lips. Oh, yeah, they could both play.

Moonlight danced across his face as he moved into a sparsely decorated bedroom and set her gently on the bed. Quick fingers had his sweats shoved to the wooden floor—leaving him nude.

Wow.

The man was beyond masculine. Powerful legs, ripped abs, and broad shoulders combined to create...pure male. His cock was full and way too big. How was he real?

Her breath heated, and her skin tingled. Want and need blended until the world narrowed to Seth Volk. For a brief moment in time, he was the only thing in existence.

He gently pushed her shoulders to the bed before sliding work-roughened hands over her breasts and down to her bunched dress. He leaned over. His mouth followed his hands to lick her torso and abdomen. She shifted restlessly against him, her vision clouding.

He rumbled in pleasure while slowly tugging off her dress. Calloused fingers traced a path up the inside of her calf and over her knees to her inner thighs.

She bit back a moan.

Warm air brushed her skin when he knelt on the floor, his dark gaze on hers. "No holding back, Mia." The words were soft, the tone relentless. Whiskers scraped her skin as his mouth nipped her thigh.

Fire zipped right to her core. She gasped, shifted, and bit her lip again to keep from whimpering.

"Stubborn girl," he murmured. Then, over her panties, his heated mouth enclosed her clit.

Electricity shot through her veins. She cried out, arching her body into his mouth, needing more. God, so much more. The bedspread bunched when she tried to move closer and away all at once. He took advantage of her movements and yanked her panties off. Then, strong hands slid under her butt to trap her in place while his broad shoulders kept her legs spread.

His huge hands cupping her butt and his dangerous mouth over her clit almost sent her flying. "Seth, please—"

"Shh," he rumbled against her flesh. "The begging comes later."

Any protest caught in her throat as he ran his tongue over her with a low whisper of appreciation.

Her mind spun. The moment held too much intimacy, and the man had too much control. "Seth, I don't like this." The words may have lost some impact with the breathiness of her voice.

An open-palmed slap to her clit echoed in the night. She yelped. Pain and pleasure melded. Her ears rang, and an orgasm hovered just out of reach.

Seth levered up, his hand remaining on her mound, his face over hers, and his eyes a piercing blue. "Don't lie to me, Mia. Not here. Not now."

Keeping her gaze, he slid one finger inside her.

Heat made desire climb through her until her cheeks burned. "Not...lying," she gasped.

Dark amusement lifted his lip. "Really?" Another finger.

She swallowed loudly, her body moving of its own accord, regardless of the battle going on in her head.

He found her G-spot. His thumb brushed her clit, and the world exploded.

She shut her eyes and rode the waves with a choked whimper. Pleasure spiraled through her, pinpointing on his talented fingers. Finally, with a soft sigh, she came down, and her eyelids fluttered open.

Male satisfaction crossed his face. "Let's try again."

Her eyes opened wider as she grabbed his shoulder. "No, Seth—"

"I've got your taste, sweetheart. Right now, I just want to play. If you keep denying me, I'll make you beg for it." The wicked glint in his eyes promised that he *wanted* to make her beg.

The orgasm had taken off the edge, and reality crashed back. "I don't think so."

"I do." He shifted up her body, and his teeth scraped her nipple.

Lust shot through her so quickly her lungs compressed. A need, greater than before, flared her nerves to life. "Wait...I don't want..."

"What don't you want?" He licked her skin and nipped the underside of her breast.

She blinked rapidly while her nipple turned diamond-sharp, wanting him. Needing him. "This is too much," she gasped. "I want—"

"To stay in control," he whispered, tracing her ribs with his lips.

"Yes." She took a deep breath. Thank goodness he understood.

"No." Another sharp slap to her clit and sparks flashed behind her eyes. The need to orgasm lit her skin on fire. Her entire body short-circuited, and her brain fuzzed.

She didn't like this. Well, she *shouldn't* like this. Her body, however, didn't agree.

His mouth soothed the erotic pain, the gentle heat such a contrast to the cold smack that her thighs trembled. The man was playing games way out of her experience. Her body seemed to love it...while her mind struggled for reality.

This was beyond sex.

He moved back down her body, and his whiskers scraped her skin as he sank his teeth into her inner thigh. Marking her. Pain and pleasure became indistinguishable. She'd wear his bite for a week.

She gasped. "Don't mark me."

"Too late." Then he got serious. His hands, his mouth, his whiskers, his talented tongue...all moving, all creating such pleasure she could only writhe and feel.

Ten minutes, a hundred, a lifetime passed as he continued driving her higher, torturing her, making her do nothing but accept the raw pleasure he gave her. The world centered around Seth Volk and what he was doing to her. Deep down, in the tiny portion of her brain that still worked, she knew with certainty that had been his intention.

She didn't care.

His rough tongue flicked her clit again—just hard enough to have her pleading. Not enough to orgasm. Incoherent gasps panted from her, full of need—and demand.

Suddenly, his strong hands gripped her hips and shoved her up the bed. He stood, sliding over her, covering her. Tangling his hands in her hair, he slanted his mouth over hers in a soft, gentle kiss.

Her legs shot around his hips, her feet hooking together. Desperation caught on a sob.

She rubbed against him, trying to force him inside her.

His kiss continued, slowly, so much in control.

Grabbing his ass, she clutched her nails into impressive muscles.

He growled, levering up. "Slow down. I don't want to hurt you."

"You're killing me," she panted. "Enough."

A vein stood out in his neck while his shoulders vibrated as he kept control. Sweat dotted his forehead. "Slow."

Oh. So he didn't want to lose control. She clutched harder, the unspoken challenge tipping her lips. Her butt lifted as her feet pressed him against her. "Now, Seth."

His entire body hardened...stiffened as he tried to keep control. The impressive muscles in his upper arms tightened and vibrated.

Her smile even felt dangerous. Keeping his gaze, she licked his bottom lip. His sharp intake of breath spurred her confidence. Then she bit.

Hard.

His mask of control dropped. A fierce growl ripped from his chest and sounded entirely too real.

Grabbing her hip, lifting her off the bed more, he plunged into her with enough force to ram the headboard against the wall. Plaster flew.

Pain ricocheted through her body, only to be quickly overcome by a feral pleasure—a spiraling so intense she could do nothing but accept it. She breathed out on a whimper and just held on.

Out of control, he pounded. So hard, so fast, more plaster flew into her hair.

The unbreakable grip on her hip tightened. He yanked her up every time he plunged deep.

His hard shaft filled her, slamming nerves with an impossible friction. He'd given her such pleasure, there was no doubt he was *taking* now. Taking whatever he needed…whatever he wanted.

That thought threw her into an orgasm so powerful she shut her eyes and cried out his name. He somehow thrust harder… deeper…prolonging the rippling waves throughout her body until she wanted to beg. Beg him to never stop.

His speed increased. Dropping his head to the crook of her shoulder, his entire body shook as he came. The suddenness of his eruption threw her into another orgasm that had her legs gripping his hips strong enough to bruise her thighs.

Finally, he slowed. Then stopped. Yet they remained joined.

Sweat slicked their bodies. Her heart beat so hard she could barely breathe. He panted, his massive chest rising rapidly.

His hair brushed her cheek.

She could only blink. Too much emotion, too many feelings tore through her…way too quickly. A small part of her wondered if she'd always wear Seth Volk just under her skin. This was beyond sex.

He inhaled. Firm lips brushed against hers in a kiss so gentle that tears sprang to her eyes. When he lifted his head, the question in his dark eyes mirrored the one in her heart.

What in the world had just happened?

CHAPTER 20

The wind threw pine needles against the windows with an angry ting. Mia settled more comfortably into Seth's warmth as dawn arrived. He'd insisted that she stay the night, and after several hours of mind-altering sex, she'd been too worn out to refuse. She'd never slept all night in a man's arms.

Too much intimacy.

Too much risk.

His heat surrounded her as he slept quietly, his arm banded around her waist as if afraid she'd disappear. The hard muscles in his chest supported her back. Every self-protective instinct she owned whispered for her to slide from the bed. But if she moved, he'd awaken.

She wasn't ready to face him yet.

Plus, for one quiet moment in time, she felt safe. Physically, anyway.

So she lazily scanned the bedroom. His room held a huge bed with a dark gray bedspread and two dressers. A couple of pictures sat in frames on top of one—snapshots of Seth's family. Black and white photographs of old-time miners lined the wall. The room was nice but sparsely decorated.

Serenity and a sense of peace overcame her. Her eyelids finally fluttered closed.

Drifting between reality and illusion, her mind relaxed enough to throw her into the dream she usually managed to avoid.

Suddenly, she was fourteen again, bouncing in a rusted truck over a trail too rough to be called a road. The wool blanket covering the ripped seat scratched her bare legs. Her threadbare jean shorts failed to provide much protection.

Her new foster father gripped the wide steering wheel with a hairy hand. His other hand held a beer can half-full of tobacco spit. He dripped more brown into the can.

She coughed. "I don't understand where we're going."

Harold shrugged, his big belly bouncing with the truck. "I need to check on something."

Trees rose on each side of the trail, and branches scraped the truck's underbelly. Mia had only lived at the new house for a week, and something was off. Another girl named Betty lived there, and when Harold had announced that Mia was going with him on his job, Betty had started crying.

Something was definitely wrong. Mia swallowed. Confusion had her staring at the forest while her stomach cramped.

Harold finally stopped the truck. Silence surrounded them. Setting his can on the dash, he smiled with stained teeth. "Now, you earn your keep."

That's what she'd figured. He reached for her, and she kicked him hard, grabbing the door handle. Panic had her scrambling from the truck and running into the forest. His bellow followed her as he crashed after her.

She ran along a faint trail, rocks ripping into her thin sandals.

Reaching a huge hole, she almost fell in. Her arms windmilled as she tried to keep her balance.

Harold grabbed her arm and yanked back.

Her shoulder popped, and she screamed. Pain cascaded down her arm to tingle into suddenly numb fingers. She turned to face him.

He bent at the waist, his large hands on his stained pants, trying to gasp a breath. Red filled his face while sweat poured down his pocked skin. "You're going to regret running," he gasped.

Fear made her ears ring. She angled to the side and away from the gaping hole.

He nodded. "Old well from some homestead. Take off your clothes." He stopped to cough. "Or I'll throw you in."

She slowly closed her eyes. Her arm hurt, and her heart beat so fast it was hard to breathe. Flipping her lids open, she set her stance. "No."

Delight flashed across his ugly face. "I love a fighter."

"Is Betty a fighter?" Mia slid farther away from the hole.

He shrugged. "She was. Not so much anymore."

Anger flushed through Mia until her mind centered. "I am."

"Good." He grabbed for her, and she shot to the side.

Time stopped. So many thoughts scattered through her head at once, her vision wavered. She could run. She could hide.

Or not.

Mimicking a move she'd seen on television, she kicked both legs up and into his chest. Her feet landed hard, and she fell to the ground.

His eyes widened, and his arms swung for balance. But gravity kicked in, and he plunged into the hole.

She could actually hear his bones break over his terrified cries as he fell.

Mia screamed herself awake, sitting up in the big bed.

Seth leapt over her and planted his body between the bed and the door. Protecting her.

Mia took several deep breaths.

Slowly, he turned around, buck-ass naked, confusion on his face. He lifted an eyebrow. "Bad dream?"

Mia snorted out a slightly hysterical laugh. "You could say that."

He exhaled, his shoulders relaxing. Reaching for the covers, he slid inside and tugged her into a spooning position. "Tell me about it."

Warmth and safety propelled tears straight to her eyes. "No."

"Yes."

"No."

Long, tapered fingers wandered down her arm. "Yes."

Thunder bellowed high above. Rain pelted the windows. The image of how quickly Seth had shot from sleep to defend her warmed her in a very tempting way. So, she told him—all of it.

When she wound down, he pressed a gentle kiss to her head. "What happened to Betty?"

"I don't know. The authorities moved me to another place, and then Aunt Dotty came to get me." Mia took another deep breath. "The dream doesn't show up very often anymore."

"I'm sorry. I wish I could go back and kill him for you," Seth said.

He didn't understand. Mia sighed. "I didn't have to kick him. Kill him. I could've run."

The world tilted, and Mia found herself on her back, covered by the sexiest man she'd ever touched. He smoothed her hair from her face. "You protected yourself, and you did the right thing."

"Nobody else knows the full story. I lied to the police and said he fell." Yeah. She'd just opened herself up to a world of possible hurt. As an adult, she knew she wouldn't have been charged—it was self-defense. But some secrets should stay buried.

Seth blinked, his eyes warming. "I'll protect you, Mia Stone."

They both knew he wasn't just talking about past secrets. The need to remind him that they were temporary rose strong and fast in Mia. But as she stared into his blue eyes, the words wouldn't come.

Those words would hurt too much—even if they were true.

A twist of his lips acknowledged the truth. Then they slid against hers, smooth and warm. Gently, he delved deep, taking his time. A satisfied male on a lazy morning. Arousal drifted through her blood, flowing like silk.

He stilled. Lifting his head, he glanced at the window, his body stiffening. "Damn it." Bedclothes rustled, and he reached for his jeans, standing and yanking them on.

A clamoring echoed from the main room. "Volk, get out here," shouted a man.

Mia's breath caught. Her nails bit into the sheet as she stood. "Who's yelling?"

Seth zipped the jeans and left the top button free. Gone was the sexy, indulgent male. His jaw tightened, and it threw the white scar across his jaw into prominence. "Stay here." He strode toward the hallway.

She dropped the sheet and stood. "No. What's going on?" Her dress was in the other room. Looking around, she grabbed his T-shirt to yank over her head, the soft material falling to her knees.

Seth whirled on her so quickly she stepped back. He lowered his head. "Do as you're told. Stay the fuck here." Giving her a hard look, he left.

The expletive threw her, as he no doubt meant it to. She faltered in place and waited until the front door opened and closed. Temper spiraled through her nerves as she returned to reality. The man had no right to treat her like a helpless civilian—or some homemaker from the fifties. Wooden floorboards chilled her bare feet as she padded through the hallway to the empty living room.

Caution kicked in right as she reached the door. She was a deputy right now, and Seth had been a murder suspect until recently. While he'd been cleared, it probably still wouldn't do to start town gossip. So she slid a plaid curtain to the side and peered outside.

Seth stood on the covered front porch while visitors stood in the rain. Two men holding shotguns flanked an unarmed man who instantly drew her attention. The guy was movie-star handsome with black eyes and sandy-blond hair, and the irritation covering his face only enhanced his good looks.

Seth tucked his thumbs into his jeans pockets. "What the hell do you want, TJ?"

One of the other men stepped forward. "That's Brother Jeremiah to you, asshole."

Jeremiah smiled and waved the guy back. "That's all right, Brother Miles. We know not everyone believes as we do, and that's okay." He angled his head to study Seth. "Though I have to say, Mr. Volk isn't usually so surly. Is there a problem I can help you with, Seth?"

Seth chuckled, the sound much more pissed than humorous. "Sure. Go pray for me. But do so off my property. Get lost."

"Odd. Your manners are usually much better than this." Jeremiah glanced at the window and back. "Your trucks have been going up and down our mountain all morning, and it has to stop."

The hard lines of Seth's back somehow straightened. "As far as I know, you don't own any mountains around here. However, I will check it out since you say they're my trucks."

"You know every move your people make. Something is happening tonight." Jeremiah's face settled into puzzled lines. "Though why you all head up to Howler's Ridge so often is beyond me. The fact that you have three locked gates on the road makes us nervous, Seth. Those trucks have no right passing through our protected wilderness to get to your locked gates."

What gates? Mia's breath heated. She pulled the curtain farther to the side for a better view.

Seth stiffened but didn't turn around. "Actually, we have a road easement through your land to get to ours, and you know it. The gates exist on land owned by the Volk Mining Company, so they're none of your business. As is anything we might be doing on that land."

Jeremiah's eyes sparked. "The land must be protected by all of us. We're stewards, not owners."

"Then go be a steward. I'm done with this conversation." Seth turned to go.

Miles cocked his gun and pointed the barrel at Seth.

Mia reacted instantly. Grabbing the shotgun by the doorframe, she shoved the door open. "Put the weapon down."

Three sets of surprised eyes focused on her, followed by one very pissed set. Seth looked bored, but his eyes told another story. A slow shiver wandered down Mia's spine.

Jeremiah covered the shotgun barrel and pushed down. "We don't point weapons at women." He scrutinized her bare feet and the much-too-large shirt. "I do apologize for interrupting your morning, Seth. Now I understand your change in welcoming attitude."

Miles sneered. "So Volk got himself a whore. About time."

Jeremiah reacted instantly and shot an elbow into the guy's face. Miles hit the wet leaves with a dull thud. Rage shot red into Jeremiah's cheeks. "Apologize to the lady. Now."

Miles wiped pine needles off as he stood, his face pale, his gaze remaining down. "I'm sorry."

Jeremiah exhaled and kept his focus on Mia. "We all get lost, Brother Miles. What happens when we get lost?"

"The brotherhood finds us," Miles whispered.

Seth shifted to partially block Mia. "Get the brotherhood the fuck off my property before I rip all three of you apart."

"Of course." Jeremiah reached down and retrieved the fallen shotgun. "Ms. Stone. I heard you were in town. It's very nice to make your acquaintance, and I truly apologize for the inconvenience." He shifted his focus to Seth. "Please take care of the trucks and Howler's Ridge." Jerking his head, he motioned for his cohorts to leave.

Seth seemed to vibrate in place. Mia's breath quickened.

Jeremiah had taken several steps before turning back around. "Ms. Stone, if you'd ever like to talk, I'm at your disposal." His lips turned down in apology as he gestured toward Seth. "This isn't a good path for a decent woman, especially a female warrior such as yourself."

Seth stepped forward, menace in every line of his body.

Jeremiah backed away. "Good day."

Mia waited until all three men had disappeared down the dirt lane before relaxing her hold on the gun. "Nice guy."

Seth didn't move. "Go back in the cabin. I need a moment."

A wise woman would heed the advice and go back inside. Mia had never been particularly wise. "No."

His sharp intake of breath provided yet another warning. "Mia—"

She whirled on him. "You can stop ordering me around, right now. I have no clue how this town has existed with its bullshit, backward attitude toward women, but I'm having none of it. I'll do what I want, when I want." Her ears hurt with pulsing heat. "I don't need you to shield me. For goodness sakes, I can shoot and fight…probably better than you. And…you can fucking go order somebody else around."

In profile, he looked even harder than usual. "I understand that you're trained and can take care of yourself. This is my land, and my problems, and I'll be damned if you get caught up in the mess." Slowly, he turned to face her. "I'm glad you can shoot and fight. But I guarantee it's not better than me."

The profiler in Mia rose to the surface. "Who is Brother Jeremiah?"

Seth shrugged. "If you ask me, he's the leader of some weird cult. They usually keep to themselves and seem harmless. But who knows?"

Then the cop took over. "What's Howler's Ridge?"

He blinked. "The Ridge is a beautiful spot to see the entire valley, and an excellent place for a kegger on a Saturday night. I have no doubt the kids are planning one tonight, and it sounds like they're using company rigs. That's one of the many downfalls of having a bunch of eighteen-year-olds working at the mine. I'll take care of it."

Her instincts hummed. "Why don't I go with you?"

He shut down even more. "That's all right. The kids don't know you, and it'll be better if I go alone."

"Because I'm an outsider."

He reached for the gun, his gaze intensifying. "You want in? Make sure you really want what you're asking for. Nothing is ever quite what it seems."

Including Seth Volk.

Mia relaxed her shoulders. "Whatever. I promised to take my aunt shopping in Seattle this afternoon before seeing a play. I need to go home."

"Let's find your clothing, and I'll give you a ride." He slid open the door and waited for her to precede him inside, his tone too polite.

"Thanks." Her mind spun. Seth Volk wasn't the only one who could tell a good lie.

It was time for her to head to Howler's Ridge.

CHAPTER 21

Cold metal rubbed against Mia's spine as she patiently maneuvered through brush and trees, climbing the rocky hill. The gun remained secure and provided a sense of safety, as did the Glock in her ankle holster. She kept the flashlight low on the trail and had for the past two miles after parking her car just inside the third gate to the Volk Mining property. Someone had left the gates open.

She and Pete had spent most of the day reviewing maps of the terrain and had created a plan where he'd approach Howler's Ridge from the far north, and she'd walk the three miles and come from the south.

The fact that the mine's trucks were on their own property failed to provide any probable cause for her and Pete to obtain a warrant. So, yeah, they were trespassing.

Whatever they saw would not be admissible in court.

But she needed to know. They'd form a plan to gain evidence elsewhere if something illegal was going on. Every instinct she'd developed through years of investigations told her that something was happening—something that involved her new lover.

Lover.

Seth Volk. He'd definitely acted sketchy when she'd asked him about Howler's Ridge.

He was the one person in her life she hadn't been able to get some sort of handle on. Sleeping with him had most certainly been a mistake, but a small part of her had rejoiced in the experience. She'd never felt like that—and probably wouldn't ever again. He had been right in saying the pain would be worth it. Even if she had to arrest him, even if she might've blown the entire case, the night had changed her.

Of course, if he *was* doing something illegal out at Howler's Ridge, she'd do everything in her power to take him down. Justice mattered. Her job mattered.

Moonlight cast shadows from the pine trees yet clearly illuminated her path. Firelight glimmered through the trunks ahead, and she took a deep breath of relief. Her legs burned from the walk, reminding her that she really needed to get back into shape. At one time, a three-mile hike wouldn't have made her breathe heavily.

Times had apparently changed.

Music wafted through the night, the breeze carrying a haunting and mournful tune. The trail turned to rock. She climbed cautiously, finally reaching the top. Her heart hammering, she peeked around a blue spruce and looked toward a sprawling vista about twenty feet below. A crackling fire blazed in the middle of the round area. One side was rock, one side forested, one a grassy parking area, and the final dropped into nothingness to reach what appeared from the map to be the Lonely River.

About fifty people milled around the fire, their voices hushed, their moods as somber as the music blasting from one of the mining trucks.

Mia lifted the binoculars secured by a strap around her neck for a better view.

The blood instantly froze in her veins.

Her first focus landed on Seth as he stood by his father. Her second focus stopped her breathing. Near the cliff on the river side stood two scaffolds holding two female bodies. Ruby and Mandy.

Good God. They were going to burn the bodies.

So far, her research had indicated that Seth and the town's members weren't affiliated with or descended from any known American Indian tribes, so the practice of burning bodies didn't make sense in this case.

Besides, who had stolen Ruby's body and why? The body was still evidence.

Mia lifted her cell phone to text Pete. NEED BACKUP, FOUND RUBY'S BODY.

Pete instantly responded. WAS STOPPED—NO WARRANT—GET OUT OF THERE.

Too late. As Mia watched, Benjamin Volk grabbed a torch from the fire and instantly lit both scaffoldings on fire.

As one, everyone turned toward the bodies and lowered their heads in what seemed like prayer.

She released the binoculars and tugged her gun free. Crap. She needed to get down there and stop the burning. Rushing to the right, she made out a rough trail on the way down.

Another glance at the people below stopped her cold.

Shirts, pants, and shoes hit the earth as they stripped naked.

What kind of weird religion required mourners to get naked while dead bodies burned? She halted, unsure. No way could she arrest everyone at once, and she was definitely outnumbered.

Was burning a body a crime if it happened during a religious ceremony? Probably not. But Ruby's body had been stolen, and that *was* a crime.

Indecision kept her immobile—and then shock turned her legs to stone.

Benjamin Volk's neck elongated, his jaw snapped, and he

dropped to all fours. The air crackled around him, fur sprang up along his naked body, and a wolf suddenly stood where he had been. Erik was next, and he turned into a golden-brown wolf.

Holy crap. The wolf that had befriended Mia's mother and that Mia had spent time with just last night. That had been Erik?

She'd told Erik all about her case and her feelings about it.

Everyone around him, including Seth, instantly followed suit. On all fours with black fur, Seth was larger than any other wolf. A white patch cut up his jaw where his scar was, and his blue eyes glowed in the firelight.

As one, the wolves lifted their heads and howled at the moon.

Mia choked as her lungs seized. Panic sharpened the entire world.

Benjamin's muzzle twitched, his eyes opened, and his head turned, his golden gaze landing on her. A snarl flashed his razor-sharp canines, and he lunged into action.

With a vicious bite to her lip, she turned and ran.

In several moments, he bounded onto the trail in front of her. She skidded to a stop, her eyes widening to let in more light. Death glimmered in his eyes while saliva dripped from his frightening teeth.

She settled her stance and aimed her gun at him. "Move, and I'll fucking blow off your head."

This wasn't happening. This couldn't be happening.

She shook her head, her aim remaining true. Either she'd just suffered a psychotic break, or this was happening. The people of Lost Lake were wolf shifters.

Ben pawed the ground, angling closer, his gaze on her jugular.

The air swished, and a snarling black wolf jumped between them.

Seth.

Raised fur covered his back as he faced Benjamin with a low-pitched snarl.

Ben snarled back in warning.

They were going to fight over her.

Hissing, Ben leapt for her. Seth instantly countered, a loud crunch filling the night as muscle smacked into muscle. Ben fell back several feet, and Seth landed on all fours. His back vibrated, but he didn't move as he shielded her.

Ben angled to the side, a series of low growls rumbling from his chest. Seth growled back.

Then silence ruled as the wolves stared at each other. Seth suddenly shook his head. They stared some more, and then Ben snarled. Seth snarled back.

Were they somehow communicating? Mia kept her hand on the gun, her aim on Ben. If he went for her again, she'd shoot him between the eyes, regardless of Seth's presence. Wolf shifters. Real wolves. How was this possible?

Finally, Ben turned and bounded back into the forest.

Seth turned and faced her. The fur receded on his body. He slowly stretched onto his back legs, and his features narrowed. The air popped, and he stood to his full height in human form—buck-ass naked.

And seriously pissed.

He grabbed her arm and jumped for the trail. "Run."

She dug in her feet, halting him. Her mind reeled. "No way. Explain."

He whirled on her, grabbing her shoulders, his face a hard mask. Ice swirled in his eyes. "Fucking run, or you're going to die. Ben won't be back alone, and I can't take all of them. We need to go. *Now.*"

Her body reacted to his panic, and her legs sprang into action. She followed him along the trail and into the forest where a barely visible path lay. Branches scraped her arms, and brush slammed against her calves, but she kept a firm grip on her gun. Finally, they arrived at a small clearing that held Seth's truck.

He opened the driver's door and tossed her across the seat in one fluid motion. Firing the ignition, he jerked the truck into drive and careened down the dirt road.

Mia clutched the dash, her breath panting out. "How is this possible?"

His jaw snapped shut. "What the hell are you doing on our property?"

Anger flew through her veins. "My job. One of your people stole Ruby's body, and that's a crime."

"I stole the body."

Damn it. "Great. You're under arrest."

Seth slammed the brakes and jerked the truck around a tree, somehow increasing his speed. The forest blurred outside. "You have no proof. The body is gone by now."

Plus, she'd been trespassing without a warrant. Not that the law mattered right now. "How are you wolf shifters? I mean, are you werewolves?" She did *not* just ask that question.

He snorted, and the sound was much more irritated than amused. "No, we're not werewolves. We're wolf shifters who have been on this Earth, and this continent, a lot longer than your people."

"Native Americans? I mean, the whole burning of the body thing so the spirit is released is an Indigenous custom."

He flipped on the headlights. "We're just who we are. No affiliation to any particular tribe."

She pushed herself back in the seat as the truck gained speed. "Why did you steal Ruby's body?"

"An autopsy might've revealed something different with her physiology since she's a wolf shifter." Seth glanced in the rearview mirror and hit the accelerator harder.

Mia swallowed as the lake flashed by. "Who killed Ruby? And Mandy?"

"I don't know yet," Seth said grimly.

"The silver in their throats? The lore is true? Silver kills wolf shifters?"

"Yes, but the silver has to reach our bloodstream." Seth glanced in the rearview mirror. "My people claimed the silver mines early to control some of the product."

She gulped. "So whoever killed the women knew they were shifters, thus the use of all the silver."

"Maybe. At the moment, I have bigger problems."

"Like what?" Mia asked.

He cut her a hard look before concentrating back on the road. "My job is to kill you now, Mia."

She swung the gun toward him, steadying her aim with both hands. "Excuse me?"

"As the Enforcer, my main priority is to keep our secret. To keep anybody from finding out about us. You can't know what you know," he snapped.

"Are you going to try to kill me?" Her voice shook enough to tick her off, and an odd hurt tingled down her spine.

"No." He checked the side mirror. "But protecting you from not only my pack but also the other three doesn't seem possible." His thick hair flew when he shook his head, his voice rough. "I wish you wouldn't have come out here tonight."

"But I did." She breathed out, her mind spinning with plans. "I can protect myself." As well as Gena and Dotty. They needed to get out of town and soon.

Seth chuckled, the sound dark and fatal. "No, you can't. My people will find you, wherever you go. You can't know what you do, and we both know you can't go public. Nobody would believe you." He exited the lake road, headed toward his cabin.

Mia leveled the barrel at his head. "Take me to my home, Seth."

"No." Without warning, and without turning his head, his arm shot out, and he grabbed the gun. "You go home, and you sign your family's death warrants."

Mia gasped out air. "They wouldn't kill my family just because I know your big secret."

Seth slammed on the brakes, and the truck skidded to a halt by his cabin. "They'd kill everyone you'd ever met if it meant keeping the secret." He grabbed her and hauled her from the truck, shoving her gun back into her hand. "There's only one way to save you and your family…and I guarantee you're not going to like it."

CHAPTER 22

Mia perched on the couch, her gun in her hand, her gaze on the man pacing the cabin while cocking his shotgun. He'd yanked on jeans but had neglected to clasp the top button.

She shook her head. While she was willing to listen to his plan, she'd take down his entire clan if they threatened her family. But for now, knowledge equaled power. "Okay. The cabin is secured, nobody is out there...what did you mean? How can I keep your people from coming after my family?"

He slid the curtain out of the way, his gaze on the darkness outside. "The only way to keep you safe is to make you one of us."

Her breath heated. Fog she'd been unaware of cleared from her mind. "You want to make me a wolf?" Absolutely not.

"Not exactly." Muscles rippled along his back as he moved to gaze out of the other window. "I can't turn you into a wolf. But I can mate you."

"*Mate* me?" she coughed out. What was this, some weird sci-fi movie? "You have got to be kidding me." While she had never researched such a thing, she did have an odd appreciation for urban fantasy and had read about matings. Who knew they actually existed? "Um, what exactly do you mean?"

He slid the curtain closed and turned the full force of those dangerous, multi-hued blue eyes on her. "What do you know about wolves?"

Apparently not enough. "Let's see. They're wild, there are different species, and they, uh, mate for life."

"Yes." The shotgun rested easily against his jean-clad thigh, the weapon not nearly as dangerous as the man. "We mate for life. While there may be a marriage, there's no divorce. While a mate lives, the mating rules." The air shimmered around him. "One of our strongest laws is that a mate is safe—even if he or she were human at one time. You want to live? You need to mate."

"Which means what?" she whispered.

His lids half-lowered. "I bite you during sex and mark you for life. You'd change then."

Anger and frustration heated the air in her lungs. "That's the lamest line I've ever heard to get someone into bed."

He tucked his free hand into his pocket, his eyes darkening. "Darlin', I've had you once, and I could easily have you again. If I wanted you naked and begging, I could make that happen in two seconds. You know it as much as I do."

What an ass. Of course, her nipples peaked at the dark timbre of his sexy voice. "I'm not turning into a wolf." What bizarre, crazy words to utter. But she'd seen him change into a wild animal, and she wasn't insane. Not yet, anyway.

"I already told you there's no chance you'd turn into a wolf. You'd be a mate, which means you'd change…a little," he said.

Terrific. She was a big believer in hair removal. The last thing she wanted was to grow fur on her face. "A little?"

He nodded. "Yes. Your immune system would improve to match mine, and your life expectancy would about double. Plus, your strength and speed should increase somewhat, and any other wolf out there will be able to scent me on you. Forever." A masculine, daring smile curved his lips.

"And if I say no?"

He lifted an eyebrow, losing the smile. "I'll protect you for as long as possible, Mia. But if you refuse, then you and I will both die. There's no way we can run from all four packs."

"Why?" she whispered. "Why would you protect me?"

He stilled, and his focus somehow sharpened even more on her. "I meant what I said the other night. You changed me. I care about you. More than I can explain."

She swallowed, her heart warming. There was no rational explanation for how much she already cared for him. Except maybe that she had lost her mind. "This is nuts."

A strong sigh echoed on his exhale. "Even if we mate, you should understand that my life expectancy isn't so great right now, anyway. But my family will protect you if I die."

A trembling started down her larynx. "Why would you die?"

"Ben is getting old, and both Erik and I have Alpha in our blood. Erik from Ben, and me from my biological father, who's long dead. A new Alpha has taken over that pack, so there's no room for me. Erik is the rightful Alpha of this pack, but many people think I am because of the adoption." Seth's forehead wrinkled, his lips turning down. "The pack is being torn apart, and only one of us can rule. At some point, Erik will challenge me—he can't help it. It's in his blood."

Mia jumped to her feet. "So beat him."

"I can't kill my brother." Apology as well as stubborn determination flitted across Seth's face. "Not even for you."

None of this made any sense. "Why can't you both rule?"

"We're wolves. There's only one Alpha."

"That's ridiculous," she sputtered.

"Maybe. But it's who we are," he said.

She'd like to join the pack just to change things. "How does a mating work? I mean, how does a mate's body change?"

Seth leaned the shotgun against the doorway. "I don't really know. Don't really care. Some think it's magic, some biology. It's just something we accept. Most of us are miners, not scientists. This is our way of life, and it is what it is. You in or not?"

Absolutely not. "I'm ex-FBI, Volk. Those people come after me, and they'll regret it."

His nostrils flared. "It's an honor to die protecting your pack, sweetheart. You'd have some of the best hunters and killers stalking you—ready to die for the cause."

A chill skittered down her spine. Based on Seth's military file, she knew he was one of the most dangerous hunters and trackers, as well as snipers alive today. And that was from reading between the lines. For him to be so sure, and so afraid of someone, gave her serious pause.

She cleared her throat. "What else comes with a mating?"

"Nothing." He looked her right in the eye.

Honesty shone on his face, but her instincts started humming. What wasn't he telling her? "Say we mate, and I leave you. Do I die or something?"

Danger lived in his frown. "I'd hoped that if we mated, you'd give us an honest shot. If you then left, well, no. You don't die. You just can't mate another wolf."

"So I could marry a human?"

A low growl rumbled from Seth's chest. "Yes."

If everything he said was true, there didn't seem to be a downside to being bitten by him. She'd get stronger, faster, and live longer. Even then, she didn't have to stay with him. "What am I missing?"

"I keep and protect what's mine, Mia Stone." His voice lowered to the timbre of gravel spinning in a mixer. The sentence was both a warning and a declaration.

So she did him the courtesy of returning the favor. "I chart my own path, Seth Volk. Period."

A ding sounded, and Seth yanked his cell phone from his

pocket. "What?" After listening for a moment, he shut his eyes and leaned his head against the door. "I understand. We'll be there at dawn." Ending the call, he lowered his head to meet her gaze. "My father is finishing the ceremony tonight but has your house surrounded. If we're not there at dawn, he's killing your mother and aunt."

Heat slammed into her gut. Mia shot toward the door. "I'll kill him."

Seth stopped her by wrapping both hands around her biceps. "You won't win. Not against twenty of them. They'll burn the house before letting you get to it. There's one chance, and I've spelled it out for you."

"Are my aunt and mother safe?" Her chest hurt.

"Yes. They won't even know they're being watched," he said.

There didn't seem to be much choice, and it'd give her an edge when dealing with Ben during dawn. This was so crazy. "Does mating hurt?"

"Yes."

So now he was being completely honest. Great. "No offense, but the last thing I want right now is to fuck you." She shrugged free from his hold.

"How about I fuck you, then?"

The coarse language matched the lust leaping into his eyes. Her abdomen warmed instantly, and her cheeks heated. A dangerous mixture of anger and desire rippled through her veins. "This might be the biggest mistake you've ever made."

"Of that, I have no doubt." His hand encircled her nape, drawing her closer even as he kept one hand on the gun. Warm lips wandered against hers, gentle and somehow sweet.

She grabbed him with her free hand, jerking him closer and deepening the kiss. Gentleness was the last thing she wanted— this was a logical move without emotion. Frankly, even though she'd seen him turn into a wolf, she wasn't so sure this whole mating situation held any truth. Maybe his job was to distract her.

Shoving him, she wrenched free. "I need to call my mother."

Keeping her gaze, he hit a number on his phone. "Go ahead."

The phone rang several times, and then Dotty sleepily answered. "For goodness' sake…what?"

Mia sighed in relief. "Hi, Aunt Dotty. Sorry to wake you, but I wanted to check on you and Mom."

"We're fine, sweetie. Your mom played with her wolf for a little while, and then she went to bed. Cute little thing is still on the deck asleep." She yawned loudly.

Dread iced through Mia until even her eyes chilled. "Um, okay. Well, I'm going to, uh…"

"You're a grown-up, Mia. I'll judge you at a later date. Night." Dotty hung up.

Mia slowly handed the phone back to Seth. "Your brother is on our deck in wolf form, but Dotty seemed fine."

Seth's jaw hardened. "Your family is safe until dawn. You have my word."

That would have to do, now wouldn't it? "You need to know, if I do this, it's only to protect my family. I have no intention of tying myself to anyone for life."

He smirked. "If I mate you, we're tied for life whether you like it or not."

"Only in your world. Not mine."

A veil dropped over his eyes. "True. But I'm hoping you'll stay in my world. At least give it a chance."

Why? So far, his world sucked and was mired in the customs of a century long gone. Besides, her past had screwed her up enough that all she knew how to do was fail at relationships. "I like you, and I'm attracted to you, but that's all I have to give."

He gripped her chin, his hold firm. "You're more than what you think, Mia. Trust me."

She didn't trust anybody. Not really. "For tonight, I will."

His hold firmed, and he lowered his lips to slide against hers. "That's a start, now isn't it?"

Allowing a wolf shifter to bite her shouldn't be done lightly, but she was short on time. Aunt Dotty and Gena were in danger, and if this would save them, then she had no choice. "Yes. It's a start." At the words, calmness centered her. She hadn't meant to promise anything, and yet her heart hitched.

Raising his head, he twined his fingers with hers, slowly leading her toward the bedroom.

He brought the gun with him.

Entering the quiet room, he nudged the door shut and slid the lock into place. He leaned the shotgun against the wall and held out a hand for her Glocks, gently placing the weapons on the night table.

Guns and sex. She tried to shake her head at the absurdity of the night, but the sexy man kept her attention. Seth was tall and strong, and an intensity lived within him that matched the wild animal he kept inside. Right now, he wanted to protect her for as long as possible.

That fact drew her even more than the passion sparking through her skin.

He reached for the hem of her shirt and slowly slid the material over her head. Gently, almost reverently, he unclasped her bra and smoothed the straps down her arms. Heat flared in his darkening eyes. "You're beautiful."

She'd never felt that way until Seth had really looked at her, his expression changing. For the first time, she felt beautiful. Flattening her hands on his rippling abs, she hummed. "You're something amazing." Something beyond human, which now made sense. "So strong."

He reached for her jeans, undoing the button and sliding down the zipper. "The marking hurts, Mia. Most humans can't take it, which is why we normally mate other wolves. I'm sorry to cause you pain."

Pride lifted her chin. She was as tough, if not tougher, than any female wolf out there. "I can take it. Don't worry."

"I know you can take the pain, but I wish you didn't have to." He frowned. "Maybe you should take a painkiller or something first."

Irritation jerked her head back. "Do female wolves take painkillers first?"

He stiffened. "No."

"Then I don't need one." Her stubbornness didn't make sense, but she didn't care. Nobody would ever say that she wasn't as tough as a female wolf.

"Okay." His palm slid up to cup her breast.

Fire ripped through her core.

Thunder roared across the sky outside, and rain began pelting the metal roof. Even so, the storm was nothing compared to the whirlwind inside her. His mouth took hers. She swayed, caught in his heat. So much need—so much want. Why did she respond like this to him?

Her eyes fluttered closed, and she sighed deep in her throat. The kiss was hot, sexy, and consumed all thought.

An explosion split the night.

Seth jerked away and grabbed the shotgun.

Shock widened her eyes to let in more light, while Seth's narrowed. He lifted his head and sniffed the air. Men's bellows echoed for him to come outside.

He growled. "There are at least ten, and I smell Frank Barnby."

"You can smell individual people?" she gasped, reaching for her gun.

"Yes. They're here against Ben's orders. Probably want to kill us and then deal with Ben as heroes." Seth grabbed her free hand and stalked toward the closet. Shoving shirts to the side, he exposed a large door, which he opened to reveal a dark tunnel. He pushed her inside, shut the closet door, and fixed the shirts before following her. "Run."

CHAPTER 23

The dark tunnel opened to another secluded bay where Seth had a metal boat hidden. Fire lit the night behind them, smoke rippling up as the rain battled the blaze. Another explosion competed with the storm. He yanked the vessel free and helped her into it, slipping the shotgun under the middle metal seat.

She shivered in the rain, topless and more than a little out of breath. "They're burning your house."

"Yeah." He grabbed the oars and instantly slid into a smooth series of strokes, hugging the shoreline and rowing away from his burning cabin. "The idiots don't realize Ben will kill them for disobeying his orders—whether or not they cleaned up a mess for him. They should know that."

"I'm the mess?" She shoved wet hair out of her face and hugged her bare skin.

"We both are." Seth's jaw firmed in the dim light. He glanced at her shivering body. "Hold on, sweetheart. I'll get you to warmth and safety."

She nodded, her gun in her hand, her gaze on the shoreline in case she needed to shoot. Right now, she'd love to shoot somebody.

Lightning zigzagged across the sky, illuminating Seth's bare torso and strong face. Fury lit his eyes and caused her to pause. His voice had been so calm, but a deadly rage danced in his luminous eyes.

She shivered again, this time not from the rain. "I'm sorry about your cabin."

His eyes cut through the night as he focused on her, still rowing rhythmically. "I'm not angry about the house."

"Oh?"

"No. I'm angry they came after you when you're under my protection. I stated the fact calmly and made it known to all. That's unforgivable." His deep voice held no mercy.

She swallowed and blinked rain off her eyelids. "You can't kill them all."

He didn't reply.

Thunder rolled again, and the rain increased in power. Waves slammed against the hull. Seth swore and angled toward the shore. Jumping out, he dragged the boat across a beach. "Jump out." He reached a hand to help her.

Once she'd steadied, he grabbed the gun. "Looks like we do this the old-fashioned way."

Mia sneezed, taking his hand as he jogged into the forest. "Old-fashioned?"

"Yep." He pushed her gently against a tree. "Outside with nature."

The bark scratched her, but she relaxed her arms as the boughs shielded her. "Will they find us?"

"No. They don't know where we are, and the storm will mask our scents long enough. At dawn, we need to hurry to your house." He yanked down several full branches from a pine tree, quickly securing them into a sort of shelter. Minutes later, he'd added more branches for fullness, as well as layered the ground with soft brush.

This was nuts. She couldn't actually be thinking of doing this. With him. Right now and in the cold. Wolves were real.

Her brain could not wrap itself around her new reality, so she just watched him work with nature. Then she coughed. "You're quite the Scout."

He grinned, the smile not softening him a bit. "Yeah, that's me."

Her teeth chattered.

He reached out a hand to draw her under the boughs. "Let me warm you."

Chills racked her knees as she stumbled forward. Seth removed her soaked clothing along with his, then laid her down, moving in to cradle her. His breath heated her ear as they spooned. "Just relax and warm up."

She wiggled her butt against his groin to get more comfortable. "You're warm."

"Yeah. Wolves are warmer than people. Trust me, this is a good thing."

His heat sank into her skin, seeping into her muscles. She sighed as the shivering stopped. "I feel better."

"Good."

The rain continued beating down, but the boughs kept them dry. As she relaxed, as she warmed, a new type of heat wandered through her abdomen. Seth wrapped around her, his chest cradling her back, his groin against her butt. He was hard—and ready.

She swallowed and tried to concentrate. Her heart picked up in pace. Butterflies winged through her abdomen. Her thighs clenched, and her sex softened.

He inhaled against her neck, the arm at her waist tightening. Slowly, his tongue caressed the shell of her ear.

She trembled and pressed back against him. The adrenaline of the night, the dangerous storm, the men after them...they all created a secluded, stolen moment in time. One full of intimacy and need. "Seth—"

"Shh," he whispered, pulling her onto her back. His palm flattened against her abdomen as he rose to one elbow.

She relaxed into the soft ground. "As bizarre as this entire night has been, this is the most romantic moment I could even imagine."

He caressed up between her breasts. "You have a sweetness to you, Mia Stone, that flays me open every time." Leaning over her, his thigh settled between her legs, and his mouth wandered along her jawline. Wet heat reached her earlobe, where he nipped.

She shifted against him and slid her hands down his broad back. Heat and muscle filled her palms. "I don't think anybody has ever called me *sweet*," she murmured against his skin, tracing his collarbone with her lips.

"Then they don't see the real you." He wandered along her cheekbone until he reached her mouth.

Firm, gentle, coaxing, his lips angled over hers, delving deep and making the world spin. She dug her fingers into his hair, holding him, her tongue tangling with his. He cupped her breast and wandered down her body to tease her clit.

She gasped into his mouth and arched herself into his hand.

He leaned back, pleasure curving his smile. "You're wet. For me."

His movements were slow, but an urgency hovered over the night. They didn't have much time until dawn.

So she gave him the truth. "Yes, I am."

Desire darkened his eyes to midnight. "Good." Ducking down, he flicked her nipple with his tongue.

Fire shot straight from her breast to her needy sex. He turned his attention to the other nipple, taking his time flicking and caressing her until her mind blanked. Then he wandered down her torso to kiss her clit.

A strangled cry caught in her throat. Even under pressure, the man liked to take his time. She shifted against his mouth. "We, ah, we need—"

His lips trapped her.

This time, the cry escaped. No. She needed to be quiet. "Seth, we don't have time. What if they—?"

He slipped one finger inside her and slowly licked her sex. "We have time," he rumbled against her.

Her eyes rolled back in her head. Need kept her in place as her mind spun. Then one thought had her focusing. Wait a minute. "Whoa, there. You don't bite me...I mean, you don't mark me—?"

"No." His thick hair brushed her legs. "I don't bite you here." He nipped her thigh. "Or here." He nibbled on her hip bone. "Or here." His lips enclosed her clit just as his finger brushed against her G-spot.

The world exploded as an orgasm roared through her with an intensity that made tears spring to her eyes. She rode out the waves, her body shuddering, her mind filled with him. Finally, he allowed her to come down. Her chest heaved, her ears rang, and her breath panted out, but every muscle was relaxed.

He kissed her mound softly and slid his hand under her butt to reach her lower back. With a sharp lift and a quick twist of his wrist, he flipped her onto her hands and knees.

She stilled. Soft brush filled her palms when she tried to keep her balance. Her mind sharpened as a dark desire flared awake in her nerves. "Wait, Seth. I don't do this—"

"You do now." Hands on her hips gripped her, holding her in place. "This is how it has to happen, Mia."

A quivering rippled through her abdomen at his dark, authoritative tone. Her body flared to life while her brain flashed warning signals. She'd never trusted a man enough to turn her back on one, much less let one take her like this. Vulnerability quickened her breathing until her lungs ached. "No, I—"

"Yes." He angled over her and reached around to palm her

breast. His thighs brushed the backs of hers, and he tweaked her nipple at the same time his tongue traced her ear.

She trembled in need, her fear momentarily forgotten. Desire coursed through her and pinpointed right where his cock waited at her entrance. "Don't hurt me." Not for a second did she mean physically.

"Never. I'll never hurt you." He paused, his body vibrating against her, so much strength and muscle held in check. His dangerous fingers tapped down to tug gently on her clit. "I'll stop if you want."

Flames shot through her entire body as her nerves short-circuited with so much need her eyes swam. "Don't...stop. Please...don't...stop."

The hand on her hip flexed, and he pushed inside her, one inch at a time, letting her body accept him. Finally, he was fully inside her, pulsing.

Oh, God.

He warmed her from within, so hot, so large. Holding her in place, he began to move, slowly at first, and then with a speed that fluttered her lids shut. Pleasure cut hard through her, too intense to allow for anything but total immersion.

His thighs shoved hers farther apart. A strong hand banded under her chin, lifting her head, keeping her firmly in place.

She couldn't move if she wanted to.

He hammered into her, his stomach against her back.

Faster.

Harder.

Stronger.

"Now, Mia," he whispered in her ear.

A blast of heat spiraled from her core, shooting through her torso and limbs. Intense waves of raw pleasure rippled through her as all sound, all sight, all thought disappeared into insignificance. Too powerful to be termed an orgasm, the flash of light enveloped her, and she cried out his name.

Sharp canines sank into her right shoulder, the pain catching her second cry in her lungs. Her eyes flashed open. On pure instinct, she struggled to escape the hurt.

He held her tightly, his teeth piercing tissue and muscle until embedding in bone. With a low growl, his jaw snapped shut, and his teeth met in the middle. He pounded into her—taking as he marked.

Tears ripped into her eyes. She gasped, coughing out pain.

He stopped moving and ground against her, his entire body stiffening as he came. Slowly, he relaxed around her. His teeth retracted.

She cried out as they scraped back through her flesh. A shudder racked her body.

He withdrew and tugged her to the ground, pulling her onto her back so he could cover her. Gentle hands smoothed the hair from her face and wiped away her tears.

He kissed her. "I'm sorry I hurt you, Mia. I'm so sorry."

She nodded and took several deep breaths. "I'm all right." But she wasn't. Not even close.

CHAPTER 24

Mia settled her stance and peered around the tree. Pinks and golds lightened the eastern sky as the sun peeked above the mountains. The wind had banished the clouds, but the rain had drenched the ground. Her boots offered stability, her gun gave her security, but her shoulder burned like a brand.

Just before dawn, Seth had retrieved her go-bag from the trunk of her car, so she'd have clothes and a weapon for this meeting. Apparently wolves could travel distances faster than she'd imagined.

Wolves. This wasn't a dream. Last night had really happened, and a wolf shifter had bitten her to the bone.

So far, she didn't feel any different. Maybe Seth had been full of it and had just wanted to bite her. Of course, those canines had reached much farther into her flesh than ordinary teeth could without causing serious damage. Her orgasm had been incredible, but that could've resulted from an adrenaline rush and gratitude at still being alive.

But there was no discounting reality. Right now, her only focus had to be on protecting her family.

As she took in the ten men silently waiting near her deck, she wondered how long she'd be alive. While none of the them appeared to hold weapons, as wolves, they probably didn't need them. The cabin lay dark and quiet in the background. Hopefully, Gena and Dotty would sleep through whatever was about to happen.

Mia gripped her weapon with sure hands and slid into view.

Seth stood next to her, still barefoot, still only wearing jeans. An animal in human form.

Barely.

Relief crossed Benjamin Volk's face as he gazed at his son. So he had heard about the cabin being burned down. Hardening his expression, he widened his stance while the other men remained passive and stoic behind him. His eyes burned, and he kept his gaze on Seth. "I'm sorry it has come to this," he murmured.

Seth angled his body, shielding Mia slightly. "I won't allow you to kill her." His tone was absolute, with more than a hint of a growl.

That was *so* not how this was going down. Mia maneuvered from behind him to face the crowd, her weapon pointed between Benjamin's eyes. "Try it, Ben."

The men around Benjamin shifted slightly, and one cast a quick glance at the other.

Seth didn't move. Were they that afraid of him? It was two against eleven, and a couple of the men appeared more cautious than angry. Just how dangerous was Seth Volk that a bunch of wolves feared him?

She swallowed but kept her aim true on their leader.

Erik, his gaze sober, stepped forward to stand by his father. He had Seth's size, but his expression was more concerned than anything else. "There has to be another way to fix this. Nobody needs to die. I'm sure Mia will sign a confidentiality agreement."

How odd. Seth's brother was trying to protect her. Too bad she might have to shoot his father.

Benjamin's brow wrinkled, and he sneered. "We're not accountants. Don't be stupid."

So. No confidentiality agreement. Good to know. Mia relaxed shoulders that had suddenly tensed. If she squeezed the trigger, her aim needed to be true.

Erik snarled, suddenly looking every bit as dangerous as his brother. "I repeat. Nobody needs to die here, especially an innocent woman."

"I agree," Seth said. Then he waited.

Benjamin frowned, indecision quickly crossing his face only to be smoothed out. "There is no other way."

The breeze picked up, ruffling Mia's hair.

Benjamin lifted his head, and his shoulders shot back. His nostrils flared. "You're fucking kidding me."

As one, the other men followed suit, a series of growls coming from a couple of them.

A wide smile brightened Erik's face. "Congratulations, Bro."

"Thank you," Seth rumbled. "Any questions?"

What was going on? The hair rose on the back of Mia's neck. She kept her aim true, her stance set. "Care to explain, Seth?" she muttered.

"They smell me on you...and you on me." Pure, male satisfaction tilted his lips in something too pissed-off to be a smile. He focused on his father but raised his voice enough to include the group at large. "I'm available right now if anybody wants to challenge me. Otherwise, accept my mating and stay the hell out of my way."

Benjamin flashed sharp canines. "You'd challenge me over her?"

"In a heartbeat," Seth said without hesitation.

Warmth followed quickly by unease slithered through Mia's skin at the declaration. Possessive and absolute, the tone didn't hint at the temporary nature of their relationship. Or union. Or whatever a wolf mating turned out to be.

A wolf mating. How freaking odd.

Erik's smile didn't wane. "I'm not challenging you. I like her." Then he did sober. "But she's human." He looked her over, head to toe. "Should we get her to one of our doctors?"

Doctors? "Why do I need a doctor?" she asked.

Seth angled his head toward her, keeping his gaze on the threats. "I told you. Mating isn't easy for humans."

"I can handle it," she said. So far, she felt fine.

Erik lifted his chin. "If you need help and can't find Seth, call me. I'll come right away." He rattled off a phone number.

Well. That was sweet.

"This won't do," Benjamin snapped.

She cleared her throat, her gun on Benjamin, her gaze on Erik. "This is the last, and I mean *the last*, time you use my family to threaten me. If any of you comes near my family again, I'll take you out…with…silver…bullets."

Erik lifted one eyebrow. "I was protecting Gena, not threatening her."

Mia gave a short nod. "Keep it that way."

His eyes twinkled. "She's my friend. I always protect my friends, and I have every intention of continuing to do so." He shoved his hands into his jeans pockets. "Plus, now we're family." His chuckle rode the breeze. "Also, I believe you'd better tell your mate about the threat to you from the man in DC."

"Shut up." Benjamin exhaled slowly. "Does your woman understand our laws?"

"Yes," Seth said.

His woman? Laws? What laws? Mia cut a hard look at Seth but remaining quiet seemed wise. Taking on so many men would be a considerable risk, and she couldn't put Gena and Dotty in such danger.

Benjamin eyed Mia, his jaw firming. "She is human. You can reverse this."

Mia jolted. "You can?"

"No," Seth said. "There's no reversal. Period." His jaw might as well have been made from stone.

Instinctively, she looked at Erik. He seemed to be the one most willing to actually discuss the situation.

He shuffled his feet. "Sometimes, it takes a few good bites to fully convert a human to a wolf mate. I figure it's just because of the different genetics. Each time can be...difficult."

"I'm sure we got it in one," Seth drawled. He hooked his thumbs in his worn jean pockets. "I'm getting bored. Either attack or get the fuck off this property."

Benjamin reared back. "We'll discuss this and the burning of your cabin once we're back at the ranch. Be at the homestead in fifteen minutes." He pivoted toward the road.

One of the men grabbed his arm. "Wait a minute. We can't just let her live."

Faster than sound, Ben whirled around and grabbed the guy around the neck, slamming him to the ground. The sound of his head bouncing off the deck ricocheted through the morning as the wood splintered. "Question me again, and you die." His lips twisted in a snarl.

Mia tightened her hold on her weapon. Adrenaline flooded through her, making her lightheaded. That was new. Why was she dizzy?

The downed man gasped and then nodded. When Ben released him, he shoved to his feet, blood pouring from his temple. Without another sound, Benjamin took his leave, followed by the other men.

Except Erik.

He slowly crept toward Mia. Genuine amusement lit his eyes, though a wild glint glowed deep within that she hadn't noticed before. He smiled, suddenly appearing much younger. "Welcome to the family. I always wanted a sister."

Seth sighed.

Erik lost all levity as he looked at his brother. "I'll help you protect her. On my honor." Then he grinned again. "A human FBI agent sister. I never would've dreamed this one up. And, Seth, she's probably in danger from a human in DC, just FYI." His laughter trailed on the wind as he turned and jogged into the forest.

Mia lowered her weapon. "If I find out Barnby or anyone else who burned your cabin is dead, I'm going to arrest your father for murder."

Seth shrugged, turning to face her. No expression hinted at whatever was going on in his head. "What danger was my brother talking about?"

"The partner of the guy I shot," she said. "There's been another killing in Kentucky, and that's all I know. One thing at a time, Seth. I will arrest all of you if necessary."

"I'm fairly certain you'd need some sort of proof to arrest somebody, Deputy Stone."

Now didn't seem to be the time to inform him she had every intention of arresting Barnby the second she finished checking on her mother. Hearing the man yell out to Seth before the flames had engulfed the cabin gave her excellent probable cause to bring him in. She took a deep breath. "What laws does your father want me to understand?"

"Just one. Don't tell anybody about us."

Yeah, like anybody would believe her anyway. "Not a problem."

Seth shuffled his feet, tracing a finger down her face. "Are you all right?"

Actually, her head hurt, her shoulder burned, and her skin prickled. Her body warmed from his gentle touch, and desire spiraled through her abdomen. "I'm fine."

"You're going to have a physical reaction to the marking, sweetheart. Hopefully not too extreme, but most humans have a difficult time." Concern furrowed his prominent brow. "Let me help you through the process."

"What if one bite didn't do it?" Curiosity filtered through the odd sensations bombarding her.

"Then we'll do it again," he said, his eyes glinting.

She cocked her head. "Just hypothetically, what if a human doesn't take a mating the first time. Does it go away?"

He ruffled his dark hair. "No. It never goes away, but they wouldn't fully transform. It's my understanding that it's a weird limbo situation that is never comfortable."

Well, that sounded just great. She sighed.

He cupped her face. "Let me help you. Come home with me and spend the day relaxing. I'll even make you breakfast. We can figure out the situation with the killer in Kentucky."

It was shocking how tempting a day of domestic bliss with him was to her. She needed time to think. "Thanks, but I have work to do." Without question, she required distance from the sexy wolf and his devastating touch. "Unless you want to tell me who murdered Ruby and Mandy." She needed to solve their murders before going back east.

He dropped his hand to his side. "If I knew, I'd tell you. Now you can at least understand that we'll take care of the situation. The human police force needs to leave it be."

"That's not going to happen." Even if Mia agreed, which she certainly did not, Pete would never drop the case. "I'm still going to do my job." She still felt like Mandy's death was her fault.

Seth rubbed his chin while irritation filtered across his handsome face. "You're a stubborn one. Things are different now. We're different. You'll need to learn to trust me and work with me. Ever heard of compromise?"

Discomfort made her hands tremble as she tucked the gun into her jeans. "Um, no. Besides, things aren't really different. I'm still mostly human. You're, well, not...this isn't forever."

"This could be forever, and you're not human. I marked you and felt the change." He grasped her arms, vulnerability darkening the blues in his eyes. "We could have forever."

Panic increased her breathing. They weren't on the same side, and she was a crappy bet. Besides, no way could she live in the backward world the wolves had created in this little town. "No. Seth, trust me. Don't give me your heart."

He released her, his eyes softening. "My heart? Jesus, Mia. You already have my soul." Then he turned toward the forest and didn't look back. "Call me if you have any trouble with the transition." Several broad strides later, he disappeared from sight.

Transition?

CHAPTER 25

Mia stood outside the door of the station's single interrogation room while taking several deep breaths to calm her seizing lungs. Chills swept through her, and her stomach cramped.

Pete shoved keys into his pocket and glanced at his phone. "My pals in DC didn't find any other similar crimes, and bad news on the court file for Eddy Johnson. Somehow, it's lost."

Mia huffed. "That's convenient."

"Right? Also, the recording from the ATM camera should be in my inbox any minute. Let's hope Ruby is on it. Maybe whoever killed her is on it, too. We can watch it after you interview Frank Barnby."

Mia's brain pounded. Her body didn't seem to be enjoying the transition, whatever that meant. "Thanks for bringing Barnby in for me." She'd called Pete right after she'd checked on her mother and Dotty. Both women had slept through the entire standoff taking place outside the cabin at dawn.

Pete nodded. "Barnby didn't even make a fuss when I brought him in, just said he heard that you and Volk had died in a fire and didn't know who started it. Cocky bastard."

Mia forced a smile, her grip tightening on the manila case file. "He thinks I'm dead, huh?"

"Oh, yeah." Pete failed to return the grin. "Uh, though, what *were* you doing at Volk's place last night?"

"Questioning him about Mandy," Mia smoothly lied. "Then things went south from there."

"Good thing he had an escape ready." Pete hitched his pants over his belly. "Though I find the entire situation weird."

If he only knew. "I'd like to take Barnby alone," Mia said.

"Fine with me. He's handcuffed to the table, so he won't give you any problems." Pete frowned. "You feeling all right? You're kind of flushed."

Nausea swirled through her belly. "I'm fine. Probably fighting the flu."

"Oh." Pete stepped back. A rueful smile slid across his face. "Keep your distance, then. I don't need to get sick."

Mia rolled her eyes and opened the door to the small room. Worn bricks lined all four walls, and the only window was a small square in the door. The room also lacked surveillance equipment, unlike larger city or FBI interrogation rooms.

Barnby sat cuffed to the table, a bored expression on his face. At seeing her, his jaw dropped open.

She shut the door and took a seat across the scarred wooden table. Reaching into her pocket, she drew out her phone to place it on the table. But she didn't push the record button. "Surprise, Frank."

He jerked back, his cuffed hands jingling the silver.

Mia smirked at the pure silver cuffs. "Yeah, I wouldn't want to be you, Barnby. Attempted murder of a police officer carries additional jail time in Washington. Jail time away from pretty Lost Lake and its big moon."

His gaze hardened. "You didn't see me."

"Nope, but I heard you and am more than willing to testify about it." She dropped the manila file on the table. "So is Seth."

All color slid from Barnby's face.

Mia pursed her lips. "Oh, yeah. Seth is alive, too. He smelled you and heard you right before you lit his home on fire." She tapped her fingers on the table. "You know, I feel like he's more infuriated by the fact that you tried to kill me, since he made that archaic claim that I was under his protection."

Barnby swayed.

"Yep. Is it a big deal to kill someone's woman in your society?" She opened her eyes wider, going for his jugular. She didn't like it, but she knew how to get to him. "Seth and his daddy are pretty darn pissed at you. Your job at the mine is probably *terminated*." As was his life, if Seth had anything to say about it.

Barnby shook his head. "You don't understand. I can't go to jail. I need to leave town and now."

"Oh, I *do* understand." Mia leaned toward him, lowering her voice. Maybe this would work, maybe not. "Take a whiff."

His forehead crinkled as he frowned and inhaled deeply. Shock froze him in place. "Holy shit."

Her body warmed. "I'm your only way out of here. Talk to me."

Then he threw back his head and laughed, the sound obnoxious in the small room. "This is awesome."

Mia kept her face a calm mask. He was laughing? She couldn't let him know he'd just thrown her, so she remained perfectly still. "How so?"

Barnby glanced at the closed door and leaned toward her. "The Volk family Enforcer mating a human? Not only a human, but a cop? His *daddy* will rip out his throat before the next sunrise."

Mia's vision wavered as a blast of nausea ripped through her stomach. "Seth can take care of himself."

Barnby tilted his head to the side. "You feeling okay, bitch? Looks like the transition is starting."

"Never felt better," Mia said calmly, swallowing to shove bile back down her throat. "It's my understanding that the risk is to the human when she mates a wolf. Right?"

Barnby shrugged. "Wolves mate wolves—especially Alphas. Somebody like you would weaken the bloodline, which weakens the entire pack. Of course, Seth will never be Alpha, so you probably just tied yourself to a dead man. Even if Ben doesn't kill him today, he will eventually—or Erik will when he takes over...which more than ever will happen now. Even Seth's supporters will turn away now that he's mated...you."

Sweat sprang up along her spine. The tissues in her throat thickened. "You do realize that not only did you commit attempted murder of a cop last night, you tried to slaughter Seth's mate. Alpha or not, he'll kill you." As she forced out the words, the truth of them chilled her blood. Yet satisfaction filled her as Barnby paled again.

He sniffed, his gaze darting around the narrow room. "I want my lawyer."

"You can call him." Mia stood and locked her knees to keep from falling over. "You have one chance. Work with me, and I'll protect you."

Muddy brown eyes took her measure. "Work with you how?"

"Tell me who killed Ruby and Mandy."

His face hardened. "What exactly do you think an Enforcer does?" Barnby's lip twisted. "You sure you want to know?"

"Of course, I want to know." Her breath quickened. "Who killed them?"

Barnby shrugged, his eyes gleaming. "I think you already know. Seth Volk killed them both."

Fury and dread shoved the nausea from Mia's stomach. "Seth has been cleared for Mandy's murder. He'd already left town."

"He was cleared as a human. Seth Volk is all wolf, even in human form. You should know that." Barnby snorted. "Wolves travel fast, remember? Human timelines don't work for him."

Mia swallowed. Barnby was lying. He had to be. She turned and strode through the door to find Pete on the other side. "He wants to call a lawyer."

Pete nodded and gestured for a deputy to take care of it. Then Pete gestured Mia toward his office. "The ATM video arrived a minute ago. Let's go see if we can find Ruby on it."

"I'll meet you in your office." Mia lurched over to sink into the chair at her temporary desk near the corner. Pain pills rattled when she threw the aspirin bottle back into her desk drawer after swallowing two dry. If her head ached any more, the damn thing might explode. Pressing both hands on the desk, she shoved to her feet.

The walls morphed around her like those in a carnival fun house. Rubbing her eyes, she concentrated on placing one foot in front of the other until she arrived at the guest chair in Pete's office.

Both of his eyebrows rose. "You okay?"

"Yes." She glanced toward the monitor on the far wall. "Let's watch this, and then I may take the rest of the day off."

"Good idea." Pete reached for the remote perched on his desk, and the screen filled with the back parking lot of the tavern. "We have from six o'clock to midnight here." He pushed a button, and the recording began to fast forward.

About half an hour into the recording, Ruby arrived in the back lot, jumping out of an older Miata. Alone. She looked young and carefree with her dark hair swinging around her shoulders. Many other people arrived and entered through the back door... many people Mia had seen turn into wolves the previous night. Other people, ones she didn't recognize, also used the back entrance.

Her skin tingled with fever. She cleared her throat but the lump in the center remained. "I wish we had CCTV of the front entrance."

Pete nodded, his gaze on the screen as he fast-forwarded to around midnight.

The back door opened, and Ruby came into view. Laughing,

she stepped into the parking area followed by Erik Volk. He had a hand against the small of her back, and his gait was graceful.

Mia sat straight up in her seat. "Hello, Erik."

Erik laughed along with Ruby and swung her around for a passionate kiss. He palmed her butt and rubbed her against him. Finally, he pulled away and dropped a light peck on her nose. Then he said something, his gaze serious, his eyes soft.

Pete leaned forward. "Looks like our boy was in love."

Mia nodded. Wow. That was the real thing.

Ruby smiled and said something to Erik that instantly slid a huge grin across his face. With another kiss to her nose, he turned and went back into the bar.

"Interesting," Pete muttered. "He loved her."

Yeah. He had, and the man hadn't seemed to be mourning lately. Was he just that good at hiding his emotions? "What could've gone wrong between the scene we just saw and her death about three hours later?" Mia asked. Not that she hadn't seen domestic violence cases during her career.

Pete shrugged and then squinted. "What's that?" He pointed to the far right corner of the screen.

In shadow, something moved. Slowly, a man took shape as he maneuvered into the light. The bright moon highlighted Seth's face, every hard and predatory angle.

Adrenaline ripped through Mia's veins as her fight or flight instincts took control. "Looks like the brothers were competing."

On the screen, Ruby jumped back, her hand to her chest. Then she relaxed when she apparently recognized Seth.

Seth said something, and Ruby frowned. She sighed and glanced toward the closed door, resignation on her pretty face. Then, with a slight nod, she turned toward her car.

Grasping her elbow, Seth escorted her to the passenger side of her beat-up Miata. Ruby took one last look at the closed door, sorrow and an odd hope filtering across her face. Then she straightened her shoulders and slipped into the car.

Seth shut the door and stalked around to slide into the driver's seat. Within seconds, the car rolled out of camera view.

Betrayal blurred Mia's vision. She stood as nausea rippled through her gut. "Bring him in," she said before hustling to the door. Hopefully, she'd make it to the bathroom before puking.

Damn Seth Volk.

CHAPTER 26

Seth fought the very real urge to lunge across the desk and punch his father in the nose. "I mated her, and I'm keeping her."

Ben rolled his eyes. "That woman has no intention of being kept, and you damn well know it. You mated her to save her... because you love her. That green-eyed human grabbed your heart, and you're never getting it back." He smiled. "She's a gutsy one, she is."

Seth swallowed and leaned back in his chair. "It sounds like you admire her."

Ben shrugged. "I do. She's feisty, fragile, and female. I like her. She reminds me of your mother."

The world had just stopped spinning. "I'm confused."

Amusement lifted Ben's lip. "Get used to it."

Erik cleared his throat from his position by the mantel in the study. "So, uh, what's the plan now?"

Ben lost his smile. "Now we have an even bigger problem than before." His eyes darkened with sobriety. "Most of our people will want your head on a spike because you mated a human. Your mother's people won't like it, and I've always been concerned they'll come after you so you can never challenge their current Alpha."

Seth's head jerked back. "You're concerned?"

"Of course." Ben narrowed his eyes. "You might be the most stubborn son of a bitch alive, but you're my damn son. I don't want anything to happen to you."

Seth's mouth opened, but no sound emerged. He slid suddenly sweaty palms down his jean-clad legs. "I don't understand. You know Erik needs to be Alpha, and there's only one way for that to happen."

Ben slowly nodded. "I know. Our people will only accept him. But I thought we'd have some time to figure out where you could go—somewhere safe. Now, I have to figure out where both you and Mia can go that's safe." Despair lived in his frown. "So far, I have no solution."

If Ben had turned green and said he hailed from Mars, Seth would've been less surprised. "You're not my father."

"Yes, I am. I adopted you, and you're mine." Ben shook his head. "Damn stubborn boy."

Denial fought with hope in Seth's chest. "You only adopted me because my mother insisted upon it."

Ben grimaced. "I know. That's true. But within a week of you living here, you became my son. I meant it, and I'm proud of you. You're mine, Seth. Period."

The shock at the words wasn't nearly as strong as the shock coursing through Seth at how much he needed to hear the words. "I, ah, thanks." Memories rushed into his brain, so many, so fast. The hours Ben had spent teaching him to fight. To drive. To play sports. The pride in the old man's eyes when he succeeded.

Ben really did care.

Thanks was a stupid thing to say. "I mean, I, uh, love you, too."

Erik chuckled. "You two are just freaking fantastic with the mushy words."

Ben rolled his eyes. "Spare me from know-it-alls."

Seth rubbed the scruff on his chin. "I think I've been out of it lately."

Benjamin's gaze softened. "It's the Alpha blood in you wanting to come to the surface. You've both kept amazing control of yourselves."

Seth rolled his neck. "Thanks."

Benjamin nodded. "You're just lucky I'm healthy, and our opponents won't be throwing you two jackasses in an arena to fight it out for Alpha quite yet."

Seth needed to find a safe place for Mia, so that never happened.

Erik turned on him, all amusement gone. "I think it's time you told me what you were doing with Ruby, Seth."

Ben reached for a cigar. "Yes. It's time to clear the air."

"I agree," said a voice from the doorway.

Seth jumped up and placed his body between the door and his father. He'd been so involved in the discussion that he hadn't heard or smelled the sheriff. Pete stood at the door, gun drawn.

"Well, hello, Sheriff."

Pete nodded. "You need to come downtown with me, Seth. Mia and I have some questions for you."

Seth stilled. Mia was at the station? The woman had to be sicker than a dog from the transition. She needed to go home, and now. He growled. "Let's go."

Ben grabbed his phone and started dialing. "Don't say a word until your lawyer gets there." Then he chuckled. "Mia had you arrested. Yeah, she's just like your mother."

Seth failed to see the humor in the situation. When he reached the station, he and his mate were going to have a little talk. From now on, she'd damn well take care of herself...and stop arresting him.

While he'd never act as Alpha of a pack, an Alpha he was. His mate needed to understand what that meant.

* * *

SETH STRODE through the front door of the police station and right to Mia's temporary workstation. "You need to go home. Now."

Pete walked behind him. "You got this?"

"Yes. I'd like a moment with Mr. Volk." She stood. "Seth, come with me." Her head hurt, but she hid the pain and strode to the interrogation room that only had the one window in the door. Once inside, she shut it and turned to face him. "Now is your last chance, lover. Did you kill Ruby?"

Fire lit his eyes while his lips compressed into a dangerous line. Warmth assailed her as he stepped into her space.

Instinct ruled as she raised both hands to ward him off. "Back off, Volk."

He towered over her with at least an extra foot of height. At least an extra hundred pounds of muscle. And without question, a much more dangerous temper. "After the other night, how can you ask me that?"

Doubt had her clearing her throat, yet she tilted her chin. "The other night was just sex. Now answer the question."

He stilled. The air shifted with just enough pressure to kick her heart into gear. A low growl rumbled from his chest. "It was more than sex."

"Grow up. Sex is sex." Showing softness would wrench away control of the moment. So, she yanked the knife from her back pocket. The silver glinted with a knowing power under the fluorescent lights.

His instant smile was the angriest expression she'd ever seen. A shiver wound down her spine to chill her entire body. When he stepped forward, she took an unwilling step back.

Seth eyed the knife. "You'd stab me, even knowing what that would do if you got it to my bloodstream."

"Yes." She met his gaze squarely as she bluffed. The best

trainers in the world had taught her how to evade and lie, and she was good at it. But no way did she want to see him suffer such pain.

He shoved his hands into his pockets and moved until the knife rested against his abdomen. "Prove it."

As dares went, it was a good one. "I don't want to harm you if I don't have to. Just answer my question."

"I'm going to count to three, Mia, and you'd better stab me."

The man actually wanted to writhe in pain. Temptation rose to teach him a lesson, to teach him she'd meet any dare. But her hand began to tremble on the weapon. She tightened her grip. "What happens at three?"

"I take the knife away from you." Matter-of-fact, his voice failed to mask the pissed-off hue of his multi-colored eyes. "One."

She slid back, twisting her hand just enough for a better angle on the weapon. Her breath heated while adrenaline shot through her veins. "Don't push me."

He mirrored her step. "Two."

She couldn't let him take the knife. For all time, he'd doubt she meant what she said. "Last chance. Back the fuck off, Volk."

"Three."

They moved at the same time. Mia shot the knife down to pierce his thigh just as he swept out his arm. The blade ripped through his jeans and then clattered across the floor. Blood dotted the way.

He grabbed her arms and flipped her around.

With a hiss, she slapped both hands on the brick wall and shoved back, but he was quicker. Heat and muscle plastered against her back, holding her in place. His hand swept down her front, shoving her arms down so she faced the wall.

Trapped.

A relentless arm banded around her waist, holding her in place. Seth's free hand clutched her hair at the nape and tugged her head to the side, exposing her jugular.

Quick breaths panted out as her lungs compressed, and she tried to fight. Fury spiraled heat into her cheeks when she couldn't move. Her mind cleared as she waited for him to make a move she could counter.

Sharp teeth sank into her neck.

Pain flared her nervous system to life. Her eyes opened wide. It wasn't a normal bite. Worse yet, raw desire commingled with the rage heating her blood. She tried to jerk away. "You fucking wolf. Get your canines out of me."

The deadly points retracted, and his rough tongue soothed the wound. "As I recall, you like me inside you." Anger rode the low tone while warm breath brushed her neck.

What was wrong with her that this show of dominance was turning her on? "That was a mistake."

His voice roughened even further. "Don't like fucking an animal, sweetheart?"

"No."

His hold tightened. The hard line of his erection pressed into her back, and she fought a groan.

A low chuckle whispered along her skin. "Liar. I may be an animal, but I can smell your need, Mia Stone. I could mount you right here, right now, and you'd fucking beg for more."

Fury shot her head back, and she twisted to throw an elbow.

He released her waist to clasp her throat, keeping her head against him. "Not nice."

"Let go of me."

"Not yet. First, we get a couple of things straight." A sharp fang nipped her earlobe before he licked his way around the shell.

Her knees began to tremble—and not from fear. Not even close. "We're in the police station," she breathed to remind them both.

"Keep that in mind. I don't give a shit where we are. Any time you draw silver on me, I'll react. There's something between us, and it's time you understood the rules."

Rules? She jerked her head and nailed him in the lip. His low hiss made her smile. "If I scream, the sheriff will come running."

Another male chuckle. "If you scream, the sheriff will know you can't handle a suspect all by yourself, little girl. We both know there's no way you'll scream."

If she could inch to the left, she could hook a foot around his leg. Slowly, she slid her foot to the side.

"No." He yanked her back in place. "Here's the deal. We're together, like it or not. And next time you pull silver on me, I swear to whatever God you believe in, every time you try to sit for the next week, you'll regret the silver."

She paused and frowned at the brick wall. "You can't be serious."

"Deadly."

"I'm a trained agent, Volk."

"Then I strongly suggest you don't try to use silver against me, Deputy." He flipped her around, his body keeping her in place. "You need to know; I don't give a damn where we are or who's around."

His eyes had darkened to the hue of midnight absent a moon.

She shook her head, her mind fuzzy. "You can't honestly be saying—"

"I am. You need everything spelled out for you, don't you?" He leaned until his face was only an inch from hers. "Okay. If you pull silver on me again, I will retaliate and teach you a lesson you don't want to learn. In other words, your ass will wear my palm print for a week. Maybe two if you piss me off enough."

Oh, she had to teach this jackass a lesson. "You know I could take you down with at least three different moves right now, right?"

"Maybe." He shrugged. "My training is just as good as yours. Regardless, take me down *without* silver in your hand, and we'll just grapple. You have silver, you get spanked."

Her mouth opened and then shut, but words failed her. She

cleared her throat. "You even try it, asshole, and not only will I have you arrested for battery, I'll kick your wolf-ass to the lake and back." Then she'd take whatever silver she had and shove it through his stubborn hide.

"Then we understand each other." With a hard press of his mouth on hers, he released her and stepped back.

The door opened.

Pete and Lenessee walked in. Pete's eyebrows rose, and he glanced from Mia to Seth, his hand resting casually on his holstered gun. "Everything okay here?"

"Fine." Mia shoved past Seth and reached for the stack of papers. She wanted to stay and question Seth about being with Ruby the night she died, but the room kept spinning, and she needed to throw up. Like now. "Mr. Volk refuses to cooperate. I'll let you handle him." Keeping her chin up, she swept from the room, continuing through the hallway until she reached the outside. Enough of this crap. If Seth wouldn't tell her the truth, she'd find out herself—after the world stopped spinning around her.

The transition was getting stronger. What did that mean?

CHAPTER 27

Mia stumbled into the cabin, where the scent of baked chicken nearly made her hurl. Her vision hazy, she waved a hand at her mother and Dotty, where they sat at the table, eating dinner. "I'm sick. Flu. Stay there."

Her mind spun, right along with her stomach as she crept up the stairs and fell onto her bed. Had Seth killed Ruby? If so, why? If not, why the big secret that he'd been with her that night? Mia had to get over this transition so she could think again and figure out what had happened to Ruby and Mandy.

If Seth was a killer, she'd take him down.

If he wasn't, she'd probably have to apologize to him.

Either way, if her head exploded, she wouldn't have to worry about it.

Her brain might shatter. She whimpered and yanked a pillow over her face. Flashes zinged behind her eyes. Lights shaped like sharp knives. Her blood boiled to the temperature of lava.

She bit her lip to keep from crying out and tasted copper. Minutes compounded to create hours. Her mother checked on her a couple of times, smoothing a cool hand over her neck and muttering.

Then the house went silent as nighttime fell. Blissful quiet surrounded her while her body went crazy. Dreams combined reality with imagination. In a haze, she ran through the forest in wolf form, the night alive, the colors vibrant.

Every time she woke back in her bed, she breathed out in disappointment—and pain. Agony escaped her body through every single pore.

Tears shot from her eyes to soak the sheet. Tremors racked her body until her teeth rattled.

Finally, a steady hand removed the pillow from her head and rolled her over onto her back.

She whimpered in protest as moonlight bathed her body where it streamed in from the now-open window.

"Shhh," Seth whispered, stretching out and cradling her. "Two things will help you through this: the moon and me." He wiped tears from her cheeks, the pads of his fingers rough but his touch gentle.

The shuddering subsided. Warmth cut through the chill. "What's happening?" she croaked through a mouth that might've well been filled with cotton balls.

"You're transitioning from human to mate." He stroked her arm. "Relax and let the change happen. Soon you'll be so strong, you'll be able to arrest me anytime and anywhere you want… without backup."

Ha. She'd seen how strong he was. She'd always need backup with him. "I don't want to change."

"You will as soon as you feel healthy again."

The strong scent of wild sage filled her nostrils, providing a sense of safety and peace. "How are you here?" she slurred.

"My lawyer is very good. All you had was the recording, which isn't proof I killed anybody." Seth unbuttoned her sweat-soaked shirt and tugged her arms free. The air instantly dried her.

Mia sighed as her body relaxed. "Did you kill her?"

"Of course not." He pulled off her pants and settled the blanket securely around her. "You know I don't need to use silver to incapacitate anyone. Nor do I kill women."

That statement failed to reassure her much. "You should say that you don't kill."

"I won't lie to you. I have killed and will probably do so again to protect my family and my pack."

Mia had killed to save her mother, as well. "Why are you here, Seth?"

"I'm here because a mate's presence helps with the transition. Now go to sleep. When you awaken, you'll feel better." He tugged her into his warmth and kissed her firmly on the temple.

"Why were you with Ruby that night?" she slurred, her head still hurting so badly her teeth felt like they might fall out.

"We can talk and fight about it tomorrow, Mia. Tonight, you need sleep."

Unconsciousness pulled her under, and she had no choice. Once again, wolves and the pulsing of the moon filled her dreams.

She woke with a start as dawn peeked through the window. A strong arm around her waist kept her plastered against a warm body so hard it felt like brick. Even so, they fit well together.

"Morning," he said, his voice clear and strong. He'd obviously been awake for quite some time.

"Hi," she croaked, her throat feeling as if she'd sipped acid all night. Her limbs trembled, but her headache had softened to a dull pounding. "You said I'd be stronger."

"I didn't say you'd be stronger today. Just when the transition is over." His breath brushed the bite mark on her shoulder. "The swelling has decreased a little bit. That's a good sign."

"When will the transition be over?" She tried to roll away. How could she even think this was real? That she'd mated a wolf? Oh, yeah. The incredible pain and nausea attacking her body. That was how.

"Within a week." Seth tightened his hold until she couldn't

move. "Your reaction was strong enough that one bite *did* do it, just so you know. You're fully my mate."

Yeah. She got that.

He kissed her ear. "We need to talk."

"Damn straight." She blinked several times to clear her head. The hard-on he sported that pressed against her butt softened her thighs. Now was not the time to think about sex with the man. "Where did you and Ruby go that night?"

Seth wandered his lips across his bite.

Lust slammed right to her core. "Stop that," she snapped.

He sighed. "Fine. Ruby and I had been meeting secretly for about six months prior to the month she died."

Hurt caught the air in Mia's lungs. He'd been seeing Ruby? "Oh. So she *was* cheating on your brother? Or was she cheating on you with Erik?" Just who had the main couple been in this disaster? That would be motive, now, wouldn't it?

"No." Seth exhaled. "We weren't lovers. We were friends. For five months, I tutored her so she could earn her GED."

Mia snorted. "You're a tutor?"

"Yeah. I think she thought that nobody would mess with the Enforcer, and she didn't want to put anybody else in danger. So, she came to me and asked for help. I helped her."

That was sweet—if Mia believed him. "So you tutored her so she could take the test? Did she pass?"

"She did, and then I helped her apply to colleges. She was accepted to Notre Dame, and that night, we had planned to tell my father."

Mia frowned. "I don't understand. She needed your support to tell Benjamin that she got into a great college?"

"Yes. Members of our pack—*any* pack—aren't supposed to venture away unless it's for military training or medical skills. We need numbers for strength, and our secret can never get out. Members, especially females, are not encouraged to leave home."

Seth nipped Mia's ear. "Ruby and I wanted to change that, person by person, starting with her. To do so, we had to go to our Alpha."

"So, what did your father say?"

Seth sighed. "Nothing. Ruby told me that night that she'd been meeting with an informant from the Copper Pack and had information on dissent in their ranks and who'd make the best targets to bring to our side. The girl thought she could trade information for freedom when she met with my father."

Mia blinked. "Hold on. First, what's the Copper Pack?"

Seth caressed a hand down her arm, bringing all sorts of nerves wide-awake. "There are four packs in our coalition, all maintained by mining. We're the Silver Pack. The other three are Copper, Slate, and Granite. It's simplistic but centuries old."

All right. That was interesting. "If you're a coalition, then why would Ruby be spying?" Mia asked.

Seth shifted his weight, pressing her against him. "We're a coalition out of necessity to deal with the other species and groups out there. The Copper Pack has tried to take over our land more than a couple of times, and their Alpha is getting older, as is Benjamin. A conflict is inevitable."

Mia straightened her legs, wincing as her hip joint protested. "So it's possible somebody from the Copper Pack killed Ruby?"

"Yeah, but doubtful. I don't think they have a clue there's a traitor amongst them. Ruby wouldn't tell me who it was, and I figured I had time to get the truth from her. I didn't know somebody was gunning for her." Frustration darkened his tone.

This was information Mia could've used earlier. "I am so finished with you keeping secrets."

"Then come all-in to the pack. You can't straddle the line and have one foot outside and one in, baby. It's that simple." His strong voice held no give.

She exhaled, noting that the burning in her chest had subsided. "Okay. What did your father say when Ruby told him about the informant and that she wanted to go to Notre Dame?"

"Nothing. Benjamin would've been furious that she'd been talking to an informant, and I had to get her out of that situation before we spoke to him. I planned to meet with her informant and take over or kill him, but I wanted to give her time to trust me with the name. I didn't realize she didn't have time."

Mia chose to ignore the casual remark about killing the informant. For now. "So you just said you'd both talk to Benjamin later?"

"I told her that she wasn't to put herself in danger again and that I'd have to handle that situation first before we sent her off to college. She agreed very quickly that night, saying that something had come up and she needed more time to prepare herself to talk to Benjamin. She wouldn't tell me *what* had come up, and I figured she was just having second thoughts and needed time to think about it."

Mia gasped. "Ruby found out she was pregnant."

"Yeah. That had to be what was going on. She seemed excited and nervous all at once—and, no, she did not tell me she was with child. It had to be early because I didn't even sense the pregnancy." Seth stretched out his feet. "Before you ask, my guess is that Erik was the father. And, no, he had no clue. My brother was genuinely shocked when you dropped the bomb that day at my father's house."

Mia's brain kicked into gear. Finally. "Would anybody object to Erik and Ruby having a baby?"

Seth stiffened behind her. "No."

"Seth. You just said you wouldn't lie to me. Stop lying."

He growled low. "Fine. Ruby's mother was human, which made Ruby half-human. Many wolves are purists and believe the Alpha line must be kept clean."

"Is Ben one of those people?"

"No."

"Seth—"

"I mean it, Mia. My father believes differently, as do I. Erik's baby would've been welcomed into our family, as would Ruby have been, and I still would've pushed for her to go to college if that's what she wanted to do." A buzzing echoed, and Seth tugged his phone to his ear. "What?" he whispered.

Suddenly, he jumped to his feet. "I'll be right there."

Cold wafted across Mia's skin. She rolled over to face him and swung her feet to the floor. The room spun just enough to force her to clench her teeth. "What happened?"

Seth paled until his lips appeared blue, and fire flared to life in his intense eyes. "Somebody shot my father."

Alarm propelled Mia to her feet. She swayed.

Seth steadied her. "Go back to sleep. You need more rest."

"No. I'm coming with you." She grabbed his hand, telling herself that she was a cop and investigating a shooting was her job. A tiny voice in the back of her head snorted. She was going because Seth Volk needed her.

Instinct whispered that the Enforcer who protected his pack didn't need anybody.

Except her.

CHAPTER 28

Blood scented the air with hints of copper that competed with the stench of old smoke. Mia followed Seth into Benjamin's bedroom at the rear of the massive home. While the fire damage remained in the other part of the house, a smoky haze hung in the hallway.

Benjamin lay on his bed wearing worn sweats. A myriad of bloody exit wound holes covered his chest, abdomen, and neck. All color had deserted his face, leaving his skin the hue of worn parchment. His chest struggled to wheeze out breath, and his eyes remained closed.

Erik stood on the far side of the bed, his narrowed gaze on his father, anger cascading off him. "The doctor will be back in a minute. Dad's in a coma."

Seth faltered.

Mia pressed her hand to his lower back.

His shoulders stiffened, and he shuffled closer to the bed. "Did Doc get all of the bullets out?"

"Yes." Erik scrubbed both hands down his face. "But the silver had time to take effect. Doc doesn't know if Dad will wake up."

"Who shot him?" Seth lifted his chin, his body visibly settling in a battle stance.

Erik's eyes flashed a light blue and then returned to their normal color. "I'd have figured Barnby, but he's still in jail. Dad was headed out to the shop, and someone ambushed him. Cowards. Alice heard the shots and ran outside."

"How many people know he's in a coma?" Seth gently touched his father's hand.

"Enough." Erik's eyes swirled an angry blue. "We're in deep shit."

"Yeah. I get that." Seth tucked his hands into his jean pockets.

Mia inhaled slowly. What was wrong with these guys? "Let me get this straight. Somebody shot your father with silver bullets, enough that he's slipped into a coma, and you're treating him at home instead of at the hospital?"

"There's no cure for silver," Seth said slowly. "A hospital would make no difference, and not all of the local hospital personnel are ours. Some are human. This is easier."

Mia stepped away from Seth to focus on Erik. "What about the police? Have they been notified?"

"No," Seth answered before Erik could. "No police. No investigation. We'll deal with this ourselves."

Damn it. She was a cop. Grabbing her phone, she whirled for the hallway.

She didn't make it.

Seth grabbed the back of her elbows and lifted her through the doorway. Heat filled her head. She shot both fists down and connected with his upper thighs. Emitting a short growl, he flipped her around and pinned her against the wall. Fury lit his eyes, and a vein pounded in his neck. "No police."

Her breath froze, and her muscles tensed. "We can put out a BOLO and start canvassing. I am the police, Seth."

"Not today." He lowered his head to hers, threat evident in the smooth movement. His shoulders vibrated. "Today, you're a mate."

The wolf shifted beneath his skin enough to be seen. His blue eyes morphed into wolf shape and then turned back.

No sound emerged when she opened her mouth. He was an animal. A primitive beast lived deep down at his core. A beast she had no hope of taming.

Alice hurried into the hallway, her hair a mess and panic on her face. "I just scouted around outside…there's a scent, Seth. A strong one."

He dropped Mia and grabbed the phone from her hand. "Stay here." Turning on his heel, he hurried down the hallway.

Erik brushed by her, following his brother.

Mia took several deep breaths. "Whose scent?"

Alice shrugged, gracefully gliding toward the bed. Red rimmed her eyes, and furrows marred her brow. Her hand shook when she reached out to cover Ben's.

Mia fought the urge to comfort the woman. "Alice, you're impeding what is now an active investigation. Whose scent did you find outside?"

"What investigation? You going to report that I smelled something and refused to tell you what?" Alice whispered, her voice filled with pain. "Somehow, I don't think so."

Good point. She had resources that would help find the shooter, but she *did* understand their need to keep things private. Why couldn't they work together? "Ben is strong. He'll survive." Mia assured softly.

"You'd better hope so. If not, you and Seth are dead." Alice shook her head. "That boy should've mated Emily like Ben wanted. Then he'd live and be Alpha of *their* pack someday." Anger and regret burned in her eyes as she looked over her shoulder. "You've all but signed his death warrant."

Mia stepped back from the venom as well as the words. "If Seth had mated Emily, he'd have his own pack?"

"Yes." Alice focused back on Ben. "The boy grew up an outcast and finally had a chance to belong. We had it all perfectly planned, and everyone would live far into the future. He had a chance to be...himself. Finally. You've taken that away from him."

Mia blinked. Goose bumps rose on her skin. Seth had mated her to save Gena and Dotty and, in effect, had given up his life. Why would he do that? "There has to be some way to negate a mating."

"Only if you die," Alice said, leaning over to smooth a hand over Ben's forehead.

Mia's jaw firmed. "There has to be another way."

"There isn't."

Wolves were impossible. Given her terrible night and weird dreams, there was no doubt in her mind that the mating had taken place. She still wasn't feeling a hundred percent, though. But she'd protect Seth. "What if Seth and Erik refuse to fight? I mean—"

"Then the pack will tear them both apart." Alice snorted. "They can't refuse. We need an Alpha strong enough to protect us from the Granite Pack. They'd love to destroy us."

"Why?" Mia asked. This was crazy.

"Because of Seth." Alice sat on Ben's bed. "Ashlynn was next in line at the Granite Pack, and then she left and took Seth with her. She betrayed them all. Ben basically declared war when he took her in and mated her." Alice's voice softened. "Men in love do stupid, stupid, stupid things."

History proved that fact to be true. "What if we run?" Mia whispered.

Alice turned to face her again. "You could try. But really...does Seth seem like a runner to you?"

The man might get her to safety. But no way would Seth Volk run like a coward...wolf or not. "No."

"There's your answer," she said, her eyes filling. "If Ben doesn't awaken, then..."

"Then I'll figure something out," Mia muttered, turning and heading from the room. She was a cop, and she had a job to do. No way would Alice tell her whose scent lingered outside. Seth or his brother would level with her, or she'd arrest their asses and figure out a human-type reason later. If they weren't going to protect themselves, she'd figure out a way to help them. First on her list was finding the asshat who'd shot Benjamin Volk in the back.

She held her breath through the smoky house until she reached the front porch. Seth stood at the edge, his back to her, his body tense—like a sentinel on full alert. "Where's Erik?"

"He's scouting in wolf form." Seth jerked his head toward a pile of clothing on the nearest chair.

"What are you doing?" she asked, striding to stand next to him with a view of the forest to the west.

"Planning."

The darkness in his tone froze her in place. "You're going to follow the law."

"I know."

"The *human* law," she hissed.

He lifted a shoulder, his gaze remaining on the trees, his profile strong and chiseled. "Human law is the last thing you should be worrying about."

"Yeah, about that." She swiveled and pressed her hands to her hips. The profiler in her finally woke up and tried to make sense of the situation. "What exactly is your plan?"

"Meaning?"

"I may not know you all that well, but I do know three things: you won't run, you won't lie down and die, and no way will you kill your brother."

"That doesn't leave many alternatives," he said evenly.

"You had an alternative…and you gave it up." Mia settled her stance. Her shoulders hunched against her will.

He turned slowly, his gaze warming her face. "From the first second I saw you, so earnest and brave and facing me through those bars, I lost any alternative but you, Mia Stone."

The truth in his deep tone, the absolute determination in his otherworldly eyes sped her breath. He wanted forever, and he was giving everything he had.

To her.

She didn't understand him, but against all logic, she believed him. Panic fluttered through her stomach. He deserved something she wasn't sure she could give—wasn't sure she could even identify.

Erik bounded out of the forest, his thick coat shifting over powerful muscles. Reaching the porch, his bones cracked as he stood on his hind legs, morphing into a man. "I caught the scent."

Seth stilled. "Who was it?"

"Another Barnby. Fred, Frank's brother."

"There's another Barnby?" Mia's gut clenched.

Seth flashed his teeth. "Let's go."

Frank was safely in jail, although his brother was out there somewhere. Had he shot Benjamin? Why? Mia grabbed Seth's arm. "No. We go and arrest him. He broke the law, and he'll pay." She needed to question him. Frank's problem had been with Seth, so it didn't make sense that Fred would shoot Benjamin, unless this had nothing to do with her. Who would want Ben dead and why?

Seth glanced at his brother, who was hurriedly yanking on clothes. "Get the truck. I'll meet you in a second after I deal with my...mate."

Erik nodded and ran toward the metal shop, not looking at her.

"You're going to *deal* with me now?" Mia dropped her hands. She really didn't want to shoot him, but the idea held merit at the moment.

"Yes." Seth slipped her phone into his pocket. "I know you don't understand any of this, and that isn't your fault. But Erik and I need to strike swiftly and hard against the man who dared to shoot our Alpha. If we don't, we're all dead. We'll face multiple challenges instantly, and there's no way we'll beat them all. We have to show that we're prepared to defend and protect until our father is well."

"These are *your people*." She shook her head. "You're no more than—"

"Animals?" Seth stepped into her space. "Yeah. Now you're getting it."

"I don't accept this." Law was needed for order and fairness. Vigilante justice led to trouble…wolf or not. "I won't follow these laws."

Regret twisted his lip. "As the *Enforcer*, especially when the Alpha is down, it's my job to make sure you do."

The man standing before her went beyond Enforcer to pure Alpha, whether he admitted it or not. "Are you threatening a law enforcement officer, Volk?"

"Threat? No. Just stating facts to *my mate*, darlin'.'" His tone lowered to a deadly softness. "Every move I'm about to make will be scrutinized for any weakness. As a way to take me, and thus my father, down."

She lifted her chin. "I'm not a weakness."

"So long as you refrain from challenging me, you're not."

Anger spiraled heat into her face. "You going to go all Alpha on me, wolf?"

A veil shielded his eyes. "If I do, you'll know it, Mia."

The truck sprayed gravel as Erik slammed on the brakes. "Let's go, Seth."

"Just because you caught a scent doesn't mean one of the Barnbys shot your father. You need facts, logic, and investigations to find enough evidence, and you can't just go off in anger." Mia stepped away. She really had to think about all of this. "I'm staying here."

"No, you're not." Seth lunged.

CHAPTER 29

Seth had too easily subdued Mia in the truck until they arrived at her cabin, and then he jumped out, still holding her. "I need you to trust me."

Mia steeled her spine. "I do trust you, but we need evidence before we exact justice. If it was a Barnby brother, we can't let a man get away with shooting your father, regardless of whether or not he's a wolf shifter. We all live in the same jurisdiction, and the laws matter."

Seth lowered his forehead to hers. "I know, but this is life or death. Please. Trust me."

Her heart warmed. How could she deny the request? Seth had done nothing but trust and protect her since they'd first met. She owed him that much. "I won't do anything until I hear from you."

He kissed her and returned to the truck, where they spun out and furiously drove away. Now they were heading out to take care of another pain-in-the-butt Barnby. She really didn't understand this new world. Yet what if Barnby didn't do it? No doubt everyone had already heard about the altercation between Seth and Frank, and they probably knew that she'd brought Frank in for questioning. His brother would make a good fall guy for some killer, and it seemed like intrigue surrounded the wolf world. Different packs, different alliances, different coalitions. Evidence mattered.

Weakness trembled down her legs. Her head spun. When would the transition be finished? She leaned against the side of the cabin and sucked in several deep breaths. Cramps attacked her stomach.

A car engine echoed from around the bend. She straightened.

Pete's police Mustang emerged through the trees and rolled to a stop.

She opened the passenger side door and jumped inside, slamming it. She could trust Seth and still make sure he didn't make a colossal mistake and kill the wrong guy. "Do you know where the Barnbys live?"

Pete scratched his chin. "Sure. They have a family ranch about five miles out. Why?"

Loyalties clashed. Her mind spun. Well, wolf mating or not, she was a cop. "One might've shot Ben Volk last night, and the Volk boys are headed his way."

Pete stilled. "Ben was shot? Where is he?"

"Recuperating at home. Their doctor is taking care of him." Well, that was true. "The housekeeper said that Fred Barnby probably shot him." That was also true. Maybe balancing the two worlds wouldn't be so difficult. "I think she saw him on the property but did not see him actually shoot. I was hoping you'd make this my case."

Pete freed his phone from his pocket. "Doc's good. If he says Ben doesn't need the hospital, then he doesn't. And, sure. It's your case." He speed-dialed a number. "It's Pete. The youngest Barnby was heading down to bail out his brother. Keep them both at the station for questioning. I don't care what reason you give them. Call me back when you get this message." He hung up the phone and started the ignition. "I hate that answering machine, but we just don't have enough employees."

Mia started to breathe evenly, even though her muscles still contracted from the mating. "Barnby's brother was heading to the station?"

"Yeah."

So Seth and Erik wouldn't find the guy at home. Good. Her shoulders relaxed into the leather. "To the station, then?"

Pete frowned. "No. We're interviewing Eddy Johnson today, remember? The doctors made him lucid, just for us. One-shot deal."

Oh, yeah. She'd completely forgotten about Ruby's and Mandy's cases. What was wrong with her? "Of course, I remember. Geez. I'm ready for the interview."

Pete cut her a look. "Uh-huh. So tell me about Ben Volk getting shot."

The trees sped by outside until they merged onto the interstate, and Mia gave the details she could about the case.

Pete eyed the GPS set into the dash. "Any chance the shooting is related to our current case? I mean, there hasn't been a murder in Lost Lake for decades, and now there are two murders and an attempted murder?"

"Maybe." Of course, Pete didn't know about the wolf dynamics and what taking down the Alpha could mean. But as a cop, she couldn't overlook the possibility. Also, the fact that Ruby had been meeting with an informant kept sticking in Mia's head. Just what kind of intrigue was she dealing with here?

Pete exited the freeway and headed along breezy meadows to the north. "What about Seth and Erik? Where were they when their dad was shot?"

Mia stiffened. "They, uh, wouldn't talk without their attorney." Yeah, it was a complete lie. Seth had been in her bed. But where was Erik when someone shot Ben? If he'd wanted to shoot his father, he'd know exactly who to frame. Alice had said that she smelled Fred Barnby, but what if she'd been lying to help Erik? If he were to be the new Alpha, she'd no doubt give her loyalty to him. Seth hadn't mentioned smelling anyone in particular.

"They inherit a bundle if Ben dies." Pete leaned forward to peer at the darkening sky. "I still like one of them for Ruby's murder... and Erik doesn't have an alibi for Mandy's. It seems so odd that the girls were killed just like Mrs. Volk. Too much of a coincidence."

As a profiler, Mia had to agree with that premise. "You think Erik is killing women in the same way his mother was murdered?" Creepy but possible.

"Maybe Erik is nuts. Don't psychotic serial killers do weird stuff like that? Or maybe he and Seth are working together. What's going on with you and Seth, anyway?" Pete asked.

Mia coughed. "What do you mean?"

"Come on. I'm a cop, remember?" Pete turned the vehicle down a newly asphalted drive lined by tall pine trees.

"Nothing is going on."

"Okay." Pete shrugged. "Just be careful. That man is dangerous."

If he only knew.

They parked near the front entrance, and Mia stepped out of the vehicle to survey the weathered brick building. It stood to about three stories high. An intricate iron sign spread across the second story: *Lost Asylum*.

Nobody saw the irony in the name? She shook her head.

Manicured lawns spread out on all three sides, now yellow from changing weather. An angry cloud slid over the property. Cold and darkness slithered down.

She shivered, the gun at her waist feeling secure.

Pete lumbered up the walk and shoved open the thick door. Mia followed, automatically scanning the tree line to the west. She'd never look at a forest the same way again.

Did wolves watch?

Only darkness peered through the boughs and trunks.

She turned her attention to a reception area manned by a six-foot female nurse with shoulders wider than Pete's. Complete in white uniform and cap, the woman frowned. "May I help you?"

Pete faltered and then hitched his belt over his belly, stepping toward the desk. Several empty chairs lined both walls, and pictures of the stars at midnight hung above them. One lone door stood to the right of the reception desk. "Yes. I'm the sheriff. We have an appointment with Eddy Johnson."

The nurse stared down her nose at Mia. "Who are you?"

"Mia Stone. Deputy." Mia met the woman's gaze.

"Humph." The nurse punched keys on a keyboard, frowned deeper, and hit a button near the wall. The door buzzed and opened. "Come this way."

Pete waggled his eyebrows at Mia and shoved the door open wider.

The nurse clomped down the hallway, her butt swaying like two cantaloupes in her see-through white pants. "Eddy is waiting for you in the lower reception room. It's private and quiet." She stopped in front of a metal door and pushed it open. "I must ask you to control yourselves and not to upset him."

"We'll do our best," Pete muttered, stomping into the room.

Mia followed and fought another shiver as cold air whispered over her arms. Creepy.

A man sat on a sofa facing away from them and toward a wide expanse of windows showcasing a meadow leading to the forest. A rocky mountain rose behind the trees. Howler's Ridge lived on the other side of the rise.

Pete cleared his throat. The guy didn't move.

The door shut behind Mia, and she surveyed the room. Two sprawling chairs angled toward the sofa but didn't block the windows. A fireplace gaped, empty and cold, while pictures of daisies lined the walls.

Taking a deep breath of lemon-cleanser-scented air, she eased around the sofa to take a chair. "Mr. Johnson?" she asked softly.

The man nodded. White hair cascaded to his shoulders and matched the whiskers and eyebrows on his face. He sat in a ratty, maroon-colored robe with fuzzy brown slippers. "I'm Eddy Johnson." He kept his gaze on the windows. "There's a storm coming. A big one."

Pete dropped into the other chair. "Do you mind talking to us for a moment?"

Eddy slowly turned his head to survey Pete and then turned toward Mia. Grooves spread out from his faded blue eyes that didn't look anything like laugh lines. "You're different."

She frowned. "Different? What do you mean, Eddy?"

A smirk lifted his pale lips. "They've changed you."

Mia sat back. Cold prickled down her spine.

Pete rolled his eyes. "Listen, Bub. I know they medicated you for our visit, so just relax and cooperate."

"Did it hurt?" Eddy asked, leaning forward.

Pete clapped his hands together.

Eddy jumped.

"Mr. Johnson, we need to know why you killed Ashlynn Volk so long ago," Pete said.

Eddy shook his head. "I didn't kill that pretty lady." He clasped gnarled hands together in his lap, his eyes widening as he looked around the room. Leaning forward, he lowered his voice to a raspy whisper. "Her own kind killed 'er."

What exactly did Johnson know about the wolves? "We know you were in the vicinity the night Ashlynn died," Mia said. "Did you see who killed her?"

"No." Eddy's gaze wandered over Mia's face. "You look a little like her, you know. So sad she had to die." Tears filled his eyes. "But it wasn't me."

"Mr. Johnson, how did you get the silver handcuffs you used on Ashlynn?" Pete asked.

Eddy rubbed his whiskers. "Silver is pretty. Shiny."

"Yes, it's very pretty." Mia softened her voice. "Did you use silver that night?"

"No. I never had no silver." He shook his head sadly. "If I had silver, I'd have rented a room and not lived outside. So silly to use silver on a lady body."

The breath caught in Mia's throat. "Did you see the silver on the lady?"

Eddy shrugged. "Maybe."

"Did you put the silver on her?" Pete asked.

Eddy threw out his hands. "No. I don't leave silver."

"Who left the silver on the lady?" Mia asked.

"One of the monsters." Eddy grabbed Mia's hands.

Pete leaned forward, and Mia shook her head. He relaxed but kept his hand on his gun.

Eddy's bony fingers pressed into her flesh. "Get out now. You don't know. You don't know about the beasts within the beasts. They'll take you...and they'll kill you. Just like that pretty Ashlynn."

Icy fingers tapped down Mia's spine. "What about the other two women? The ones from Seattle."

He frowned, his eyes clouding. "I didn't see the other women. Heard about them. The doctors have talked to me about them. I never saw them." His exhale was deep. "Was there silver on them?"

"Yes," Mia said.

He shook his head, and his white hair brushed his shoulders. "So sad. Silver is too expensive, too pretty to put on whores."

Mia swallowed. "Whores?"

"Yeah. The shrinks told me about the women from the city. Hookers." He shrugged. "It's too bad about the silver."

Mia cut a look at Pete, who grimaced. "Was Ashlynn Volk a whore, Eddy?" She stayed close to him.

He focused on her, his gaze wandering from her jaw up to her hair and back. "Aren't they all?"

All right. Maybe Eddy did have some issues with women. "Do women deserve to die like that? Staked to the ground?" she asked.

"Not with the good silver." He cackled. "I'm done. You're boring."

Pete stood. "We're not getting anything from him. He's a nutjob."

Eddy turned back toward the window. "I didn't used to be. Happened here." He jerked his head toward the storm gathering outside. "What I've seen outside this window—so much howling."

Pete snorted and headed toward the door. "Let's go."

Eddy cut a sly glance Mia's way. "I wasn't alone out there that night, you know."

Awareness stilled Mia in place. "Who else was out there?"

He turned back to the view. "A handsome pup with blue eyes. Very blue eyes."

CHAPTER 30

Mia pushed through the exit into the cool day, leaving Pete inside to complete the paperwork. A pup with blue eyes? None of this made sense. Seth hadn't mentioned turning into a wolf that night, although he'd been the one to find his mother, along with his friend. She had to find that friend.

She maneuvered outside and smacked into a hard male body. Shaking her head, she stepped back.

"Deputy Stone." Brother Jeremiah steadied her with both hands on her elbows. "I do apologize."

Mia took a deep breath and peered up. "Brother Jeremiah. How odd to see you here."

His smile flashed perfectly even teeth. "I work here."

The wind slammed pine needles and dead leaves against her legs. She shivered. "Excuse me?"

He yanked off a long, black overcoat to tuck around her shoulders. His tan Dockers and white button-down shirt casually emphasized the coiled muscle beneath. Sandy-blond hair was swept back from a strong face, and earnest black eyes twinkled with amusement. "I'm a clinical psychologist. May I call you Mia?"

Mia had never understood *earnest*. "Sure. How about I drop the *Brother* and call you Jeremiah?"

He nodded. "Only the folks in my commune use the term anyway. Besides, a pretty lady like you can call me anything you want."

"Are you a preacher?"

"No." He rubbed his chin and pivoted to shield her from the blistering wind. "I'm just the unofficial leader of a lot of lost folks."

Sounded like nice phrasing to describe a cult. "Does God talk to you, Jeremiah?"

He sobered. "God talks to all of us. All you have to do is listen."

"If you say so. By the way, do you treat Eddy Johnson?" Maybe she could get some insight here.

Jeremiah shoved his hands into his pockets. "I can't talk about patients. You know that."

"Just tell me if he's as crazy as he seems."

"We shrinks don't really like the term *crazy*." Jeremiah's lip quirked. "But, hypothetically speaking, someone like Eddy may be saner than we think."

Mia stilled. "What do you mean?"

Intensity swirled in Jeremiah's eyes. "I think he has seen things we can't explain. What do you think, Mia?"

"I think there's a lot in life we can't explain. What's high on your list right now?" she asked. Was it possible Jeremiah knew about the wolves?

"Nothing concrete...yet. Though I can tell you that your boyfriend is in the thick of whatever's happening in this town. Always has been, always will be."

Mia's head jerked up. "Always has been? How long have you known Seth?"

"I grew up here. Went away to college and came back with my, er, flock. To a peaceful place where we could live, grow our own food, and live by our own rules." His gaze wandered her face. "If you don't mind my saying so, I find you stunning.

Would you like to accompany me to dinner sometime this week?"

"Thank you, but I don't think so." She removed the jacket to hand to him, and his hospital ID fell out of the pocket. "Sorry about that." She ducked to snatch it off the ground and paused, reading his name beneath his smiling picture. "Dr. Bankston?" Her head jerked up so she could meet his gaze. "As in Tyler Bankston?" The kid who'd been partying with Seth the night they'd found his mother dead?

Jeremiah sighed, accepting the coat. "Yes, I was Tyler Bankston, but I am no longer. Once I was called Tyler Jeremiah Bankston, or TJ, but I've always been Brother Jeremiah at heart. I merely had to find my followers to realize that fact."

Now why would the good doctor leave town, change his name, and then return? Time to do some digging on the brother. "I see. Why did you change your name?"

"I didn't. I'm just using my middle name because it sounds more like who I am. Old-fashioned and one with the Lord." He leaned against the brick building as if he could chat all day in the chilly wind. "Then when I started our little community, others began calling me Brother Jeremiah because I give a sermon every week. You should come. I believe you'd find what you're looking for in our church."

One of her eyebrows rose of its own accord. "What am I looking for, Jeremiah?"

His smile was charming. "Peace and purpose, just like the rest of us." He tilted his head as if reading her. "And a sense of justice and truth, probably. The world you've entered needs to be exposed, and perhaps you're here to do just that."

"What world?" she challenged.

"I don't know yet, but I am going to keep digging." His gaze lightened. "Something tells me you know more than I do. Already."

She lifted her chin. "What were you and Seth doing in the woods the night you found his mother murdered?"

Jeremiah exhaled. "We snuck some hooch from Old Man Barnby and went out to the forest to get drunk."

"Fred and Frank Barnby's father?"

"Grandfather. He died a few years back. The guy made great hooch."

Connections upon connections existed in this darn town. "So you and Seth were friends?"

"No." Jeremiah's jaw firmed. "We played on the football team together and sometimes hung out. Seth didn't have friends—wouldn't let anybody get close enough to be his friend. Even before his mother died."

A pang jabbed at Mia's heart. So, he'd been lonely his entire life? That made her want to save him. Comfort him. But she needed the truth. "What did you see that night?"

Jeremiah paled. "I'm still not sure. We were drinking by the ridge, talking about the next game, and suddenly Seth lifted his head. Then he turned and ran. So I followed him. It was like he knew exactly where to go because we found his mother tied to the ground…dead."

Mia swallowed several times. The entire situation was unthinkable. "What then?"

"I panicked. I ran to town and called the sheriff."

Mia nodded, a piece of the puzzle clicking into place. If Seth had been alone, he never would have alerted the human sheriff. "What did Seth do?"

Jeremiah frowned. "I don't know. I've always wondered."

He'd probably shifted into wolf form out of pure pain. Maybe Eddy actually *did* see Seth in wolf form that night. "Everyone reacts differently to trauma. Is that why you became a, um, shrink?"

"Maybe." Jeremiah reached out and pushed her hair over her

shoulder. "I can tell you're a strong woman. But I wouldn't be able to sleep if I didn't at least give you a warning. Seth is dangerous. He was dangerous as a kid, then as a soldier, and now as a leader in the town. You should run, not walk, out of his life."

"I can handle myself." She pulled away from his hand, and her hair slid through his fingers. There was an edge to him that she couldn't quite quantify.

Jeremiah frowned. "I'm sure. But, well, Seth was a suspect for a while in the killing."

"He was with you."

"No. We met up over by the ridge. I actually stole the hooch. Seth met me there and would've had time to kill his mom first." Jeremiah scrubbed both hands down his face. "Though he didn't act like he'd just committed murder or anything. But in my time as a psychologist, I've met with perfectly nice people who'd done evil deeds."

"Psychopaths." Mia had studied plenty of them.

"Yes. They're usually charming, intelligent, and charismatic—like Seth." Jeremiah shifted to the side.

"Do you really think Seth could've killed his mother?"

Jeremiah looked away and then back. "I honestly don't know. Physically, yeah. Mentally, definitely. Emotionally? I don't know. Even back then, he was over-the-top gentle and protective of women. I guess that could be a front because if it's the truth, then it's hard to imagine him doing such a terrible thing. I've gone back to that night in my head so many times over the years, and I still don't have an answer. I don't have *the* answer."

The wind picked up, pricking along Mia's skin. "If Seth killed his mom, then who killed the other two women in the same manner?" It didn't make sense.

"His father?" Jeremiah asked.

Mia blinked, stepping back.

"I know." Jeremiah held up both hands. "It sounds nuts, but as I told you, I've spent a lot of time thinking about it. Either we had a serial killer who brutally murdered three women and moved on, or the other two kills were a cover for Mrs. Volk's murder. Or hers was a cover for one of theirs, but that isn't as plausible."

"Unless Eddy Johnson is the killer. He was convicted, right?"

Jeremiah snorted. "Yeah. He was convicted in a little courthouse in town, without much legal help, and then sent here. A nice, tidy, quick little situation."

"Did he do it?" Mia asked.

Jeremiah faltered. "As I said, he's a patient, and I can't discuss his care. You know that, Deputy Stone."

She rubbed her hands down her chilled arms. "Hypothetically, in this situation, do you think a person like Eddy could've done it?"

Jeremiah tacked his ID to his belt. "In your hypothetical, the answer is no. I do not think a person like Eddy would be the actual murderer."

Fascinating. "Do you think Eddy belongs here in this hospital?"

"Yeah, or I'd discharge him. That's as much as I'm willing to discuss a current patient with you." Jeremiah smiled, his teeth perfectly even. "Are you sure you wouldn't like to have dinner with me? I'm a great cook, or we could try a new restaurant on the other side of town. It's called Murphy's, and the food looks delicious."

"My dance card is a little full right now, but it's kind of you to ask." She gave in and shoved her freezing hands into her pockets. "Who do you think committed the recent murders?" The man was a trained psychologist with ties to the town, so maybe he had an idea.

"If I knew, I'd tell you." He met her gaze evenly, his body relaxed, and the look in his eyes thoughtful. "If Seth committed the early murders, or even just one of them, then the question would be, why start again now? What does he need to hide now? If not Seth, then who?" Jeremiah unfolded his overcoat from his arm. "I've always thought his brother was an incredibly angry person."

Mia blinked. She'd seen charming, popular, and slightly goofy in Erik. "How so?"

"Erik has a good-natured façade, but I've seen him lose his temper more than once. It's terrifying." Jeremiah stepped back as the door began to open. "The guy tore apart a gym one time at the school. They lost a basketball game, and I heard he ripped one row of bleachers out of the wall all by himself. He would've been too young to commit the earlier murders, but I'd take a hard look at him now. He's not quite right."

Did teenaged wolves have trouble dealing with anger? She couldn't imagine normal hormones plus wolf traits. Tearing bleachers away from a wall might be normal in that case. Mia stepped away as Pete strode outside, his frown cutting grooves into his already lined forehead. Apparently the nurse had given him problems.

Jeremiah held the door open wider. "Well, I have to get to work. If you ever want to meet and chat, please give me a call. That dinner invitation will remain open."

"I appreciate your take on the situation, and I might be calling you for more information." She just needed to figure out what to ask him.

"Anytime." He pulled on his coat, and something heavy dropped from the other pocket to hit the cement walkway.

Silver handcuffs stamped by Volk Mining.

"Lucky those didn't hit our feet. It hurts." Jeremiah leaned down and grabbed the cuffs, tucking them into his pocket once again.

Mia barely kept herself from reaching for her gun. It looked like she'd just found another suspect. "Why do you have those cuffs?"

His smile failed to reach his eyes. "This is a dangerous job and a dangerous town, Deputy Stone. I believe you already know that fact."

CHAPTER 31

Irritation pricked Seth's skin like wasps, and he pressed the button to roll down the window in the truck as he drove. The day had turned chilly, and he wanted to feel the bite. After searching the Barnby farm, he'd insisted on driving home, and Erik hadn't given him much of an argument. Pine trees flew by outside, and the thick weight of late summer hung in the air with a hint of smoke from wildfires a state away.

In the passenger seat, Erik calmly rolled down his window, stretched out his legs, and sighed. "Your mate probably knew that the Barnbys wouldn't be home."

"I'm aware." Seth's hands tightened on the steering wheel. He'd wasted two hours searching the Barnby farm, and nobody had been anywhere around. A neighbor had finally said that the brothers had been called into the police station, and wasn't that a pisser? The humans had gotten involved. Yeah, Seth was blamed for situations like that. He was the Enforcer, after all. Life was going to shit, and control was outside his grasp.

"I like her." Erik cracked his knuckles.

Seth jolted out of his thoughts and turned to look at his brother. When had he gotten so big? So muscled? The guy was solid with a broad chest in a blue T-shirt that led to ripped jeans. He looked like an Alpha. "You do?"

Erik nodded. "Yeah. She's smart and loyal. But man, she's fragile." His lips pursed.

"Not for a human. She's trained," Seth said, awareness settling across his shoulders.

"I wasn't talking physically," Erik murmured, watching the dirt road in front of them.

Seth slowed down for a couple of potholes the size of small Buicks. Sometimes, he forgot how insightful Erik could be. "How so?"

"She's been alone for a long time without any cover, and she's sweet." Erik shrugged. "I can't explain it because I don't really know her, but I get the feeling if she trusted you, you could absolutely destroy her. I'd hate to see that."

"I wouldn't do that." He hadn't been waxing poetic when he'd told her that she owned his soul. For his people, for *him*, that happened fast. A soul just knew. "I mated her. She's mine." The words held power and heated his chest, going deeper than right now and right here.

Erik sighed. "That's what I figured. You've never done anything by half measures." He rolled his neck. "Well, then, we need some sort of plan to keep her safe. To keep you and me and Dad safe until he recovers."

Seth showed his teeth. "*I'm* the plan until he recovers. If we're challenged, I'll rip out throats. This isn't the time for conference tables and negotiations." They were wolves. It was that simple. Yet as he said the words, the reality of the situation hit him. He wasn't going to be the Alpha of their pack, and they might be staring at the precipice of the time for the Enforcer to step back. Every ounce of energy in his body rebelled against the thought of not protecting his people.

That job would be Erik's.

Seth repositioned himself on the seat and sped up. "How do

you know about her case back east?"

"She told me when I was in wolf form." Erik shrugged. "She was talking more to herself. Said she doesn't know if it's a copycat. If not, then somebody is after her."

"I'll take care of the threat after we settle things here," Seth murmured.

Erik nodded. "Thought so. I'll help if you need it."

"Thanks." Seth's blood roared with the need to lead, and his mind tried to shut that down. He attempted to banish the feeling of the warning buzzing through him. Enemies would be coming for them soon. "Are you ready, brother?"

Erik turned to look at him, his eyes sizzling. "Well, now, there's the rub." Wisdom shone in his deep eyes. "We're in a cluster of fucks. Dad is ill, you've mated a human, and my girlfriend, the female pregnant with my pup, was brutally murdered, showing I didn't protect her. In addition, the world is waiting for you and me to fight to the death to lead this pack. So no, brother. I'm not fucking ready for any of that."

Against all rational thought, Seth barked out a laugh. "You do have a way of defining a situation." His gut churned. "I could take Mia and run. Maybe if we got far enough away, nobody would try to take us out." The idea of leaving his pack, deserting his world, ripped through him with jagged claws. But to protect her, he'd do it. He'd do anything.

"You're too strong," Erik said mildly. "I could be deadly enough to keep our pack in line, but your birth pack will always be coming for you—probably from the shadows. You're a threat to them."

"I'm a threat to you," Seth muttered. "From the outside looking in, for people who don't really know us, I'm a threat to you and this pack."

Erik wiped a hand across his eyes. "The attack on you will come from outside, not inside our pack. As I said, you're too strong. If you took an oath to continue as Enforcer, you'd be fighting your very nature. Even I can feel it, and the wolf inside me sympathizes."

There could only be one Alpha. Seth hid a snarl and then calmed himself. "I made my choice, brother. I mated a human instead of Emily, which took away any opportunity I had to lead another pack." He didn't want another pack. He loved this one, even though he'd only belonged on the fringes, no matter how kind most members had been to him. "I'd do it again."

"I know, and I agree," Erik said.

Something inside Seth relaxed for the first time. A hard ball of anger, frustration, and loneliness disintegrated. "You do?"

"Yeah. I learned a lesson with Ruby, and I messed up. I should've mated her and given her me. All of me. Now I can never do that, and I'll always wonder what could've been. Life is short. People are fragile. If you have Mia, if you love her, don't let her go." Erik turned to watch the trees again. "Or you'll regret it for the rest of your life."

Seth exhaled. He'd missed these times with his brother. When had they stopped spending time together? Most of his good memories throughout his entire life included Erik.

Erik's phone buzzed and he looked down to read the screen. "Dad is out of the coma. Thank goodness."

Seth felt something in his chest relax, and he shot off a quick text to his errant mate with the good news. She'd want to know. "We still need a plan."

"Someday," Erik agreed. "Dad is going to get better and will be back to form in no time, so now I'm not too worried about it."

A scent caught Seth's attention, and he turned his head to the trees. Then another joined it. He drove around a corner, and two trucks, mud coating their tires, blocked the road. He pulled to a stop. "You might want to get worried. Right now."

* * *

Mia finally took the time to tell Pete all about Mandy's diary and that she'd known that Erik was the father of Ruby's baby. "She was out to prove it and had started tailing him."

Pete turned toward her. "Seriously?"

Mia sighed. "Yeah. She had a plan and even had a rough drawing of the Volk house and points of entry. I don't know if she executed it. Apparently Ruby worked a side job of cleaning houses in the area, and Mandy tried to follow in her footsteps just to investigate. Thought that maybe Ruby had stumbled onto something doing her job...or Erik had gotten pissed about the baby and killed her." The poor kid. That was nuts, although decent investigative tactics. "Did you know Ruby cleaned houses?"

"No," Pete said.

"Maybe it was only for pack members," Mia mused. Why hadn't anybody mentioned the side job? She was getting tired of being on the outside of all the information in this town.

Pete glanced at her. "Pack?"

Shoot. Mia scrambled for an explanation. "You know, the whole Volk Mining Company and them owning the town. Seems like a pack of miners to me."

Pete snorted. "That's a fair assessment."

Whew. All right. "Either way, my guess is that Mandy stumbled onto something in her poking around. She would've made a decent cop if she'd ever been given the chance."

"Shit," Pete muttered, pulling to a stop in front of the station.

Mia should probably give the diary back to the family. "Exactly." Erik was still her strongest suspect. She needed to talk to him alone, without anybody flanking him. How could she make that happen?

The office was chaotic when Mia and Pete walked inside.

A wide deputy with blond hair and a full beard looked up from fetching some mail off the floor. "The Barnby brothers escaped." A bruise extended along his jaw, and his nose was bleeding. "They're stronger than they look."

That was because they weren't human. Mia sighed. "Any idea where they were going?" Her gut told her they'd flee the entire area, considering Seth probably wanted them dead.

"No." The deputy wiped blood off his chin. "I have BOLOs out and am prepared with an arrest warrant." He looked her over. "You seem to be feeling better today. I'm glad."

"Thanks." She did feel better and kept checking her skin for fur. None. Only a diminishing headache and perhaps more energy than she'd become accustomed to having. Would she get stronger? So far, she didn't feel like she could lift a Volkswagen or anything, but it was nice that the fever had dissipated. "I think it was just a stomach bug." She nearly choked on the lie.

Pete scratched his head. "What now?"

She paused, looking around the reception area. The Barnbys would be long gone, especially if they'd shifted to wolf form. Seth and Erik were no doubt busy searching for the duo, which left Benjamin alone. "I think I'll go out and talk to Benjamin again." Without his sons present, freshly out of his coma, he might slip up and talk to her.

She tapped her finger against her lip. "Seth didn't kill Ruby and Mandy, but Erik is a good contender." Especially since impregnating Ruby might've hurt his chances at becoming the pack's Alpha. Maybe. She still didn't quite grasp the politics of a wolf pack—of Seth's wolf pack.

Pete wiped off his brow. "Yeah, but Erik would've been what? Around twelve years old when his mother died? He would've been too young to kill anybody like that. So you're saying the recent murders were him actually copycatting how his mom died? That's sick."

The headache returned, humming inside her temples. So much for the reprieve. "I don't know," she admitted.

"Me either."

She sighed. Erik would've been a twelve-year-old *wolf*, not human. Did that mean he would've been strong enough to kill at that age? Only if he was a stone-cold psychopath. Was he? He was handsome and charming, and many psychopaths hid in plain sight.

Pete studied his deputy. "You okay going alone? I have to settle things here."

"Yeah." She preferred it, actually. It wasn't like she could talk about wolves with Pete around. "I'll have a nice chat with Ben and meet up with you later. Let me know if you find the Barnby brothers." They were probably to Florida by now.

"Great." Pete hitched up his belt and moved to survey the damage to his station, tossing her his keys. "Keep her under fifty."

Mia hurried back outside, noting clouds rolling in from the south. Dark and swollen, their underbellies promised an oncoming storm. She shivered.

The rain started to drop with fat flops on the way out to the estate, and Pete's car grumbled with power beneath her hands. Maybe she could take a drive after the interview and open the throttle. The vehicle wanted to fly, and she did like to go fast—with cars, anyway.

In the stormy day, the Volk mansion looked wounded with the burned-out part being drenched. Smoke still hung low, and the smell of smoldering wood encompassed the entire area. Darkness filtered between the surrounding trees, embracing the storm with a hint of threat. Of danger.

She stepped out of the car and fought a tremble. With a smooth motion, she released her weapon from her purse to tuck at her waist. Regular bullets should slow down a wolf shifter, at the very least. She had to get her hands on some silver ammunition.

The skies opened up with a gleeful clap of thunder, and rain plummeted down. It plastered her hair to her face, and she ducked her head, running toward the front door.

She halted.

The door was slightly ajar with a wide crack through the heavy wood at the base.

She drew her gun, her hands steady. "Benjamin? Alice?" she called out.

Nothing.

Exhaling to calm her nerves, she nudged open the door.

A body lay inside, face down, black boots facing her. Competing with the stench of smoke, the coppery smell of fresh blood smashed into her senses.

CHAPTER 32

Seth stopped the vehicle. "I'll handle this."

"The hell you will." Erik was already jumping out and heading toward the eastern tree line.

Seth growled and followed his brother, slamming the door loudly. It wasn't time for anybody to step up as Alpha of his pack. While he wasn't as certain as Erik that Ben would heal, the rest of the world would have to believe that Ben would be in top form in no time.

Lightning zapped the earth ahead, and ozone assaulted Seth's nostrils. The rain started to fall, hard and fast, punishing him. He followed Erik through swaying trees as the wind whipped pine needles up into his face. It was as if Mother Nature didn't want them to proceed.

He didn't like it, either.

They emerged into a clearing surrounded by thick trees.

Seth had already smelled the wolves. Even so, with the Alphas of three packs as well as two Enforcers congregating in a relatively small space, the sense of power and danger rode the wind.

Hard.

He stood next to his brother, acutely aware of the trees behind them. "We couldn't do this inside a coffee shop?" he asked dryly, ignoring the rain berating him while clocking the biggest threats. If things turned bloody, he'd go for Jackson Tryne first. Jackson was the Alpha of the Granite Pack, a solid mountain of a man—and Seth's biological second cousin or something like that. He attended alone, apparently not seeing a need for an Enforcer.

Seth had to admire the arrogance, even if it did leave the Alpha without somebody to cover his back.

Philip Nightsom, Alpha of the Slate Pack, stood next to his Enforcer, a guy with death in his black eyes.

Seth admired that, as well.

What caught his attention next was Yago Yassi, the head of the Copper Pack. The guy was well over three hundred years old, his skin sallow, his eyes sunk so deep it was hard to determine the color. He was fading fast, and rumor had it there was an internal fight for who'd step up. What exactly had Ruby Redbird discovered? Had her investigation led to her death?

Seth appraised the leader. There was no way Yassi had the strength to shove drill steel through anybody's neck. That didn't mean a member of his pack hadn't taken care of the young woman for him. Seth's gut disagreed, though. It just didn't feel right.

Philip stepped forward, his Enforcer keeping pace. "Rumor has it Ben is on his deathbed. You two need to settle things."

In other words, a fight to the death.

"No," Seth said quietly.

Yassi cleared his throat and stretched his vulnerable neck. "We can't allow you and Erik to remain in one pack, Seth. You know that."

"Too much consolidated power?" Erik drawled.

Yassi cut his gaze to Erik. "Yes."

Fair enough.

Jackson Tryne lounged against a tree. Did they have the same eye color? Seth tried to banish the curiosity about his blood relative, especially since the guy would try to rip out his throat if given a chance.

Tryne looked around. "The point is moot. You're both Alphas, and I can feel your power from here. Neither of you will be able to follow or obey...anybody. Not once Ben is gone."

Erik's hand curled into a fist. "Our father will be fine, so I suggest you watch your tone, Tryne. He might want a piece of you for dinner just to complete the healing process."

Seth subtly shifted his weight to halt his brother's threat. There was no need for that yet, especially since Ben might not regain his health. Even so, he made sure nobody else noticed the movement. The last thing he needed was the other packs finding dissent in his. Even if there was some.

Yassi stared at Seth. "We don't want you. You should know that."

Seth let an eyebrow rise. "Gee, Yassi. That kind of hurts my feelers." Was the guy insulting Seth or implying that Erik would be easier to work with—weaker than Seth? Or both?

"Why?" Erik asked.

Leave it to his brother to make people say the quiet part out loud. Seth set his feet.

Yassi had apparently figured that diplomacy at his age was a waste of time. "Seth's a rebel with ties to two packs. That's untenable to the rest of us. Plus, you're much more reasonable, Erik. Our pack can work with you."

Reasonable meant weak in their world.

Erik growled, and the rumble cascaded across the clearing. Even the skin along Seth's nape prickled. Yeah, his brother was turning into one badass Alpha.

Seth cocked his head and studied Philip. "What about your grand plan of handing over your daughter to me? In that case, I would've had ties to three packs."

"Two," Tryne said, his voice a low rumble. "The second your mother left, she cut all ties with my pack. Period."

"Agreed," Seth said. His loyalty was to the Silver Pack, Ben, and his brother. And now Mia. That was enough. "Philip? You didn't answer my question."

Philip shuffled his feet in the rapidly muddying grass, his gaze hard, and his lips pressed together.

Amusement took Seth, and he chuckled.

Erik planted his hands on his hips. "What's funny?"

Seth shook his head. "Philip was appeasing Dad. There was never any chance of a *merger* between our packs."

Philip nodded. "That's true. Not about the appeasing part, though. Your father is an old friend, and I just wanted him to figure out for himself that you couldn't lead our pack. You're too unpredictable, Seth. I'd never give you my daughter."

Seth let his teeth show. "Your daughter could easily lead your pack herself and isn't yours to give. You might want to remember that fact before she rips out your jugular and proves it to you." He'd always liked Emily, and the idea that Philip thought he could pass her on to anybody just pissed him off.

Philip's chin lowered. "As nice as it is that you've gotten all modern, Alphas are male. Plus,"—he held up a hand before Seth could respond—"Em doesn't want it. At all. My replacement has been chosen already, and he'll do a fine job."

Seth snorted. "Please, tell me you're not talking about your nephew. Victor couldn't lead a search party in desperate need of a beer…while standing in the middle of a tavern." Vic was the only blood relative of the right age to take over.

"Watch yourself, Enforcer," Philip snapped as his own Enforcer took a step forward. "Or we'll help your pack make the right decision."

Energy cascaded down Seth's back. "Anytime. I'm free now."

Tryne straightened to his full and impressive height, his face as solid as any rock. "No. Out of respect to Ben, you have one week.

Either he's back on his feet and strong, or one of you has taken control, and the other is gone. Unlike Yassi, I don't care which one. Good luck." With that, he turned and disappeared into the trees.

The rest of the pack leaders followed suit, leaving Seth and Erik alone in the stormy clearing.

Erik looked at him, his gaze intense. "We have to get Dad strong. Now."

* * *

MIA CROUCHED and felt for a pulse in the Volk bodyguard's neck. Nothing, and his blood coated the floor, with the back of his head showing trauma. Somebody had shot him several times, and she'd bet anything they'd used silver bullets.

She stood and called it in, requesting backup. Then she edged her way through the house, silently clearing each room. Her heart thundered in her chest, but she kept going, falling back on training. Her treads were silent on the stairs as she headed up, and she cleared the landing before proceeding. A bedroom door creaked when she nudged it open, and she winced but followed through. "Alice," she hissed, rushing for the woman who lay curled up on the red-stained carpet.

Blood covered the front of Alice's flowered dress when Mia turned her over. "Help me," she wheezed.

"It'll be okay." Mia searched her for injuries, not seeing any bullet holes. Instead, raw and deep scratches marred the woman's neck, the side of her face, and down her torso. "Is there any silver in you?"

"I don't think so," Alice said, her breathing shallow, and her eyes filled with pain. "They just attacked with claws and fangs."

Sirens sounded in the distance. "Who?" Mia asked, drawing a throw blanket from the bed to drape over the woman before she went into shock.

A tear leaked out of Alice's swollen eye. "The Barnby brothers." She jerked. "Benjamin. Where's Benjamin?"

Mia patted her shoulder. "Hold on. Help is coming. I'll find him." She stood and moved back into the hallway, her gun secure in her hand again. Using her boot, she shoved open bedroom doors, one by one, until she reached a wide door at the end of the hallway that stood partly open.

Using her hip, she opened it the rest of the way, swinging her gun inside.

Benjamin lay on his back on the blood-soaked carpet...his throat ripped open to the floor. More bullet holes dotted his upper torso, and part of his upper lip had been clawed off. One silver bullet lay next to his right ear. His eyes were wide and glassy, his skin pale, and his life gone.

Mia swallowed, her stomach lurching. The claw marks down his sides were deep and fierce, jagged and wild. She scouted the remainder of the room for the Barnby brothers, but they were long gone. Blinking, she slowly backed out of the room, careful not to disturb any of the blood on the doorframe.

Seth. She bit back a sob. He'd be devastated. How was she going to tell him?

A ruckus sounded downstairs. "Mia?" Pete bellowed.

"Up here. We need the paramedics up here. Now," she yelled back, returning to Alice's room. The woman was breathing better, but the cuts still looked deep on her face. "You'll be okay."

She coughed, her entire body shuddering. "Benjamin?" she whispered.

Mia stilled, her mouth working but no words emerging.

Tears filled Alice's eyes.

Heavy footsteps sounded on the stairs, and then Pete led in the paramedics.

Mia stepped out of the way. "Benjamin is dead in the farthest bedroom," she whispered.

He nodded and turned, heading down the long hallway.

The paramedics, one tall blond woman and another shorter dark-haired guy, worked on Alice and carefully loaded her onto a stretcher to carry downstairs. She remained quiet in her injuries, her eyelids closed, and her wounds deep.

Mia watched them go.

"Dad?" Came a loud bellow from downstairs.

Mia jumped toward the stairs, but Seth was already taking them four at a time. His eyes glittered as his gaze raked her. "Where's my father?"

She grasped his elbow and tried to stop him, but he shrugged her off and hustled toward Ben's room. Once inside, he stopped cold, his hard body outlined by the storm-darkened day outside the window. He breathed out, staring down at his murdered father. The moment stretched on, a heavy silence blanketing the house. Then his head snapped back, he turned, and he pinned her with his gaze.

She couldn't move. Not an inch.

The hard angles of his face set into feral lines. He turned and stalked toward her, holding her captive with his gaze alone. "Who?" His voice was guttural and animalistic.

The saliva in her mouth dried up. She could only stare at him, her body frozen in place. This was the part of himself he'd warned her about. This *animal*.

His nostrils flared. "You *will* tell me."

Erik bounded up the stairs and leapt around the banister, his hair ruffled and panic in his eyes. "Dad?"

Seth slowly shook his head.

The sound Erik made was one of pain. Deep, gut-wrenching, soul-killing pain.

The look in Seth's eyes matched that sound. Then a different look entered them. One of death.

Erik grabbed his arm. "Alice said the Barnbys attacked them. I talked to her before they put her in the ambulance." He blinked. "But she didn't say that Dad...that he..."

Seth was already running down the stairs.

"Seth!" Mia yelled, moving to chase after him. She reached the landing, Erik burst past her, and she barreled outside into the wild rain.

Within seconds, both Volk brothers disappeared into the storm.

CHAPTER 33

The rain battered the Volk's roof, beating ferociously in an attempt to get in. To get at her. Mia curled up on the sofa in the living room by the entryway, a fire rumbling in the fireplace, a blanket over her legs. An untouched cup of tea had gone cold on the table next to her.

She glanced at her watch again. It was after midnight. After signing off on the removal of Benjamin's body, she'd made her reports at the precinct, checked on Alice, called her mom to say she'd be out all night, searched unsuccessfully for Seth, and finally just decided to wait for him back at his father's place, considering his cabin had been blown up. He had to come back here, right?

The urge to go upstairs and clean all the blood tugged at her, but right now, she was exhausted. Just a little sleep and she could take care of the problem.

She curled up, her head on the sofa back, her gaze on the flickering flames. Her eyelids fluttered closed, and she breathed deeply.

A noise had her sitting straight up perhaps an hour or so later. Maybe more.

Seth stood tall and broad in the doorway, soaking wet, steam coming off his T-shirt. His eyes had morphed to the dark blue of a winter night sky, mysterious and lethal. His black hair curled over his collar, and his jaw looked like it was made from chiseled stone.

His chin slowly lifted, and his eyelids dropped to half-mast.

She stopped breathing, her heart breaking for him, and her instincts warning her not to move. To still in place, just like prey caught in a predator's hunting grounds. Her skin electrified, and her body softened, while her heart rammed against her rib cage in a futile effort to be set free.

He slowly, deliberately, shut the door and silenced the storm.

She finally broke free of his spell, turning and setting her feet on the wooden floor. "Did you find them?" It was useless to pretend she didn't know exactly where he'd gone.

"No."

She clasped her hands in her lap. "Seth, I'm so sorry—"

"No," he said, holding up his hand. "No. Just…no." He kicked off his boots, his voice rough and hoarse. "The mourning comes later. After."

She sucked in air. "After? After what?"

"Vengeance," he said, ripping his shirt over his head and dropping the wet mess next to his boots on the slate floor.

Her mouth opened and then closed. It was useless to remind him that she was an officer of the law. The dwindling fire caressed the brutal planes of his chest and ripped abs, and her breath caught in her lungs for a different reason. "Where's Erik?"

"Still looking." Seth scrubbed a rough hand through his hair, scattering droplets to the slate. "We lost the scent near Portland, and I think they got on a boat. We'll find them, but it'll take more than our noses."

Using a boat was a decent idea. The brothers probably headed up to Alaska. If they were smart, they'd keep going and never stop.

Although from the look on Seth's face, they were as good as dead right now.

She couldn't handle this. This new world, these new rules that violated the oaths she'd taken to protect, this male she couldn't stop wanting. It was all too much. She stood and inched toward him and the doorway where she'd left her boots. "I just wanted to make sure you were all right." When she reached him, she awkwardly patted his bare arm, feeling heat and muscle. "I know you don't want to mourn, but I'm so very sorry."

Only one sharp jerk of his chin showed that he'd even heard her.

She released him and moved for her boots, her abdomen alight, and her heart hurting like she'd been stabbed with an ice pick. Gathering her strength, she shut her eyes and breathed in. Then she let instinct rule, turned, and plastered herself against his back, hugging him around the waist and fastening her hands to his abs.

His entire body stiffened. "What are you doing?"

Tears gathered in her eyes and slid down his skin. She kissed his spine. "Grieving with you." Whether or not he wanted her to do so.

His chest hitched.

Then he turned, breaking her hold. "Go home, Mia. I can't be soft right now."

She wasn't a woman who took risks with her heart. With her soul. Oh, she'd hunt a bad guy and dive into a deadly forest with a gun to find a sociopath, but giving herself? With no guarantee that she wouldn't end up in tatters of pain? No. Not her.

So when she stepped into him and slid her hands up his bare chest to his neck, she knew *exactly* the amount of agonizing pain she was inviting. Even so, the possibility of easing his pain, just the *possibility*, was enough for her. For once. If he couldn't cry, she would. "It's okay, Seth," she whispered, tears tipping over her bottom lids to her cheeks. "You don't have to feel anything right now." She was hurting enough for them both.

"You need to go," he ground out, his hands wrapping around her biceps and holding her in place. "I'm off. Not in control."

"I've never wanted you in control," she said, leaning forward to place a gentle kiss right above his heart. "Not with me. Not when we're us." The words came from somewhere deeper than the moment and she let them out, not holding back. Not now. Not when the very air around him swelled with pain. And anger. So much *fury*. If there was a way to ease him, she'd do it.

The bite mark on her neck pulsed and ached, burning with need.

"You should go." His eyes glittered, and he looked down at her mouth, his tension sharpening the world around them. "You're still human—mostly. Don't let me hurt you."

Instinct ruled her. She didn't understand it, but her body heated, and challenge rose hard and fast inside her. Somehow, she *knew* what he needed. What *she* needed. "Oh. I didn't realize you wanted to crawl away and lick your wounds." She broke his hold and moved for the doorway, barely able to breathe.

He was on her before she bent for her boots, flattening her against the door, his body unyielding behind her.

Her nipples hardened to sharp diamonds against the wood, and her knees nearly gave out on her. She tried to swallow again, but her throat had stopped working.

"I know what you're doing. Stop it," he growled. "Put on your boots and take your sweet ass home. I'll deal with you tomorrow."

She shoved him back with her hips and turned, fumbling for the doorknob. "Deal with me? I don't think you're Alpha enough, dog boy." When his eyes flared in surprise, she took advantage, yanking the heavy oak open to reveal the punishing storm. Then, going all-in and almost instantly regretting it, she pivoted and took out his knee with a precise kick to the side.

He went down onto his other knee.

Then she ran.

* * *

Rain splattered her face and smashed her hair against her skull, but she careened right into the storm, pivoting for the forest. She had seconds to seek shelter. Her socks stuck in the mud, so she lifted her knees high, pumping her arms for all she was worth.

They both needed this. What, she wasn't completely sure. Hopefully this wasn't a horrible mistake.

She ran down a trail between trees, their boughs protecting her somewhat from the rain. Then she turned, finding a barely there trail and dodged left, weaving and winding, going on instinct.

Seth's bellow of her name catapulted through the storm. Her body shivered from head to toe.

She gulped and slowed, taking another turn and becoming more strategic. The entire forest smelled like pine and spruce, hopefully masking her scent. If he wanted her, he'd have to earn her.

The wind pierced the shelter of the boughs, seeping right through her shirt, making her shiver. Yet she persisted. The hair on the back of her neck prickled. Quickly, she turned but saw nothing.

Yet she knew he was there.

She kept going, paused, and then stilled. Waited. Breathing quietly.

He stepped out from behind a tree ahead of her, his eyes burning an unholy blue in the night. Rain sluiced over his bare chest, molding his jeans to his muscled legs, his black hair wild in the wind. "What the hell are you doing?"

She wasn't sure. Not even close. "You want me?"

Slowly, he nodded, heat swelling from him.

"Then you're gonna have to earn me," she said, meaning every word. Nobody had ever come close—except this wolf.

"You should reconsider," he said, his voice gritty.

She took a step back. "Too late." Much too late. So she turned and ran. Hard and with every ounce of strength she had. She caught sight of him up ahead, again, and slid in the mud to turn.

His laugh rode the wind, arrogant and angry.

She ran harder.

He played with her, forcing her to twist and turn, keeping her running. Finally, she emerged in a small field set against the rocks and pivoted to watch him prowl from the tree line.

He'd *herded* her there.

Standing her ground, her legs wobbling from the run as well as fear, she let her teeth show. "That all you got? Wolf?"

The animal danced just beneath his skin. He changed in that moment. Oh, he was still human, and most people wouldn't have noticed, but he'd bitten her. He'd mated her. She saw the second the wolf took control.

Using her last bit of strength, she swiveled in the rain and ran full-out for the trees.

He caught her around the waist, spinning and throwing them both to the wet earth. He landed on his back, cradling her on top of him, protecting her from injury. Then he rolled them over. "You have lost your mind."

She bucked and fought, scraping her nails down his arm. "I lost my mind the second I met you," she snapped, her head ringing, and her body on fire for him.

"Good." He stood and yanked her up. "Let's go inside."

It was the safe move. The right move. "No." She kicked him in the knee again and ran to the trees.

She almost made it.

This time, he took her down to all fours, shredding her shirt with what felt like claws. Her bra was next. She huffed out air, the rain cooling her skin, her head reeling. "Seth," she whispered.

"Too late." He used those deadly claws to destroy her jeans and even her socks. Then her panties shredded, leaving not one mark on her skin.

Desire ripped through her sharper than those claws, making her pant. Was it healthy to want somebody this badly?

"Is this what you wanted?" He flipped her onto her back, bent over her, his body hot...and naked. When had he ditched his jeans?

"Yes," she panted, rain splattering up from the ground. "I want all of you." If she was going to be the mate of an actual wolf, she needed them both to understand that she was strong enough. More than strong. "You with me?"

"Yeah, I'm with you." He half-lifted her, his grip bruising. Then he kissed her.

Hard.

Her head swam, and she kissed him back, grabbing onto his hair and never letting go. She poured everything she had, everything she wanted into him, knowing he'd take it and make her safe. Then he flipped her back around.

She landed on hands and knees, her head dropping. Rough hands grabbed her hips. His hold was unbreakable, and the air quieted around him. She waited, wet and ready. Needing him in a way she'd never understand.

Tightening his hold, he plunged inside her and pulled her back. Shock filled her and then she was climbing, desperately, as he pounded into her hard and fast, out of control. Her nails dug into the wet grass, and she held on, her eyes shutting, feeling everything she'd ever wanted.

Everything she hadn't known existed. The female inside her, the one mated to a wolf, howled.

She screamed his name as the first orgasm cut through her, but he didn't stop. Not for a second. Then she was climbing again, panting and searching, gasping for that release. The storm, the rain, the danger all spiraled away into nothingness. There was only right here and right now and Seth Volk.

His mouth nudged her neck, and then he struck, those deadly fangs piercing right where he'd marked her before. She cried out, the world silencing as her entire body exploded into a climax that took everything she had.

He held on, pounding harder and then ground against her, her name a muffled sound on his lips. His fangs slid from her flesh and he licked the wound clean. The strength in her arms gave out, and she fell, caught instantly by him. He pulled out and stood in one graceful movement, taking her with him. She blinked. Overcome. Then he lifted her against his chest and walked back through the storm, holding her safe and secure.

Completely.

CHAPTER 34

Around dawn, the rain slowed to a persistent patter, no longer punishing the ground. Seth lay on his childhood bed, one leg out of the covers, his mate snuggled against his side. His eyes remained open as they had all night. Her soft breathing in sleep soothed him, and he allowed himself these precious unguarded moments with her. Her scent of vanilla and lilacs dove deep into him, providing comfort.

He'd been lost the moment she faced him so bravely beyond those jail bars, her strength only enhanced by the vulnerability glimmering in her stunning eyes.

His Mia. A woman who should've been born in a different time—a flame of fire in a dark world.

His chances at seeing her change through her long life, seeing her create life, seeing her fight injustices, were not good. But he knew, without a doubt, that Erik would protect her with his life.

His brother. Seth loved them, and he'd kill or die for them both.

Without hesitation.

He smelled the wolves before he heard them. His body went on full alert, and he gently slid from the bed, careful not to awaken Mia. She murmured and curled into a ball, her long hair splayed out on the pillow. Silently, he pulled on ripped jeans and a worn black T-shirt before padding downstairs for his boots.

Rolling his neck, he strode out into the rain, walking toward the nearest garage, where they'd gathered. Most of the males in the pack, as well as some of the females stood waiting, all still. "You've heard."

Ralph Fulsome stepped forward, his chest wide, and grief for his daughter still in his eyes. "We're sorry about Ben, Seth. He was a good Alpha, and he'll be missed."

Seth jerked his head in acknowledgment. There were at least fifty males present, and while he was good, nobody was that good. If they wanted him dead, he'd be dead. But they'd go with tradition and want Erik to fight him. Probably. "We'll have the funeral for him tonight," Seth said, glancing at the lightening gray clouds. Rain slid down his face, and he allowed the drops to cool him.

"We want the fight afterward," Ralph said, apparently having been elected to do the speaking.

Seth lifted an eyebrow, letting the predator inside him show. "You want me dead that badly?"

Several members shifted their feet, and many looked at the ground.

Ralph faced him directly. "Nobody wants you dead, but what's the alternative? Plus, you might win."

Anybody who even remotely knew Seth understood that he'd never kill his brother.

"You could leave. Take Mia and go," Susan Pake said quietly, her blond hair up in a bun and getting wet. She was around forty, a widow with three kids who could shoot better than any wolf Seth had ever met. "You could find a good life."

Seth nodded. He'd be living without a pack, without his people. Though to stay with Mia, he'd do it. She mattered more than all else, although a part of him would always feel cut out and raw.

The scent of lilacs hit him, and his wolf stretched awake. He turned just his head to see Mia on the doorstep, dressed only in his flannel, her legs bare, and her hair curling wildly down her back.

"Seth?" she called, looking cautiously at the assembled group.

He swallowed. "Go back inside. I'll be there in a minute." It didn't seem like anybody would challenge him right now.

She studied the group, faltered, and then threw her shoulders back. Barefooted, walking over rough grass and rocks, she headed right for him, her eyes on fire.

He couldn't breathe.

She reached him and slipped her hand into his, facing his pack by his side. Small, fragile, unarmed, she barely reached his shoulder yet didn't hesitate.

Everything inside him warmed, swelled, and settled.

His mate.

His wolf sprang fully awake, prepared to devastate any threat against her. The pack studied her, admiration entering the eyes of many. Susan even smiled.

He should tell Mia to go back inside, where she was protected, but she was making a statement, and he felt like it was safe enough to do so right now. "We're leaving tonight," he told her. Their chances weren't good on their own, not with other packs out there wanting him taken out, but he would take the chance with her.

Her hand trembled in his, but her expression remained calm. She stared out at the assembled people, not flinching, her chin held high.

Pride filled him, along with heat. He looked directly at Ralph. "I'll see everyone tonight at the ceremony for Ben. For now, get off my property."

Ralph blinked and made a hand motion. Silently, the members of his pack disappeared back into the woods, and the atmosphere thickened as several must've shifted.

Seth kept Mia's hand and strode through the light rain to the house, where he shut the door behind him. "That meant a lot. You standing by me."

She wiped rain off her face and looked up at him. "I'll always stand by you."

He brushed her hair away from her shoulder. "In a situation like that, don't do it again." He kept his voice pleasant while his wolf agreed deep down.

She met his gaze evenly. "Excuse me?"

How could he explain that his primary goal at all times was to provide her with safety? He was an Alpha, even without a pack, and she was his mate. It was that simple, yet she was human and didn't understand. "We had no idea what we were facing, and in that situation, you stay covered." He kept his voice level, knowing she didn't understand and hoping she would at least try and not make him show her in a way neither of them would like. She'd given herself to him during the mating and more specifically, the night before in the storm, and that meant something. Everything.

"Seth? I'm trained."

"Not against wolves," he said. "Obedience doesn't come easily to you, and I understand that, but my patience isn't limitless."

Those eyes flared. "Oh, sweetheart. Don't even try it."

Yep. This would be more difficult than he'd considered. He sighed. She smiled. "I've given you fair warning," he said.

"You have." She leaned up and kissed him. "Now. I have things to do, big bad Alpha."

Unfortunately, at some point, she would likely force him to live up to that title with her. He kissed her back, taking the reprieve.

For now.

* * *

After the pack exited the Volk property, Mia headed to her cottage, promising Seth she'd be safe. They still had a killer, maybe more than one, out there. The Barnby brothers were on the run, and Ruby's and Mandy's murderer was still close. She had to do her job and find the psychopath who'd taken their young lives. She knew, without a doubt, that Seth wasn't the murderer.

What about Erik?

After a hot shower, she strode into the kitchen of her cottage to see her mom and Dotty waiting for her at the kitchen table. "I'm sorry things have been so crazy lately," she said, accepting the cup of coffee from her aunt.

"Romance will do that," Dotty said dreamily.

Romance? Right. That word didn't come close to describing Mia's current situation. She was mated to a wolf, which was stronger than any marriage, but they'd only publicly been on one date. Blending her human and now wolf worlds would take some time, and gut instinct told her that Seth wasn't the patient type when it came to her. "Hmm." She took a seat.

Her mom rolled her eyes. "We know you're with Seth, and while it's fast, I can't really judge." The woman had been married multiple times. "But you shouldn't get too serious until he makes some type of commitment."

Mia coughed into her coffee cup, barely keeping the liquid from coming back up. Did a deep bite and partial immortality count as a commitment? "I'll keep that in mind," she agreed.

"How are the cases going? I was so sorry to hear about Benjamin Volk," Dotty said, twirling her mug in her bony hands. "His death was announced in the paper this morning."

"Not good," Mia admitted. "I know who killed Ben, but they're on the run. I still have no idea who killed the young women." Her mind reeled. She was missing something. A piece to the entire puzzle didn't fit, but she couldn't quite figure it out. What was it? The thought nagged at the back of her brain, scratching her.

Gena looked her over. "At least the flu is gone. You're glowing." She sighed. "Young love. There's nothing like it."

Love. Mia sipped her coffee. While she'd made light of Seth's veiled threats earlier, she was aware that he'd meant every word. She wasn't a woman who kept herself safe at all costs. She was a cop, and she hunted predators—or at least she had until she left the Bureau.

Who was she now? Well, she was still hunting killers, at least for the time being. She stood. "I have to get to work. Are you two doing all right?"

"Yep. We've joined a Mah Jong club in town," Gena said proudly. "We're both getting out in the world. Slowly."

Mia paused. "Oh, Mom. That's fantastic." Were things really getting better? Maybe moving to the cabin by the lake had been the best thing they all could've done. But now, they had to leave. Or at least, she did. They were just getting settled in. "I'm proud of you both."

Dotty hitched her bulk back in the chair. "Get to work, Mia El. You have killers to catch."

True statement. Mia suited up with her gun and badass boots, taking her car to the hospital. The smaller Glock felt solid against her ankle.

She had to wind through several hallways to find the woman, but finally she walked into Alice's room.

The woman sat up in bed, eating what looked like pistachio pudding. Bandages covered her neck and part of her arm, and the swelling on her face had already gone down. Her eyes were vacant, and she ate robotically.

Mia walked inside and handed over a flowering plant she'd purchased at the small hospital gift shop. "You look like you're healing quickly."

Alice jolted and then set down the pudding, her gaze on the plant. "Thank you."

Mia sat in the one guest chair, its leather already soft from what appeared to be years of use. "I wanted to run you through the night again."

Alice sighed and looked at the white blanket covering her. "I told you everything." Tears gathered in her eyes. "Benjamin...he was so brave. Even though he was injured, he tried to save us. To fight." Her nails shredded the cotton. "It wasn't fair. He could've easily taken both Barnbys just a week later. They knew that. They struck when he was down. Cowards."

Mia nodded. "I agree." She sat back and studied the woman. Wolves healed faster than humans. Something to look forward to —if she gained that ability. "How did they get in the house?"

Alice pursed her lips as if remembering. "They rang the doorbell. Jay answered it, like usual, and I heard a fight. Then the firing of a gun." She lowered her voice. "Seth came to visit me here earlier and confirmed the bullets were silver. The coroner in town is one of ours, unlike the one in Seattle."

That explained how easily Seth had thought he could get Ben's body for the ceremony tonight. Mia patted Alice's hand, stopping the ruination of the blanket. "I figured." The bloody mess stuck in her head. "They really fought first, though. Why didn't the Barnbys just shoot you all?"

"Wolves like a good fight." Alice sighed, putting her head back. "Bastards thought they could take me out without silver. Or..." Her voice lowered and saddened. "The pricks just didn't want to waste the bullets on me." She looked at the bandages. "There was a time I could've taken both of them without any help. So long ago. Getting older sucks." Her eyes took on a faraway look. "Although, Frank...he said something. Something weird."

"What?" Mia leaned forward, her interest piqued.

Alice shook her head, her gaze searching. "What was it? Something that stuck with me." She breathed out and closed her eyes. "Something about women and necks. About shutting us up for good." She swallowed, her eyes opening again. "I don't know. It just struck me as odd."

Mia nodded, her mind spinning with the new information. "Agreed. Do you think Frank knew either Mandy or Ruby?" There was no doubt that the silver through the throat had stopped all sound for the female victims. Had Ruby's death merely been one of opportunity? And Mandy's because she'd discovered something?

"Sure," Alice said. "It's our pack. Everyone knows everybody."

Mia glanced at her watch. "What about Ashlynn Volk? Did Frank know her years ago?"

"Yes," Alice said. "In fact, if I remember right, the Barnby family was opposed to Benjamin marrying outside our pack. They were rather vocal about it."

Determination flowed through Mia. Frank Barnby was looking like a good suspect, finally, and it'd be a relief to clear Erik if she could. She had to find him and talk to him first. "I'll let you rest, Alice."

Alice reached for the pudding. "I'll see you tonight."

Mia stood, pausing. "Tonight? You can't leave the hospital."

Alice's eyes blazed. "Ben and I have been together for more than a decade, and although we never mated, that's as close as I've ever come. Nothing can keep me away from his ceremony." Her gaze lanced over Mia's exposed bite mark. "You know exactly what I mean."

Mia touched her neck. Yes, she did. Exactly.

CHAPTER 35

Mia pulled up the zipper on the black dress, her heart heavy. Her phone rang, and she reached for it on the dresser. "Stone."

"We have another one," Kurt said.

She jolted. "Another one?"

He was quiet for a moment. "Yes, Mia. We have another victim."

Oh. She'd forgotten all about the other case. Then the words registered. "Another sex worker in a dumpster?"

"Affirmative, and this time the woman was missing for at least forty hours and was strangled." Sounds of typing came over the line.

Mia struggled to concentrate.

"I need you here on this."

"I can't. Not right now." There was too much going on, and Seth needed her support. She'd never given her loyalty in such a manner, but he deserved it, and she couldn't turn away from him. Perhaps she could get him to move with her back to the DC area once Gena was healthy, and she could resume her job with the FBI. But not right now. "I'm working on, well, another case."

Kurt snorted. "Nothing is as important as this case."

"You're wrong." She tucked the phone against her ear and reached for her gold earrings. "Sorry, Kurt."

"When can you help?" Frustration coated his words.

She fastened the other earring into place. "I don't know. I'm sure the Kentucky authorities can assist you." Although he'd never admit it, she had been a better agent than Kurt. Perhaps he couldn't catch this guy without her.

"This killing was in Lincoln, Nebraska," Kurt snapped.

Mia straightened, her mind spinning. "He's moving?"

"Yeah. Looks like he's headed west."

Where she was right now. It could be a coincidence, or maybe not. "Get techs on tracing the line between the kills. Find out if there's a main interstate or such, and then get back to me."

"You're not calling the shots here," Kurt said.

"Then stop asking for my help," Mia said reasonably. She had too much on her plate right now, but she'd focus on this when she could.

Papers rustled over the line. "Do you or do you not want your damn job back?"

She blinked. Did she? "I think I do, but I can't come back right now." Once she helped Seth find a safe place, then maybe she'd return. Right now, she needed to figure out her place with him, and she had to help him. "I'll call when I can." She clicked off. Now there was no choice but to bring Gena and Dotty with them when they left.

Just in case a killer was making his way toward her.

* * *

THE FIRE BURNED, smoke rising high to rest against the underbellies of the swollen clouds at dusk. For now, they held their contents, but the heated wind promised an oncoming storm —another one.

Seth stood, feet braced, watching his father's soul climb into the heavens from the scaffolding that he and Erik had silently built together.

His people, or what had been his people, were all silent as they witnessed the end of this life for their Alpha. The rolling smoke obliterated their scents, but he felt their hurt and strength. His chest felt hollow, and the world around him seemed altered. More like the shadow of a moving object. Was this grief? So much anger boiled inside him that it was difficult to tell. His vengeance would be slow and painful when he found his father's killer—after he got Mia to safety.

Alice stood closest to the burning flames, her bandaged body looking fragile. Tears streamed down her still-bruised face. Her pain was palpable even through the thickened air. Why had she and his father never mated? It was a pity, and now it was too late.

Seth's body ached, and his wolf wanted to strike. He'd recognize the people around him in a darkened room. He knew their scents. While he'd never been in the center of anything, this was his home. He'd miss his pack.

Mia slipped her slender hand into his again, offering comfort. Offering herself. She barely reached his neck, yet he could feel her resolve. Her strength.

The embers began to die down before Seth caught his brother's eye. Erik stood a pace away, watching his father, his chest forward, head up, his heart breaking through the breeze with a scent of such sorrow it banished the smoke. But gone was the lost kid or the fun-loving party animal. A fully formed and furious Alpha stood in their place, ready to exact vengeance on anybody who crossed him.

Seth would miss him most of all. They didn't share a biological father, but they'd spilled and commingled enough blood through the years that they *were* blood. *True blood.*

Erik's eyes had darkened with pain. He lifted his chin.

Seth did the same.

Voices stirred to the right of the pyre, and Seth turned, his body freezing. Frank Barnby walked out from behind a tree, a gun pointed at Mia's head. "We need to talk."

Seth instantly plunked her behind him, shoulders back and chest broadened so he'd take any bullets. His growl reverberated across the distance.

Erik edged toward them, moving swiftly and gracefully from the other direction.

Frank swallowed, his jowls moving, his broken arm still in a sling. His hair was greased back, and dirt marred his shirt as if he'd been hiding under a rock. "You need to listen to me."

"I need to rip off your head," Seth said, his calm voice at direct odds with the fury beating through his chest and boiling his blood.

Erik kept coming, death in his eyes, his movements coordinated.

Snarls erupted all around, but everyone stepped back out of deference. A couple of wolves pushed pregnant mates toward the tree line, but even those females were snarling and looked like they wanted a piece of the Barnby brother.

Frank blanched, his meaty mouth moving, and sweat rolling down his face, even though the day had cooled. "I didn't kill Ben. I'd never do that."

So Fred had shot their Alpha. Seth let his fangs slide free. Good to know. "You tried to burn down his house."

"I did not. It was just a warning. A gentle one that it was time to pass the torch." Barnby snorted a snot bubble back up into his bulbous nose. "The pack is in flux because of you two, and somebody had to do something." The last came out as a whine.

Fury centered Seth. "You *did* burn down my cottage with my mate in it." He sounded more animalistic than human now. "I clearly explained that she was mine, and I said she was under my protection." He looked around at the various pack members just waiting for Erik to take off his head. "My vow was absolute, and I will retaliate before any other business is handled. Say whatever prayer you need to, Barnby. You've got twenty seconds."

"With the fire, she wasn't your mate yet," Frank said, shuffling his large boots in the mud. "Honest. Please—"

A squawk sounded behind Seth, and he partially turned to see Fred yank Mia up against his chest, a gun to her neck. The man jerked her purse free, which held her weapon, and tossed it behind him into the trees.

Damn it. Seth had put her against a tree, not smelling anybody.

Her eyes were wide. She swallowed, her gaze caught his, and she calmed. Trusting him.

Seth slowly tilted his head. "Apparently, your brother wants to precede you into the afterlife, Frank. I'm happy to oblige him." The smoke had covered Fred's scent. His eyes were wild, his hand shook, and his terror filtered through the oxygen. He was a foot taller than Mia and had the perfect angle to destroy her brain. Panic tightened his features.

Seth turned to face him more fully, his claws extending at his sides. "Let her go, and I'll make your death fast," he promised. Nothing but Mia existed in his mind—in his world. "Draw one drop of blood, and you'll beg for what'll feel like forever." He let the killer inside him, the one he had once tried to banish, be fully visible.

Fred paled to the color of chalk. His mouth moved, but no sound came out.

Seth stalked closer to him, his chest filling with the power of the wolf. Behind him, Frank cried out in pain.

"Got his gun," Erik said almost casually.

Seth didn't care. Right now, his mate was in danger. "One chance, Fred."

Fred pressed the barrel harder against Mia's soft flesh, and she levered up onto her toes, gasping. Fear wafted from her, along with determination. Even so, she kept her focus on Seth, waiting, faith glimmering there. She angled her leg back, no doubt to hook

Barnby's knee and take him down. He shifted his weight, halting her.

Wolf instincts were better than a human's.

She swallowed and stilled, her gaze remaining on Seth. His woman trusted him to save her from one of his own, and he would. Always.

"You're doing great, Mia. Just breathe and trust me." He kept moving.

Fred shoved so hard with the gun that Mia winced, trying harder to stand on her toes. "Everything we've done was for the pack. For the good of the pack."

"You shot my father," Seth said quietly, moving closer.

"Just as a warning, and not to kill. I didn't kill him," Fred whined. "He survived the bullets as well as that silly fire at his home. I was just trying to make a statement that he needed to choose an heir and smooth things over for all of us."

Seth let the animal take over inside him. Instincts would rule. "Let her go. Now."

Fred's jowls worked furiously. "This wasn't our fault. You don't understand. We have to make this right." His eyes widened, and his desperation this close smelled like sulfur. "It's all her doing. Mia Stone. She's human. Everything was fine until she got here. Don't you see? If you won't save everyone, then we will. This is for our pack." His finger tightened on the trigger, and his shoulders settled as if he'd made a decision.

Seth moved instantly, faster than any animal alive. He shoved his hand between the barrel and Mia's flesh, pivoted, and twisted his wrist so the weapon flew through the air. In one smooth motion, he shoved his mate to the side and slashed out with his claws, digging deep into Fred's neck, ripping down, and then back up. A quick side-swipe had the bastard's head rolling off his body and beneath a huckleberry bush.

Mia gasped, stumbling back, her neck already bruising. Her eyes widened on the body as it flopped to the mud and fell sideways. She held a hand to her neck, paling until a thin blue vein showed on her temple.

A collective murmur rolled through the onlookers. Wolves were fast, but Seth was in a category all his own.

He turned for the next threat, only to pause at seeing Frank's head roll across the mud, Erik's claws out and bloody. A spray of red covered Erik's chest and lower jaw, and if anything, he looked bored.

Seth had taught him that expression.

Erik focused and looked at Mia and then at Seth, giving a short nod.

Seth did the same. His brother had been there for him when he needed it, and he'd never forget it. Making sure he'd sheathed his claws, he reached for Mia and dragged her against his side. She shook violently but stood straight, her feet solid on the ground. "Anybody who touches her dies. Alpha or not, pack or not. Period."

Nobody dared challenge him.

Ralph Fulsome looked down at the headless bodies. "So who killed Ben? Which one of them?"

Erik set his stance. "To take down our father, even though he had been shot several times the day before? It had to have been both of them."

Seth didn't much care at this point. They'd burned down his cabin, set fire to his father's house, and then threatened Mia. They deserved the deaths they'd received. "They don't get the pack funeral."

Again, nobody argued.

Alice kicked Fred's leg and then stumbled toward the trees, her head down, her shoulders stooped. A bite mark still showed on her neck, and the scratches and bruises from the fight with the Barnbys were still raw and painful looking.

The skies clapped with thunder, and then the clouds stretched and opened wide like the mouth of a snake. Water poured down in rivulets, not drops, squelching the fire and drenching the spectators.

"Under a tree." Seth nudged Mia toward the tree line, motioning for Ralph to cover her back.

The man nodded, moving to her side.

For two beats, nobody spoke. A couple of the younger wolves looked at each other and shuffled their feet. Everybody else just looked at the brothers in the circle of death.

It was time.

Seth walked toward his brother in the middle of the clearing, steam rising from his clothing. They'd discussed this while building the scaffolding for the pyre, and even though Erik had argued, Seth was holding strong. He'd said his goodbyes then, leaving to set plans in motion during the afternoon. It was done. He didn't even have the thought of vengeance to keep him going any longer since the Barnbys were dead. Somebody else would have to solve the recent murders, and Mia wouldn't like that.

It was unfortunate because she was leaving whether she liked it or not. He'd take her entire family if she wanted, but she needed to be protected, and he couldn't provide that here.

Not any longer.

He reached Erik, and they turned to face the pack. Erik would become the Alpha, and Seth would take Mia somewhere else. Somewhere nobody could find them. Maybe the wilds of Alaska. "It is time," he said to the pack. To his people.

This was going to hurt.

CHAPTER 36

Mia stood next to Alice, her heart hurting. She understood the plan, but she wasn't sure how she'd get Gena and Dotty to agree to leave the small cabin. They had a choice, and she'd respect whatever that was. If they stayed, Pete would take care of them. But maybe they'd want to come with her. Though if they did, was it safe? Seth hadn't seemed to think it'd ever be safe for them away from a pack.

Seth faced his people so bravely, his hard body in all black, his face in strong, compelling lines. Dangerous ones—all angles and fury and power. "I am not going to fight to be Alpha."

"That's unfortunate." Erik's expression was inscrutable, and his clothing matted to his hard body. "The pack needs an Alpha."

Seth didn't flinch but tension rolled around him. "Knock it off," he muttered. "We discussed this."

A second later, Emily Nightsom stepped from the forest behind the still-smoldering wood. She paused, and Erik stalked toward her, turning back to face his brother. "This pack needs an Alpha, and it'd be sad if it were anybody but you."

Seth studied Erik. "What are you doing?"

Erik took Emily's hand. With their blond hair, they looked like two powerful gods. "Well, it's like this…"

Emily's hair was in an intricate braid, and she wore black slacks and a white sweater with no weapons—no visible weapons, anyway. "Remember how my father hinted that he'd like to use me as a bartering chip for a merger?"

Seth gave a short nod.

Emily showed her teeth, looking beautiful next to Erik's roughness. "And remember how he didn't mean it and was just trying to use me as a pawn?" Anger glowed in her dark eyes.

Seth glanced at his brother, but Erik's expression remained impassive.

Mia's breath heated.

Emily smiled at Mia. "Well, I decided to take some control. While I have no interest in being the Alpha of the Slate Pack, Cousin Vic is a moron who'll get us all killed. Erik is an Alpha, and we reached our own agreement." She leaned into Erik. "Turns out we're quite compatible."

Alice kicked a rock next to Mia, her breath panting out.

Seth cocked his head. "You want this?"

Erik nodded. "Yeah. I want this." He looked down at Emily. "I might need to challenge Cousin Vic, and I'll try not to kill him, but whatevs." He grinned, the rain running down his face to his shirt. "Philip has some good years in him yet, so there's no hurry on this. But it's convenient to have a plan. Right, brother?"

Seth's breath steamed through the rainy air. "Erik. I can't let you—"

"It's done," Erik said. "This is our decision, and we've made it." He winked at Mia. "Just think how irritated the other packs will be with our alliance. Things are going to get interesting."

Seth snorted.

"This can't happen," Alice hissed, her hands tucked into her jacket.

Mia frowned. "Why not?" What was she missing?

Alice sucked in air. "Seth is not of our blood. It matters. Erik matters. We need a true blood, and only Erik fits that rule."

Mia paused, the thoughts coiling through her brain like sparking wires. Silver bullets. Gashes and pain. Fury. She turned on the woman. "They didn't use silver on you."

Alice blinked. "I know."

Why? No. That wasn't the question. "They used silver bullets on Ben and the bodyguard."

Alice's face turned a mottled crimson. "I know."

"But why beat them? Even if wolves like to fight, that doesn't make sense." If the Barnbys had decided to kill their Alpha, they wouldn't have ripped off his lip or face in a fight. Those were rough markings. Defensive ones? A true fight. "They would've just shot him."

Alice pulled out a shiny silver gun with a wider-than-normal barrel. Mia didn't recognize the brand. "Move. Now."

People angled closer, eyeing the gun, several emerging from beneath the safety of tree boughs.

Seth came at them from one angle, while Erik covered the other, Emily on his six.

Mia looked right into Alice's eyes. She was getting tired of people pulling guns on her. "The Barnbys weren't even there."

"No." The woman's lips turned down. "They were going to die anyway after they set fire to both Ben's and Seth's homes, especially since you were the target. Plus, the moron shot Ben the first time just to make a point. Their deaths aren't on my hands."

"But Ben's is," Mia said softly, the puzzle pieces finally clicking into place. "You fought with him, full-out, and then you shot him. What would make a male like Ben fight you? Hurt you like this?" The woman was still bruised.

Erik stopped, spraying mud. "You killed Ruby."

Several people gasped.

Alice turned to face him, her eyes rabid as she looked around as if she couldn't find a spot to focus on. "You need to take your rightful place. Benjamin and I got into a fight about you, Erik. About you and Seth. He was torn up, and he shouldn't have been." She looked down at the gun. "Things were said."

"Like what?" Mia asked.

The older woman's lips trembled. "He said he didn't love me. That he never had." She looked wildly around. "I loved him. And I love this pack. It's so clear that you are meant to be the Alpha, Erik. I'm glad Ruby is dead. You need a purebred wolf for your mate, and now you've found one. Be the Alpha here with Emily. Let Vic take over their pack. It's what your father would've wanted."

"My father wanted his family to be safe," Erik snapped, shock sizzling in his eyes. "You killed him. Why?"

"We started fighting," Alice said, tears streaming down her face. "He was so cold, like he didn't care at all. Told me to butt out, as if I wasn't his true mate. I am. I lost it. Attacked him!" she screamed.

Seth's jaw went slack. "I thought you loved him."

"I did," Alice said, sniffing loudly. "He was still injured from being shot before, or I wouldn't have had a chance."

Mia inched closer to the woman. "It's time to tell the whole truth, Alice." It was obvious the woman just couldn't face what she'd done. She'd killed Ruby and then Mandy in a desperate attempt to protect Benjamin and the pack in a way they didn't want. "Let it all out," Mia said.

"You need to die, too," Alice said. "If it's the last thing I do on this Earth, I will protect this pack."

The woman was certifiable. Mia angled to the side, gulping when the gun barrel followed her. "You and Ben started fighting, you started losing, and then you shot him."

Alice nodded, tears flying. "Yes. He gave me no choice. I ran down the stairs just as Jay was coming inside from a run, so I had to shoot him, too. Then I clawed him up to make it look like he fought."

They'd had it exactly wrong. Mia took a deep breath. "You loved Benjamin."

"Yes," Alice said, her shoulders sunken, her lips lax. "For years, I loved him."

"Is that why you killed Ashlynn Volk?" Mia asked, tying the ends together.

Alice pressed her lips together. "You don't know what you're talking about. I was too late to save Ben then. But I can save the pack now. I'm not alone, you know. Plenty of us want the rightful Alpha to take over." Her finger twitched.

Mia jumped away from the trees, and pain exploded in her right side.

Another gun fired, three times from the woods.

Mia went down, almost in slow motion, turning toward the trees. Pete stood there, gun out. How had he found the group?

Mia's head hit a rock, and stars exploded all around her.

Alice fell hard, rolled, and fired wildly. The bullets hit Pete, and he flew back, out of sight.

Mia screamed his name as darkness tried to take her. Seth slid on his knees through the wet grass, cradling her head.

Then nothing. She fell into unconsciousness with a soft sigh.

CHAPTER 37

Seth sat in the chair next to the hospital bed, his face in his hands. His whiskers burned his palms, but that was nothing compared to the pain thrumming through his temples.

Mia stretched beneath the blankets.

His eyelids flew open, his gaze narrowing on her pretty emerald eyes. "Hi."

She blinked, her gaze slowly focusing on the hospital room. Then she peered down at the bandage around her upper arm. "How bad?" she croaked.

He stood and poured her a glass of water. "Flesh wound with the bullet grazing you. Silver bullet. There's enough of me in you, enough of the mating, that the silver will scar." He handed over the cup. For the rest of their lives, she'd wear that mark. Proof that he hadn't protected her.

She struggled to sit, and he helped her, using her good shoulder. "I passed out from a simple flesh wound?" Horror filled her voice.

Against all rational thought, amusement tickled through him. "No. You hit your head on a rock and have a slight concussion.

But it was the silver that short-circuited your system, to be honest."

"Oh." She looked down at the hospital gown. "Please tell me you haven't called my mother or aunt."

"I have not," he said easily, sitting again and taking her free hand. "It's well after midnight, and they should be asleep. Figured we didn't even have to tell them if you didn't want."

Relief crossed her features. She frowned. Then she jerked up. "Wait. Pete." She pulled her hand free and tossed back the plush blanket. "Pete. Where is he? Is he okay?"

Seth kept his hand gentle but firm as he planted it on her good shoulder and pressed her back against the pillows. "Pete took three bullets to the upper left shoulder and is sleeping peacefully in the adjacent room. All three went right through his body as if they didn't want to hurt him." The surgeon had just stitched the guy up and then went home. "He'll be fine and can probably go home tomorrow."

She settled, her gaze returning to Seth's face. "How did Pete even get up there?"

Seth sighed. "Apparently someone called the fire in, and since he remembered my people being there before, he did his job and investigated. He shot Alice to protect you, not knowing that human bullets wouldn't take her down for long."

Mia blinked. "I'm so sorry, Seth. Alice—"

He nodded. "I know." Never in a million would he have thought the woman capable of something like that.

"She loved your father to a scary degree. Did she finally confess to your mother's murder?" Mia shook her head. "To think she also killed those women from Seattle, just to cover her tracks. Then Ruby and Mandy."

The whole idea churned like acid through his stomach. "She didn't confess to anything. Wouldn't say the words."

Mia blinked. "Where is she? You have her contained, don't you?"

"She's dead," he said simply, meeting Mia's gaze, which turned a deep green.

Her mouth opened and then closed. "Tell me you didn't."

He gently caressed her chin. "Are you asking as a cop or my mate?" It was a fair question.

One she took proper time considering. Finally, she exhaled. "As your mate. I won't take action, I promise."

"Claire Fulsome killed Alice, knife in throat," Seth said, reliving the moment. "Alice shot Pete and went down from his human bullets, though bounced up almost instantly. Claire was behind her husband and heard everything. She believed that Alice had killed her daughter, and she went for the kill. I'm not going to exact any punishment. Period."

Mia looked toward the doorway. "The system is in place for a reason. Vigilante justice isn't the way to go."

"A mother avenged her daughter's death," Seth said. "As the Alpha of the pack, it's my decision what happens next. I've decided, and it's over. Claire will be left alone. Tell me you understand."

Her long lashes swept up and she studied him. "I understand," she said softly. "This time."

Good enough.

She picked at a loose string on the blanket. "So, you accepted the Alpha position, huh?"

"I did." He cocked his head. "You okay with that?"

"Yes." She pressed her lips together. "What about Erik? Can you see him with Emily?"

Seth shrugged. "Not really, but they have time to figure things out. Her father isn't going anywhere for a while." He didn't see them together, but who knew what could happen? Here he was, the Alpha with a mate—a human cop, no less—and nobody could've predicted that. In fact, they probably had a challenging road ahead of them, and not for a second had he forgotten that she might have a human criminal after her.

For now, he was going to enjoy the fact that they were both alive and had a decent chance of staying that way.

She set down the glass. "Let's get out of here."

Sweeter words had never been said.

* * *

AFTER A GOOD NIGHT'S sleep at Seth's house, Mia headed over to Pete's cottage to fetch him some decent clothes. It was the least she could do. Her arm ached like somebody kept poking her with a needle, and she'd scratched at the bandage enough at breakfast that Seth had threatened to wrap it with duct tape.

Then pack members had started arriving with gifts to show their support. More than half of the pack was on Seth's side, so that was a good thing. But that left a lot of unhappy wolves, as well as distrust from the other packs.

The rain had disappeared, leaving a sunny summer day with a bright blue sky in its wake. She breathed in the fresh air, her windows down. First, she'd take clothing to Pete and thank him for trying to save her life. Then she'd give him the story about Alice dying from his bullets, which the coroner would back up. After that, she'd go home and talk to Dotty and Gena about her feelings for Seth and admit that they were dating. They'd have to go out for a while, just for the human population in town.

The idea of courting was kind of sweet. She grinned. Would he bring her flowers?

Something told her that Seth would go all out—even with the gifts.

She parked the car at Pete's silent cabin and walked past untended flower beds to the front door, which was locked. A quick glance around had her finding his spare key beneath a rock by the first step. The guy was nothing if not predictable.

The hair on the back of her neck stood up. She looked out at the quiet trees, not seeing anything amiss. Shaking it off, she used the key and walked inside the cabin, sneezing instantly. The place was a bachelor's dusty dream. Leather furniture, newspapers stacked wherever, a couple of empty bottles of beer on the table. A stack of mail perched on a side table with several pieces falling onto the floor.

She shook her head. The guy needed a cleaning service. She picked up the mail and stacked it, kicking a pair of his shoes toward the mat.

Then she took the only hallway to his bedroom, passing a guest bathroom that she didn't examine. He had a big bed—unmade. She sighed. "Pete." What a total bachelor.

She flipped on the light, noting more dust and more unopened mail on the dresser. A sound outside caught her attention, and she stiffened, listening. Nothing. Was probably the wind.

There were two doors to the right of the room, and the first was open to a small bathroom with dirty clothes littering the floor. If she were a decent friend, she'd clean the cabin and do some laundry for the guy. Maybe after she picked him up at the hospital, she'd help him clean the home. Yeah. That was a good plan. He had tried to save her life, after all.

She snorted and opened the closet door, hoping he had something clean to wear.

Her hand fumbled on the wall and she turned on the light, sighing in relief at seeing a few pairs of clean jeans hanging below a bunch of T-shirts to the right. His uniforms were lined up to the left.

Straight ahead was a smaller dresser with letters and cards scattered across it. She stopped cold at seeing the blown-up and framed picture above it. A lump settled in her throat. She walked toward it, her heart hammering, her head all but exploding. A much younger Pete sat on a dock at the local lake, his arm thrown carelessly around a stunning young woman with unreal blue eyes.

Seth's blue eyes.

Ashlynn Volk. Mia shook her head, trying to make sense of the photograph. They were both young, and it had to have been taken before Seth was born. Why hadn't Pete said anything about knowing her? About knowing her well enough to keep her picture in his closet for all these years? A quick look verified that the cards and letters were from Seth's mom, poems and notations of love—young puppy love.

Mia's phone buzzed in her pocket, and she shrieked. Damn it. "Hello?"

Silence came over the line. "You sound funny. What's wrong?" Seth asked.

Mia rapidly backed out of the closet, shaking her head, trying to convince herself that the photograph didn't mean anything. Her butt hit the dresser, and the pile of mail wafted to the floor.

Her mind reeling, she leaned over and picked it up, stacking everything back in place.

A plain white envelope sat on top, addressed to Pete with a written return address for Ruby Redbird. Her stomach cramped. She ripped open the envelope to find a cleaning bill.

Ruby had cleaned Pete's home.

She'd probably seen the picture of Ashlynn Volk.

Oh, God. "It's Pete," she whispered, her stomach clenching so hard she could barely breathe. She turned to run, barreling through the cottage and throwing open the front door.

Pete stood there, bandage over his shoulder, gun in his hand. He sighed. "I really wish you hadn't come here, Mia."

CHAPTER 38

Mia slipped her phone into her back pocket and then held up both hands. "Pete?"

He gestured her inside with the gun, following her when she retreated. "Sit down." His gray hair was mussed, and his belly bulged in the light blue scrubs he'd obviously borrowed.

She sat on the sofa, still reeling. "I don't understand."

He slammed the door, his gaze and aim not leaving her. "Why?" His voice rose, and his eyes glittered. "Why did you come here?"

"I was getting you some clothes," she whispered, her body shaking. How was this possible?

He made a noise, one of frustration, and paced by the coffee table. "Everything was perfect. Just perfect. And what now?" He gestured widely with the weapon.

If she rushed him, she'd have to take him down fast. She gulped. "You said you've had a hunting cabin in this town for years. It was more than that, wasn't it?"

He nodded, his hair standing on end. "Yes. My family spent summers here, and I kept the cabin to hunt and fish throughout my life."

Okay. She couldn't think. "You knew Ashlynn Volk."

"Tryne," Pete snapped. "Her name was Ashlynn Tryne, and we were in love. I left for college, and she got married. Damn near broke my heart."

She wed Seth's biological father. Did Pete know about shifters? "Then she had Seth, and her, um, husband died." Mia's phone was still on. Was Seth listening, or had he started to come for her? She had to get Pete into handcuffs before Seth arrived, or Seth would kill him. "Then you came back?"

Pete nodded. "Yeah. I never stopped loving her. I came back, and we dated, but she also dated a few other people. Then I had to go back to the city. I promised to return for her, and she sent me a letter saying that she was marrying Benjamin Volk, and that he'd be a good father to her boy."

Mia watched the gun. "A letter, huh?"

"Yeah. That was in the days of letters," Pete said quietly. "I was on a case by then and couldn't leave right away. She got married again, and I tried to forget her. Tried to get past it. I heard she had another kid, and it about killed me. I stayed away for as long as I could. But one year, on vacation, I was in my hunting cabin. I went out for a walk, and there she was."

Mia couldn't breathe. "You fought."

"I'd been drinking," Pete admitted, sounding as if he were actually relieved to be able to talk about it. "I tried to kiss her, told her I still loved her, and she pushed me away. Said she loved her husband and that he was what she needed." He shook his head. "I lost it. Shoved her into a tree, and she broke her neck." Tears filled his weary eyes. "Snapped like a twig. I didn't understand it. It happened so fast."

Mia drew in a breath. Did a broken neck kill a shifter? If not, Ashlynn would've healed herself. She had two boys by that time who needed her. "Why the silver?" Her voice was hoarse. Did he know about shifters?

He shrugged. "She'd driven up there, around the mine, in a

mine truck. I found the silver in there, stamped with Volk Mining, and I just did what I had to do."

Mia gagged. How had she not known Pete at all? She'd trusted him with her life—more than once. "What you had to do? Make the crime look like some psychotic bastard committed it?" When Pete didn't answer, she continued, her entire body chilled as if she'd just emerged from ice. "The other women? The ones from Seattle?"

"Having more deaths than one, all ritualistic, pointed any case in the direction of a nutjob serial killer." He threw up his hands at her stunned silence and then quickly lowered his gun hand again. "I'm not a serial killer, Mia."

She barked out a laugh without any humor. "You've killed multiple women, Pete. That's the very fucking definition of a serial killer."

Sweat dotted his brow.

"Ruby and Mandy?" she pressed, needing to hear it all.

He set his stance, his gun hand steady. "Ruby cleaned my house, and I told her to stay out of the closet. Even locked it. One day, I forgot, and she saw the picture. The stupid girl challenged me about it. I didn't have a choice." He gulped. "Then I came back one day and found Mandy crawling out of a window. She'd been retracing Ruby's steps and broke into my closet. Brat."

Mia paused. "Wait a minute. Mandy's temp indicated she was killed while we were at the ball in Seattle."

Pete preened. Actually preened. "Yeah, about that. I might've pulled a fast one with the tech out there that night. It was almost too easy, and everyone just took my word for it."

Mia stared at him. He'd killed all of these women because he'd wanted to do it. She'd bet her life that he'd killed in DC, as well. A guy like him didn't just stop.

He blanched. "Don't look at me like that. I made a huge mistake with Ashlynn, and then I tried to atone for it all those years. I did a lot of good."

"Then you came back here and killed two more girls," Mia hissed. It was just a coincidence that he used available silver—to kill wolf shifters. The man had no clue. "One of your victims was pregnant, and one wasn't even old enough to vote."

Pete's shoulders sagged. "It's not my fault."

Right. Mia carefully scooted to the edge of her seat. "Why me, Pete? Why did you call me in?" A rock settled in her stomach.

He sighed. "I figured you'd find a suspect, and we'd make it stick. An outsider from DC would give credibility to the case. Also, well, you weren't exactly at top form. Still aren't. I didn't think you'd figure it all out. Not really."

"I didn't," she admitted. "If you hadn't been shot, I'd never have been in your closet." She peered up at him. "Why would you come back to Lost Lake?"

"I still feel her here," he said quietly. "Ashlynn. When I decided to retire, I thought I'd be closer to her here." He shook his head. "The picture in the closet was dumb, but I couldn't let it go. Couldn't let *her* go. That picture has been with me my entire life."

He really was sick. Mia pressed a hand to her stomach. "The Barnby brothers were a perfect setup."

Pete nodded. "Yeah, and they just disappeared. It was perfect. They're still gone, and we could've pinned the whole thing on them."

"They're actually dead," Mia said, watching him carefully. "Seth and Erik killed them for coming after family. Like me. You know Seth will rip out your heart if you hurt me, right?"

Pete scowled. "You've been on one date with the guy and you think he'll kill for you? Right."

She tilted her head. "Yeah. I really do." She sighed. "Then Alice was shot and killed." Well, shot and stabbed, but Pete didn't know that. "I thought she'd killed Ruby and Mandy."

"It was perfect," Pete lamented. Then he steeled his shoulders. "All right. Get up. I promise this won't hurt."

She didn't move. "All the suspects are dead, Pete. What's your plan here?"

"Seth," he admitted. "Or Erik. Not sure. Either way, one of them will be arrested for your murder, which will look suspiciously like the other deaths. Guess we were wrong about the Barnby brothers, as well as Alice." A tear leaked down his roughened skin. "I'm really sorry about this."

"Me, too." Gathering her strength, she lunged across the coffee table.

* * *

SETH HEARD the gunfire just as he burst through the front door in wolf form, his senses bright, and his fury raw. He'd listened through the line just long enough to catch what was happening, and then he'd shifted into wolf form to travel faster. Colors and smells hit him so quickly he skidded to a stop, his claws leaving deep wounds in the wood. Mia and Pete wrestled on the floor, magazines and newspapers scattering. The smell of blood, lilac, and vanilla threw Seth into a frenzy.

Growling, he jumped into the fray, sinking his fangs into Pete's neck. He lifted the man, dragging him away from Mia.

She scrambled back on her butt, her legs working furiously to propel her. Blood spurted as she moved.

Pete screamed, his gun hand lifting.

Seth knocked it away with one paw, growling and snarling. Driving his fangs even deeper, he dragged his prey over the wooden floor and out into the sunny day.

Pete screeched like a wounded animal, his legs and feet thumping over the porch and down to the overgrown yard.

Seth leapt into a run, and several of Pete's bones audibly broke as they hit the ground. His shoes tore free, along with the bottom section of his pants. He screamed and cried, but Seth didn't stop, the animal inside having taken over completely. Within minutes, he reached the place of his mother's death. There, he dropped Pete like a sack of raw potatoes and backed away, snarling and growling. Wanting to kill but allowing nature to take over.

Pete clutched at his bleeding neck, trying to shove parts of his throat back into place. He sobbed and crab-walked back until his head hit a tree, his eyes wide and panicked. Then he forced himself to sit, his head wobbling on his neck. The smell of death was all over him—as was the stench of terror. A sensation he'd probably caused in too many people, so many helpless women, and deserved to feel himself.

Seth stretched open his mouth wide and called for wolves. Real ones. Then he stretched out his neck and shifted, going from wolf to man in slow motion. Letting Pete see just what he'd unleashed.

Blood gurgled out of Pete's mouth, and his eyes widened. He pissed his pants and cried, snot mixing with the blood. "I didn't know," he croaked, air flowing through his wounds.

"You do now," Seth said, watching him tremble and futilely try to keep his lungs working.

"I loved her," Pete croaked.

Seth stared impassively. "Too bad. You're definitely not going where she did in death."

Pete shuddered several times, fighting the pull, his life slowly leaving his body. Finally, he stopped moving, his eyes glassing over. His injured hand fell to the ground, and he slumped into a lump of nothingness.

Seth stood there with the blood of his mother's killer staining the dirt red. There might not be peace, but there would be justice.

When he'd heard Mia's panicked voice over the phone, he'd nearly lost his mind. Everything had become clear in that second. There was only Mia and getting to her. At the thought, Seth turned and started back the way he'd come, leaving the bastard alone and dead in the woods. A nearby pack of wolves, just animals, had heard his call and would come eat the corpse until there was nothing left.

It was a fitting end for a monster.

Seth ducked his head and ran, letting the forest fly by on either side of him. How badly was Mia hurt? She'd been alive and moving, so it couldn't be too bad. Leaping across the porch, he slid in blood to reach her, gentling himself instantly before touching her. "How bad?"

She held her hand over her right thigh, blood oozing between her fingers. Shock glistened through her eyes. "Shot once. I think the bullet is still in there."

He leaned down and lifted her, holding her tight. "You'll be okay." She had to be. She was his life.

She slid her arm over his shoulder. "You're naked, Seth."

Like that mattered. "We really have to stop getting you shot." He tried for levity, but his voice came out a deadly growl.

She snuggled into his chest, her cheek against his heart. "I knew you'd come for me."

"Then why didn't you wait before attacking the psycho holding a gun?" He stalked outside to her car.

"Just doing my job," she said, her voice slurring.

Yeah, they'd have to figure that out later. For now, he needed to get his mate to a doctor.

Again.

CHAPTER 39

One week after being shot again, Mia sat on the back porch of Seth's house as kids played water sports on the lawn and people milled around colorful picnic tables laden with too much food. At least half of the town, wolf and human, had gathered to celebrate Seth taking over Volk Mining. Half of the house was still burned, but bright tarps covered the damage.

Gena sat quietly in her chair next to Mia, a glass of lemonade in her hand. "I don't know about being around this many people."

Dotty snorted from Mia's other side. "It's okay, Gena. We can leave anytime you want."

Gena's expression smoothed out. "Okay. Just knowing that makes me feel better."

Dotty sighed, looking out at the forest. "I'm still so sad about Pete being killed in that hunting accident. Poor Pete."

"I know," Mia said. The coroner had helped to cover up what had really happened to Pete, and the town was sad but satisfied with the explanation of a hunting accident.

Gena sipped her drink. "I don't think the sheriff should shack up with the local mine owner. Just saying. Are you thinking of running for sheriff?"

"I don't know," Mia murmured. How could she? She knew too many of the town's secrets, and she never wanted to be part of another coverup. Hiding Pete's death had been hard enough on her. Yet she wanted to be a cop again.

Dotty eyed her. "You're not planning on going back to DC, are you?"

"I don't know," Mia said. "I was hired as a shrink in Seattle, but there's a case I've been asked to consult about." She caught a glimpse of Seth's frown before he could hide it. Even though he was across the lawn, playing darts with members of the pack, his hearing was that of a wolf. Of course, he'd heard everything.

She lifted her chin. "I haven't decided." There hadn't been another murder, but this killer wouldn't stop. And she had to know if this killer was Delaney's partner, or if it was somebody new.

Seth turned and faced her head-on across the distance, his eyes a warning of deep blue. A shiver wound through her entire body, landing in several interesting places along the way.

Dotty sighed. "That is one fine man."

"He's more than that," Mia said honestly.

Gena patted her good leg. "More than fine. Yes. Totally hot."

Seth's ears turned red.

"So's his brother," Dotty said, gesturing to the horseshoe pit where Erik played against Emily. "I heard a rumor that since Seth has started running the Volk mines, Erik may take over Emily's family's mines. Is that true?"

"Don't know," Mia said. "I think Emily might take over, or they may do it together. It's too early to tell. Besides, what's the rush?" The two did seem to be having fun together, but more like friends. Her gaze caught on the tall male lounging against a tree who had Seth's eyes. Jackson Tryne. Seth's cousin and the Alpha of the Granite Pack. His gaze was heated, and it was planted firmly on Emily. Interesting. "Plus, life can throw us curveballs, right? Who knows what will happen next."

At that, Seth turned, grabbed two glasses of champagne from a table, and loped gracefully toward her. His movements were determined and even relaxed, but a sense of powerful tension emanated from him. He reached her. "Mia? A word?"

"Sure." She ignored Dotty's grin and accepted the champagne, walking down the deck and around the side of the sprawling house with him. "What's up?"

They reached a wooden porch swing mounted between two trees, and Seth motioned for her to sit.

She did, taking a drink of the expensive bubbly.

He tossed his to the side, letting the glass bounce on the rough grass. "You're not going to hunt a serial killer alone." His eyes were the blue of a darkened sky right before a storm as he faced her.

"Because I'm your mate?" She tilted her head back to study him, her body flushing.

"Yes." He glanced down the private drive where Brother Jeremiah and his flock were staging a protest regarding Pete's death. They weren't buying the official story of the hunting accident. "We have plenty of problems here to occupy your time."

That appeared to be the truth. "Are you going to be challenged?"

Seth lifted one powerful shoulder. "Probably. It's important to me that you're safe if that happens." He sat next to her and plucked her up, settling her on his lap, facing him. "I haven't had a chance to tell you what it meant to me. I mean, having you standing by my side."

She placed her hands on his broad chest, feeling his heart beat beneath her palm. "Yet you always try to stand in front of me."

He grinned. "Only if danger is coming for you. That's my rightful place, baby."

She blinked. "Seth."

"Yeah." He kissed her, leaning back. "Forget your fears and any sense of caution that you don't need. I'm never gonna hurt you,

Mia Stone. I may hold on too tightly, and I may insist on your safety, but I'd cut off my own arm before I harmed you."

"I know," she whispered, lost in him. Lost in his touch and his words.

He kissed her again, going deep, surrounding her with warmth. Then he released her as the swing gently swayed, controlled by his long legs. "We're mated."

Her heart heated. "I know." She didn't feel stronger, but the colors around her vibrated with intensity and a sharpness she'd never experienced before.

"Stay with me. Let's tackle all of the oncoming challenges together."

Temptation stirred within her.

His gaze darkened. "I love you."

She sucked in air. "But—"

His grin was wicked. "I know. We haven't been together long and all of that. But I don't lie, and I don't play games. I've loved you since the first time you faced me so bravely and tried to get into my head. You're smart and sweet and so lost I feel found with you. I have to say it. I love you, Mia Stone. Period."

Everything inside her burst wide-open. It didn't make sense. Or maybe for a wolf, it did. She cupped his angular jaw, letting the shadow of his whiskers tickle her palms. For the first time in her life, she didn't know how to hold a part of herself back. So, she didn't. "I love you, too." Her voice was soft, the words strong.

His eyes flared, and his lips curved. "There we go."

She couldn't help but smile. "It's not going to be easy. A lot of issues are coming for us."

"I know." He pushed her hair away from her face. "I'm yours. Always. Our lives start right now. It's going to be an adventure."

Of that, she had no doubt. She'd taken the predator she'd seen through the bars and made him hers.

Forever.

***

See what Seth and Mia are up to next in ALPHA, and read it first as WOLF, SEASON 2 in Kindle Vella—starting October 2, 2022!

Book 2, Alpha then will be available on March 27, 2023.

The Silver Pack wolves are back in an explosive and sexy romance as a new leader shows everyone, including his mate, what the word ALPHA really means!

As the new Alpha of the Silver Pack, Seth Volk is committed to his people and his duty with a deadly focus. As such, enemies are coming for him from both within and outside the pack, determined to end him before he truly gets started. Even so, there's one female for him in life, and he guards her above all others with a singular determination that both intrigues and infuriates her.

Mia Stone was a trained FBI agent thrust into this world of immorality with centuries long enemies, a patriarchal structure, and shifting alliances that has her biting not only her lip but her mate. When a killer from her past makes a move toward her, she's more than ready to meet him and take him down, although she'll have to get past Seth to do so. Her loyalty is absolute, but the Alpha is about to see her temper in full force. Of course, a true wolf always bites back...

WANT MORE PARANORMAL GOODNESS? Check out Garrett's Destiny! Here's a quick beginning:

Garrett Kayrs settled his bulk in the booth, reaching for a glass of beer from the iced pitcher on the table. Raucous laughter poured throughout the diner as motorcycle clubs converged on the way to a festival. Not one he and his brothers were attending, but they were along for the first part of the ride to camp for a weekend.

"Would you stop frowning?" Sam Kyllwood snapped from across the booth, his green eyes showing irritation.

"I'm not," Garrett growled, frowning at his friend.

Honor Kyllwood, Sam's mate, slapped him on the arm. They'd been mated for over three years, and she was definitely one of the best-natured people Garrett had ever met. "You two behave. Garrett, I'm sure you'll find somebody to play with when we get to the campground and, Sam, give him a break. It's the first time we've gone on a ride in years that he hasn't had a female on the back of his bike. He's lonely."

Sam cut the pretty woman a look, his powerful body protecting her since he'd positioned her next to the window. "The last woman he dated tried to rob you—at knifepoint."

Honor chortled. "Yeah, but I kicked her ass. Those training sessions have gone well."

Garrett hid his grin. She was correct. He'd been searching for the right female to ride behind him for years, consumed by the quest, and he hadn't found her. Prophecy claimed she'd be dangerous, even deadly, and would probably try to kill him. It was time to get on with it.

The beast inside him, one that had slumbered beneath the surface for so long, was now stretching awake. Pissed off and ready to kill. At least now he had a job to do when they arrived at the campground.

The outside door opened, and a vision walked in. Well, more like the girl next door. She wore a frilly green blouse, white capri jeans, and sexy tan wedges that showed off her dainty pink toenails. It was autumn, and she should have been wearing a jacket. A slouchy bag looked heavy over her fragile shoulder. Her auburn hair curled down her back, and an air of pure irritation emanated from her.

Looking like an indignant kitten, she stomped right into the middle of the diner, next to Garrett's table, not seeming to realize she'd walked into a den of wolves.

The man behind her definitely noticed. Young, slick brown hair, pressed beige pants, and thousand-dollar loafers on his feet. He looked around at the various motorcycle club members sitting in different areas of the diner, all hungry, all possibly dangerous. "Let's get out of here," he muttered.

The kitten turned, her hands going to her waist. The scent of something fresh and sweet wafted from her. What was that? "You just don't get it." She leaned toward the man, anger turning her peaches-and-cream complexion into cherry-blossom pink. "The answer *was* no." She swept out her arms. "The answer *is* no." She clapped her hands. "The answer will always and forever, until the *time of the rapture*, be no." She threw her arms up. Then she shook her head. "I quit."

The man reared back. "You can't quit."

"I just did," she sighed. "I'm out. I'm not finding what I need in this job anyway." She nodded, her shoulders stiff in the flimsy blouse. "I'll send your father a nice email later today tendering my resignation. Please extend my gratitude to him for the employment opportunity." She turned away from him.

The man made the mistake of grabbing her arm.

Garrett was up in a second, towering over them both. "Let. Go."

The man jerked back as if he'd been punched in the gut.

A slight gasp came from the kitten.

Probably one of pure terror. Oh, Garrett knew what she saw. He was six and a half feet of raw muscle in a torn and dirty black motorcycle-club jacket, with shaggy hair to his shoulders, a couple of bruises across his jaw, and cracked knuckles he hadn't bothered to heal after a fight the night before.

He cut her a look and then rocked back on his heels.

Her crystal-clear blue eyes were full of delight . . . and wonder. "You," she whispered, reaching out to touch his whiskered jaw. Her tongue darted out to lick her luscious bottom lip. "It's you." She tilted her head, adoration in her liquid gaze.

The touch shot straight to his balls, making him throb in a way he hadn't in years. He growled low.

Then she withdrew.

"No." He didn't know what he was denying, but he didn't want her to stop looking at him like that. Nobody in his entire life had looked at him like that. With adoration, need, and . . . hope? More than anything, he wanted that touch again.

The blush blossomed into full-on rose, and she clapped her hand against her bag. "I, ah, um, I'm sorry." She frowned. "That was, well, that was . . ." She looked around, no doubt noticing that every gaze was focused on her. She shrugged delicate shoulders and looked up at him as if forcing herself to meet his gaze. Black lashes, natural and thick, enhanced those incredible eyes. "I apologize."

"Let's go," the man said, backpedaling toward the door.

She frowned at him. "No. Go away, Aster. I'll find my own way home."

Aster looked around, paling. Then the asshole left the kitten in the den of wolves.

Her hands fluttered together. "Oh. Well." She caught sight of the empty row of barstools at the counter and started to move that way.

"No." Garrett angled his body just enough to stop her. He was at least a foot taller and a hundred or two pounds heavier than she was, basically making him a solid wall. "How do you know me?" There were many bounties on his head, but there was no way the kitten was a bounty hunter. He could read people well enough to know that.

She glanced down at his monstrous boots and took a deep breath before looking up and meeting his gaze. "I don't know you." Then she smiled, and sure as shit, it was like the sun had appeared over the mountains after the rainy season. "That was weird, and I apologize. There's no way I could know you, correct?"

"Right." He grasped her arm, careful not to bruise her. "You're sitting with us."

"No, I—"

He nudged her into the booth, putting his body between her and the rest of the bikers in the place.

It was time for some answers.

Garrett's Destiny

AFTERWORD

If you need to talk to someone, here are some resources that are available all day, every day.
Please know you are not alone.

The National Suicide Prevention Lifeline
The National Suicide Prevention Lifeline provides free and confidential emotional support to people in suicidal crisis or emotional distress.
Telephone: 1-800-273-8255
For Deaf & Hard of Hearing: 1-800-799-4889
Online chat: suicidepreventionlifeline.org

ACKNOWLEDGMENTS

Thank you to:

Tony, Gabe, and Karlina for being such a fun and supportive family;

Asha Hossain of Asha Hossain Designs, LLC for the fantastic cover;

Chelle Olson of Literally Addicted to Detail for the wonderful edits;

Stella Bloom for the perfectly pitched narration for the audio books;

Liz Berry, Jillian Stein, Asa Maria Bradley, and Boone Brux for the advice with the concepts for this new series;

Caitlin Blasdell, for being my incredibly hard working agent;

Anissa Beatty, for your hard work as my perfectly organized assistant and for being such a great leader for Rebecca's Rebels (my FB street team);

Thanks to Rebels Kimberly Frost, Heather Frost, Madison Fairbanks, Suzi Zuber, Asmaa Nada Qayyum, Amanda Larsen, Karen Clementi, and Karen Fisher for their assistance.

Thank you to Writer Space and Fresh Fiction PR for all the hard work.

Thank you also to my constant support system: Gail and Jim English, Kathy and Herbie Zanetti, Debbie and Travis Smith, Stephanie and Don West, and Jessica and Jonah Namson.

ABOUT THE AUTHOR

New York Times, USA Today, Publisher's Weekly and #1 Amazon bestselling author Rebecca Zanetti has published more than sixty novels, which have been translated into several languages, with millions of copies sold world-wide. Her books have received Publisher's Weekly and Kirkus starred reviews and have been featured in Entertainment Weekly, Woman's World, and Women's Day Magazines. Her novels have also been included in Amazon best books of the year and have been favorably reviewed in both the Washington Post and the New York Times Book Reviews. Rebecca has ridden in a locked Chevy trunk, has asked the unfortunate delivery guy to release her from a set of handcuffs, and has discovered the best silver mine shafts in which to bury a body…all in the name of research. Honest. Find Rebecca at: www.RebeccaZanetti.com

ALSO BY & READING ORDER OF THE SERIES'

I know a lot of you like the exact reading order for a series, so here's the exact reading order as of the release of this book, although if you read most novels out of order, it's okay.

THE ANNA ALBERTINI FILES

1. Disorderly Conduct (Book 1)
2. Bailed Out (Book 2)
3. Adverse Possession (Book 3)
4. Holiday Rescue novella (Novella 3.5)
5. Santa's Subpoena (Book 4)
6. Holiday Rogue (Novella 4.5)
7. Tessa's Trust (Book 5)
8. New Anna & Aiden Book - TBA

LAUREL SNOW SERIES

1. You Can Run (Book 1)
2. You Can Hide (Book 2)
3. You Can Die (Book 3 - 2023)

DEEP OPS SERIES

1. Hidden (Book 1)
2. Taken Novella (Book 1.5)
3. Fallen (Book 2)
4. Shaken (in Pivot Anthology) (2.5)
5. Broken (Book 3)
6. Driven (Book 4)
7. Unforgiven (Book 5)
8. Unforgotten (Book 6)

REDEMPTION, WY SERIES

1. Rescue Cowboy Style (Novella in the Lone Wolf Anthology)
2. Christmas story 2022 (subscribe to newsletter)
3. Novellas 2&3 in summer 2023
4. Book # 1 launch in 2024

Dark Protectors / Realm Enforcers / 1001 Dark Nights novellas

1. Fated (Dark Protectors Book 1)
2. Claimed (Dark Protectors Book 2)
3. Tempted Novella (Dark Protectors 2.5)
4. Hunted (Dark Protectors Book 3)
5. Consumed (Dark Protectors Book 4)
6. Provoked (Dark Protectors Book 5)
7. Twisted Novella (Dark Protectors 5.5)
8. Shadowed (Dark Protectors Book 6)
9. Tamed Novella (Dark Protectors 6.5)
10. Marked (Dark Protectors Book 7)
11. Wicked Ride (Realm Enforcers 1)
12. Wicked Edge (Realm Enforcers 2)

ALSO BY & READING ORDER OF THE SERIES'

13. Wicked Burn (Realm Enforcers 3)
14. Talen Novella (Dark Protectors 7.5)
15. Wicked Kiss (Realm Enforcers 4)
16. Wicked Bite (Realm Enforcers 5)
17. Teased (Reese -1001 DN Novella)
18. Tricked (Reese-1001 DN Novella)
19. Tangled (Reese-1001 DN Novella)
20. Vampire's Faith (Dark Protectors 8) ***A great entry point for series, if you want to start here***
21. Demon's Mercy (Dark Protectors 9)
22. Vengeance (Rebels 1001 DN Novella)
23. Alpha's Promise (Dark Protectors 10)
24. Hero's Haven (Dark Protectors 11)
25. Vixen (Rebels 1001 DN Novella)
26. Guardian's Grace (Dark Protectors 12)
27. Vampire (Rebels 1001 DN Novella)
28. Rebel's Karma (Dark Protectors 13)
29. Immortal's Honor (Dark Protector 14)
30. Garrett's Destiny
31. A Vampire's Kiss (Rebels-1001 DN Novella)
32. Warrior's Hope - 2023

STOPE PACKS (wolf shifters)

1. Wolf
2. Alpha
3. Shifter (TBA)

SIN BROTHERS---BLOOD BROTHERS

1. Forgotten Sins (Sin Brothers 1)
2. Sweet Revenge (Sin Brothers 2)
3. Blind Faith (Sin Brothers 3)
4. Total Surrender (Sin Brothers 4)

5. Deadly Silence (Blood Brothers 1)
6. Lethal Lies (Blood Brothers 2)
7. Twisted Truths (Blood Brothers 3)

SCORPIUS SYNDROME SERIES
**This is technically the right timeline, but I'd always meant for the series to start with Mercury Striking.

Scorpius Syndrome/The Brigade Novellas

- 1. Scorpius Rising
- 2. Blaze Erupting
- 3. Power Surging - TBA
- 4. Hunter Advancing - TBA

Scorpius Syndrome NOVELS
1. Mercury Striking (Scorpius Syndrome 1)
2. Shadow Falling (Scorpius Syndrome 2)
3. Justice Ascending (Scorpius Syndrome 3)
4. Storm Gathering (Scorpius Syndrome 4)
5. Winter Igniting (Scorpius Syndrome 5)
6. Knight Awakening (Scorpius Synd. 6)

MAVERICK MONTANA SERIES

1. Against the Wall
2. Under the Covers
3. Rising Assets
4. Over the Top
5. Bundle of Books 1-3

Made in the USA
Monee, IL
06 September 2022